MATERIAL EVIDENCE

A CAIRNBURGH MYSTERY

BILL KIRTON

BLOODY BRITS PRESS

Ann Arbor and Alnmouth

2007

Bloody Brits Press
PO Box 3671
Ann Arbor MI 48106-3671

BLOODY BRITS PRESS FIRST EDITION
First Printing July 2007

First published in Great Britain in 1995 by Judy Piatkus (Publishers)
Ltd of 5 Windmill Street, London W1

Printed in the United States of America on acid-free paper.

Cover designer: Bonnie Liss (Phoenix Graphics)

Bloody Brits Press is an imprint of Bywater Books

ISBN 978-1-932859-32-4

For Mum and Dad, far too late

Cairnburgh, Scotland

1995

Chapter One

"Forty-seven separate stab wounds," said Carston, "and that's only on page four."

His wife Kath looked up from the photographs she was sifting through.

"What?"

Carston turned the page of his newspaper.

"Forty-seven wounds. Five different cases but they all did it with knives. Two lovers, one homosexual, a wife and an antiques dealer. Homosexual came off worst. Twelve wounds in the bum, seventeen in the chest. Not necessarily in that order. The antique dealer ..."

"Shut up, Jack," said Kath, picking up a yellow packet and starting to take more photos from it.

"Just professionalism. Trouble with you is, you don't take an interest in my job," said Carston.

"Totting up stab wounds isn't your job."

"It is sometimes."

"Not in the paper, it isn't. Not other people's cases. And not when we've just had liver."

"Small-minded, that's what you are. Sad, really. Unable to see the wider issues. Don't understand perspective."

Kath put down the photographs and looked at him again.

"Have you been at that cocaine your drugs people lifted last week?" she asked.

"Chance'd be a fine thing."

Detective Chief Inspector Carston's voice tailed off as he considered what he was saying.

"I've never really understood what that means," he added, almost to himself.

"What?"

"Chance'd be a fine thing. Strange thing to say, isn't it?"

"Nothing's strange coming from you tonight. What's up?"

Carston let the paper fall into his lap.

"Nothing, love. The usual. Reading about this lot. People who were saying 'I love you darling' or something like it, probably not so long ago, now here they are carving each other up."

"I know," said Kath, in a tone that showed that she did.

She picked up the handful of photos again and started flipping through them.

"And they all say they didn't mean to kill. Like pressing a switch and saying 'I didn't mean the light to come on.'"

"Never mind that. Come and look at these," said Kath, moving along the sofa to make room for him.

Carston pushed himself up, dropped the paper in his chair and went to sit beside her.

"What've you got these out for?" he asked, picking up a shot of a couple cut off halfway up their thighs and with acres of sky above them standing in front of the glasshouse at Kew Gardens.

"I wanted to clear out that cupboard in the hall. I thought we could …"

The telephone interrupted her. She stopped and looked at Carston.

"Bye," she said.

"Might not be for me," said Carston, heaving himself up again and crossing to the door.

"Want to bet?" said Kath.

Carston went into the hall and picked up the receiver.

"Carston."

"Sorry to bother you, sir," said the caller. It was the duty sergeant at the station.

"No problem, Sandy," said Carston. "What's up?"

"Another nasty. Woman's body in a place down by the canal."

"Oh shit," said Carston. "How many holes in this one?"

"Er … Just the one, I think."

"Restrained bit of stabbing, eh? Just the once."

"No sir. Seems this one was shot."

"Well, well. Bit unfashionable, but it makes a change. Who found her?"

"Her husband."

"Aha. He did it, I suppose."

"That's for the courts to say, isn't it?"

"Don't make me laugh."

"It's thirty-six, Dyson Close. I've phoned Sergeant Ross."

"OK, Sandy, I'm on my way."

He put down the receiver and felt guilty for the small excitement that the call had lit in his head. Here he was looking forward to getting involved in exactly the sort of thing he'd just been making such pious noises about. Avoidable hypocrisy was never far away. He went back into the room, walked behind the sofa, leaned over and kissed Kath on the top of the head.

"See?" she said. "I told you. Bye."

"Sandy," said Carston. "Something's come up."

"Stop calling me Sandy."

Carston smiled.

"I'll get back as soon as I can, but it doesn't sound too promising. Could be a while."

"I'll ring my lover."

"Yes, he'll keep you company."

"Who said it was a he?"

"Don't be disgusting," said Carston as he kissed her again and went to put on his coat.

Kath looked at a snap of a much younger Carston leaning against a rock somewhere on Exmoor. His hair was thick although still neatly trimmed, his eyes looked dark, his smile generous, and the unlined features really were very handsome. Carston poked his head around the edge of the door. She looked up, held up the snap and made it obvious that she was comparing it with the original.

"Time hasn't been kind to you, my dear," she said.

"Nobody ever is," said Carston. "See you later."

Up until the Sixties, Dyson Close had been Dyson Quay. In the Seventies it was a deserted stretch of warehousing alongside which garbage bobbed in thick water. Then the Midas Eighties reclaimed

5

it, used public money and environmental conscience to scour the canal, and convinced the socially mobile that, even in Scotland, owning a waterfront property was the key to elevation. Recent repossessions had brought a little realism back into prices and, while most of the inhabitants of the Close still belonged to the increasingly rare species of Scots who voted Tory, they tended to keep quiet about it.

Number thirty-six was towards one end of the street. Outside it, the huge clutch of police cars, marked and unmarked, left no doubt that something fairly serious had happened in the building. Carston was met at the front door by Jim Ross, his detective sergeant.

"Shouldn't bother yet, sir. It's like Piccadilly Circus," he said.

"All there, are they?"

"Aye."

Carston took two steps towards the nearest car and sat against the bonnet.

"OK, what's the story?"

Ross had followed him.

"Name's Stephanie Burnham. Mid-forties. Worked for Borney and Whitcombe. Financial consultants. She's in the top room, sort of study by the look of it. Shot in the back."

"Messy?"

"Not as bad as it could be. The blood's sprayed across the floor and up the wall a bit. Some more coming out of her mouth. Nasty stuff round her bum. Must be a helluva mess inside her."

Ross gave all this information with a speed and eagerness that belied the fact that he was talking about a fellow human being. It wasn't callousness or insensitivity, just a mark of the fascination his job exerted over him. Carston had been working with him just over a year and was happy to rely on his initial summary of the crimes they were called to investigate. Jim Ross liked facts.

"What else?"

"Not much really. Not until we can get a clear look at it all. Doors and windows were all closed when her husband found her apparently. No signs of breaking and entering. The room's messed up a bit. Bit of a struggle."

"Where's the husband?"

6

"In the kitchen. McNeil's here. She's looking after him. I had a quick word. He came back about half-six. Just found her there."

"What sort of a state's he in?"

"Hard to say."

"Has he made a statement yet?"

"No, I was waiting to see if you wanted to talk to him."

"I wouldn't mind. Just to see … well, you know."

Ross turned towards the house as Carston pushed himself from the car.

"What about neighbors?" asked Carston.

Ross shook his head as he moved past the uniformed constable standing at the front door. "Next door both sides are away," he said.

"So nobody heard the shot."

"Nobody's said anything yet."

They stopped talking as they made their way through the house. There was a single, central corridor off which rooms opened on either side. The corridor was narrow and the room they turned into at the end of it was surprisingly big. It ran the whole width of the house and was obviously a kitchen and dining room combined. A young female detective constable with a pale complexion and red hair cut fashionably short was by the table. Over at the picture window stood a man around six feet tall with thinning hair and just the beginning of a middle-aged spread. His heavy cheeks were dark with stubble but the impression conveyed by his cashmere sports jacket, pale blue cotton shirt and dark gray cords was of a clean-cut, handsome man of some substance. He was holding a cup and staring out at the water of the canal at the back of the house. Ross and Carston nodded to the policewoman. Unnecessarily, she stood a little straighter.

"Mr. Burnham," said Ross, gently.

The man turned. The eyes were still staring, red and watery.

"This is Detective Chief Inspector Carston."

Burnham's eyes moved to Carston but he made no acknowledgment of the introduction. Carston slipped easily into the formula he'd had to use far too often.

"Mr. Burnham. I'm very sorry about all this. A dreadful business. Is there anything we can do for you?"

By way of answer, Burnham lifted his cup slowly and said, "No, thank you. This young lady's been very kind. Made me a cup of tea. A cliché, but welcome."

His voice was quiet, steady, only slightly strained.

Carston smiled and nodded. He walked slowly over to Burnham. The eyes followed him. He looked out at the water and nodded again to signify his appreciation of such a scene. Burnham turned to look out of the window again.

"Terrible business. Terrible," said Carston. "I never get used to what people do to one another."

Burnham gave a sudden cold, scratchy laugh.

"Try working in Sales and Marketing," he said.

The joke was incongruous, flat, rather eerie in the quiet kitchen. Carston seized it gratefully as a way to where he wanted to go.

"That's your line, is it?"

Burnham nodded.

"Calder and McStay," he said. "I cover most of the east coast."

"All right when the tourists' caravans aren't about, I should think."

Burnham's thin lips twitched a smile.

"I don't actually have to patrol the highways. I'm Marketing Director."

"Of course. Sorry," said Carston.

"Anyway, the place is all right. It's the people. My dear colleagues. That's what's depressing about it."

Carston couldn't work out whether Burnham was talking about these things to force his mind away from his wife's body upstairs or whether he was just so shocked that he'd momentarily lost his grip on the reality of what had happened.

"One of the penalties of the way we live, I suppose," he said, noticing that Ross was paying very close attention to everything Burnham said and did.

"What, being surrounded by bastards who ...?" Burnham stopped, turned to WDC McNeil and said, "I'm sorry."

"That's all right, sir," she said, with a smile that twisted one side of her mouth more than the other.

Carston grasped the nettle.

"I'm sorry to have to ask you this, Mr. Burnham, but we're going to need a statement from you. D'you think ...?"

"Of course," said Burnham quickly, not waiting for Carston to finish. "Let's get it done. I'll be under suspicion too, I expect."

Carston looked at Ross. They were both taken slightly by surprise.

"Why d'you say that, sir?" asked Ross.

"Husbands always are, aren't they? What's the figure? Thirty-five percent of all crimes against women involve domestic violence? One in five murder victims is a woman killed by lover or husband?"

The recitation was surprising, deliberately formal. He looked at the sergeant, who was clearly waiting for him to go on.

"I've read the Sunday magazines, you know," he said.

Carston was intrigued by Burnham's fluctuations and was anxious to get a statement while his mood was so expansive.

"Well, you're way ahead of us, Mr. Burnham. So, as long as you feel up to it, perhaps you'd tell Sergeant Ross here exactly what happened."

The need to confront the reality of his wife's destruction seemed to subdue Burnham immediately. He sighed, nodded his head slowly and sat at the table. Carston flicked his head at Ross, who took out a notebook, looked at his watch and wrote down the time before pulling out one of the other chairs. He took a small tape recorder from his pocket and set it on the table between himself and Burnham. The machine was simply a back-up to make sure he'd got things right. There was never any question of using what it recorded as evidence. That could only come from the reel-to-reel machines back at the station with their time codes, identification procedures and all the other gadgets that protected the interviewee.

Carston touched WDC McNeil on the arm and angled his head towards the door. She moved towards it with Carston following her.

"If there's anything you need, we'll just be outside," he said.

Burnham was sitting very still, his head bowed. When he spoke, his voice was much lower than before.

"She was pregnant, you know."

◆◆◆

9

It was after ten o'clock before the scene of crime squad were through with their preliminary photographing, filming, sifting, lifting and combing. Carston went to look at everything as they were finishing up and before the body was bagged and taken away for autopsy.

Although her face had darkened where the blood had settled in the vessels as she lay on the floor, it was still obvious that Stephanie Burnham had been an attractive woman. Ross had said she was in her mid-forties but the face was relatively unlined, and any gray that threatened to betray her had been subtly dyed from her dark hair. She was naked from the waist down and Carston could see that there was very little excess weight around her middle or on her thighs. She lay on her front, her left arm under her chest, her right trailing beside her. Her left leg was bent inwards. In her linen shirt, a small ragged hole showed black beneath her right shoulder blade.

The room had bookshelves along two walls, a desk to the right of the window, and two small armchairs on either side of the door. There was a chair tipped over near her left foot. A skirt in some heavy black fabric was bundled on the floor near the desk beside a shotgun. Some books had been pulled or knocked off the lower shelves. One of the lower window panes was cracked. Incongruously, in the corner by the desk, lay a fork and a plunger, the sort used to unblock kitchen sinks.

Brian McIntosh, the police surgeon, stood with Carston as he looked around.

"Pity," he said. "Fine-looking woman."

"OK if they're ugly then, is it?" muttered Carston.

"What's the matter with you?" asked McIntosh. "Pre-menstrual?"

"Sorry," said Carston with a small grin. "What have you got?"

McIntosh pulled at his beard.

"Not much yet. Been dead maybe eight, ten hours. Shotgun wound obviously. It's a contact injury. Whoever did it held the gun right against her back. There's bruising there, and tears around the edge where the gases blew back out of her chest. Her heart must've been just torn apart by it."

He paused, moved his finger and thumb along the line of his lower lip, then added, "Sex was obviously involved."

Carston looked at the white buttocks stained with blood and nodded.

The doctor's stroking fingers moved across his cheeks and under his chin.

"That skirt's all torn. Her knickers are under the desk there. Looks like they were dragged off her. Semen there too, I think. Can't confirm it yet though."

Carston waved a hand around at the books on the floor.

"Was she knocked about at all?"

"Hard to say till I can get at her properly. It's possible. Those marks round her anus ... And she's got a few bruises on her hands and forearms. Nothing very conclusive. One very interesting thing though. Have a look at this."

He beckoned Carston across to the body and squatted beside it. He lifted the right arm so that Carston could see the hand. It was tightly clenched. Carston squatted beside him to get a closer look.

"Never seen that before," he said.

"Not surprised. Quite rare," said McIntosh. "Cadaveric spasm. You only come across it when death occurs in conditions of high emotional tension."

"Like when somebody's got a shotgun stuck in their back?"

"Precisely."

"So what causes it?"

"Nobody knows really. It's just an instantaneous rigor. Probably means she knew she was going to die. You sometimes get it in drowning. Find bits of seaweed they've clutched at. Never seen it in a case like this before."

Carston looked very closely at the tightly gripped fist. A twist of fibrous material jutted from beneath the side of the little finger.

"I suppose you noticed that she's holding something?" he said as McIntosh got up and shook his trouser legs straight.

"Yes. Interesting, eh? Makes your job a lot easier, I should think."

"Why?"

McIntosh smiled through the bristles of his mustache and the fingers that were pushing it down against his lip.

11

"Cadaveric spasm only affects groups of muscles which have been actively working at the exact moment of death. Whatever she's got there she grabbed at as she died."

"Sounds too good to be true," said Carston.

"Nevertheless, I promise you it is," said McIntosh, picking up his case and heading for the door. He turned and spoke as he got there. "I've been in touch with Aberdeen. They'll let you have the full results as soon as they can. Mind you, they've already got three customers waiting from a joy-riding crash. Still, they said they'll do what they can."

"Thanks," said Carston.

McIntosh was already out of the room.

"No problem," he said from the corridor.

The West Grampian force was too small to have its own full lab facilities and instead had to depend on the co-operation of its Grampian colleagues for autopsy reports and full forensic examinations. It sometimes meant frustrating waits while flesh and fibers shuttled back and forth between Cairnburgh and Aberdeen but Dr. McIntosh was an established member of the north east's medical Mafia and could usually expedite examinations if cases were interesting enough.

Carston watched two constables unzipping a body bag.

"OK now, sir?" asked one of them.

Carston was still beside the body. He squatted once more, looked it over, peered closely at the right fist, then stood up.

"Yeah, OK. Take her away."

As the rough hands of the constable and his colleague were handling Stephanie Burnham in ways they'd never have been allowed to while she was alive, Carston began a slow study of the other things in the room. He knew that the reports he'd get from the experts who'd already spent the best part of two hours collecting material and information from every part of the interior would be far more thorough than any investigation of his own, but he wanted to fix the general scene so that when he read them they formed part of a coherent picture.

The books that were spread on the floor could have been knocked there by someone clutching at the shelves. They were all novels, most of them by nineteenth-century authors. Here and there on the carpet there were sharp depressions, of the sort left by the legs of chairs and tables when they've been in the same place for a long time. But these were irregular, random, offering no patterns to explain them. The blood which had been forced out of the woman's chest by the discharge had scattered across the carpet in front of her. Some had hit the wall opposite the desk. He was intrigued by the two kitchen items and couldn't for the life of him see how they fitted into the scenario.

Carston turned the pages of *Madame Bovary* as he watched the bundle that had been Stephanie Burnham being carried through the door. Ross was waiting on the landing, having stepped aside to let the two constables through with their package. Carston was slightly surprised to see him make the sign of the cross as the body passed him. It was no doubt sincere but fairly cursory and the corpse was seemingly very quickly forgotten as he came in.

"I didn't know you were a left-footer," said Carston.

"Isn't everybody?" asked Ross, slightly surprised at the remark.

"Not me. I gave up on Him after I'd seen a few cot deaths."

"Aye, I know what you mean," said Ross. "It's no so easy to get out when you're a Catholic, though."

"So I've heard. How about Burnham? Finished with him?"

"Aye," said Ross, tapping the pocket which carried his notebook and the tape recorder.

Carston headed for the door.

"OK then, come on," he said. "Let's get back and start putting it together."

Ross followed him down the stairs.

"Did he have anything interesting to say?" Carston asked as they crossed the pavement to their car.

"Bits and pieces," said Ross.

"Like what?"

"A few things. He was gardening all morning. Left here at midday. They had it off just before he went. Her idea, he reckons."

"What's so special about that?" asked Carston as he flopped into the passenger seat. Ross waited until he was sitting behind the wheel before replying.

"It's the first time in six weeks. He thought they'd given up altogether."

He shook his head and gave a deliberately loud sigh.

"What's the matter?" asked Carston.

"Imagine. Six weeks without it," said Ross.

Carston did up his seat belt.

"When you get to my age," he said, "you're lucky if you can manage it that often …"

Ross laughed.

"… and bloody grateful when you're not expected to," Carston added, smiling along with him.

Back in the office, Carston screwed his features into a grimace.

"What the bloody hell do they put in this coffee nowadays? Tastes like hamsters' piss."

Ross pulled his chair back and sat down.

"You're too sensitive," he said. "You drink too much of that wine. Ruins your palate."

Carston looked at him and shook his head sadly.

"Why d'you always talk such crap?"

"Police training college, I suppose," said Ross. "Now then, d'you want to go through this statement or would you rather talk about Brazilian blend all night?"

"Don't push your luck, Sergeant bloody Ross," said Carston, easing himself into the chair opposite him. "OK. Shoot."

Ross flipped open his notebook but instead of looking at his notes, he leaned forward onto his desk.

"He's a funny sort of guy, you know."

Carston waited, knowing that Ross would explain.

"He wasn't normal, but he didn't seem all that shocked either once he started talking. Said things about his job, the marriage, that you wouldn't expect somebody who'd just come home and found a dead wife to say … or even think of."

"What sort of things?"

"Called her a selfish bitch for a start."

"Eh?"

"Aye. Bit strong, eh? And he's pissed off at having to sort all of this out when the half-yearly audit's due at Calder and McStay."

"Bloody hell. Romantic bugger, isn't he?"

"That's the other weird thing. In amongst it all, he seemed quite …"

Ross stopped, embarrassed at having to find the right word for what he was thinking. At last, he compromised and continued.

"… well, fond of her. I don't know. It just struck me that his reactions were a bit mixed up."

"Shock?"

"Maybe."

Carston picked up a pencil and pulled a pad across the desk.

"OK. Let's have it."

Ross sat back and looked at his notes.

"Right," he said, "he's been at the races in Edinburgh all day. Left home just after twelve. It was later than he'd wanted it to be; the first race was at two-fifteen. He only just made it. He'd planned to leave an hour earlier but, like I told you, his wife wanted sex."

Carston looked at him.

"Yes. What did he say about that?"

"That was one of the weird bits. There she was lying upstairs with mincemeat for lungs and he was slagging her off for making him late for the first race. That's when he called her a selfish bitch."

"Those were his exact words?"

Ross looked at his notes.

"Well," he said, "I haven't had a chance to check that I've got it all down right yet. I got the tape … but this is the way I heard it." He began reading, his voice becoming flatter, the liveliness of his own Scottish inflexions being replaced by the halting accent of someone uncomfortable with reading aloud.

"'It was just before eleven. I'd just got in from the garden. She called me up to the study. I went up. She started giving out the usual signals. I told her I was in a hurry but she'd decided. As usual, selfish bitch. I don't know what was the matter with her. She was ferocious. Shouting. Violent. The first time for six weeks and it was as if we were strangers.'"

"Bloody hell," said Carston. "Didn't hold much back, did he? That's what I call a statement."

Ross was glad of the chance to stop reading.

"Oh aye, he was chatty enough. I tried to paraphrase what he was saying, but he didn't want to know. Needed to talk maybe. D'you want more?"

Carston sensed his sergeant's reluctance to go on.

"No, no. That's OK, Jim. Check it over, type it up and I'll read it through myself. Just give us the gist of the rest."

"Well, as I said, he got there for the first race. Left after the fourth, about ..." He looked at his notes again. "... five to four."

"How come?"

"What?"

"How come he left early?"

"Four straight losers. He was four hundred quid down. Decided to call it a day."

"I'm not surprised."

"Drove back. The roads were clear. Arrived home just after six. Parked the car, went in, poured a drink, went up to get a book and there she was. He was going to feel for her pulse but he said as soon as he touched her skin he knew she was dead. Phoned us straight away."

Ross closed his notebook. Carston nodded slowly, doodling spirals on the piece of paper in front of him.

"Mmmm," he said at last. "Anybody see him?"

"Well, I don't suppose he was alone at Edinburgh. There must have been a jockey or two there."

"Very funny. How about neighbors seeing him leave and come back?"

"We haven't talked to them yet. Anyway, they're away, remember?"

"Yes. Did he say which bookies he bet with?"

Ross thought for a moment.

"I don't think so."

"OK, that's something we'll need to ask him. We can check his story with them. I don't know how many punters bet in hundreds but I shouldn't think there are many. And we can check with the AA to see that the roads were as clear as he said. Mind you, the time he came home isn't what matters. She'd been dead a while by then."

16

"Oh?"

"Yes. McIntosh reckoned it happened around midday. Even if your pal's telling the truth about the races, he could still have done it before he left."

Ross was making notes as Carston spoke.

"D'you think he did then?" he asked.

"Wouldn't be the first time, would it?" said Carston. "Did you ask him about the gun?"

"Aye." Ross opened his notepad again. "It's his all right. He's got two, a Tolley and a Beretta."

The information made Carston forget how awful the coffee was. He risked another sip.

"Interesting," he said.

"Yeah. I asked him where they were. He took me down to the garage in the basement. He keeps them locked up in a cupboard there. The cupboard was locked and the Tolley (that's the one in the study) was missing. He reckons he's no idea who could have taken it out. He's the only one with keys."

"How about his wife?"

"Apparently not. I asked him."

Carston shook his head. Paradoxically, the neatness of it all displeased him. A pregnant wife, a husband who called her a bitch just hours after her death and made a point of telling the police that he was the only one who could have taken the gun out of its rack, something that could be conclusive evidence clutched in the dead woman's palm, no sign of any forced entry and an estimated time of death that wasn't covered by the man's alibi. Burnham wasn't unintelligent. If he'd done it, surely he'd have made a better job of hiding his guilt, even if it was only putting the gun back. Surely it was all too crude to have been perpetrated by the Marketing Director of Calder and McStay. Ross was watching him and, seeing a slight frown form on his brow, guessed at his thoughts.

"Aye. Too easy, isn't it?"

Carston looked at him and chuckled.

"OK Sherlock," he said. "Let's leave it there tonight. Get that typed up and I'll go through it tomorrow."

"D'you want me to do it now?"

"Not bloody likely. Look at the time. Your Jean'll be sending me letter bombs if she thinks I'm keeping you here."

Ross had stood and was collecting bits of paper from his desk.

"Oh, don't worry. I took her and Kirsty down to Girvan at the weekend to stay with her folks. Her sister's over from Canada."

"Topless bar for you then, is it?"

"You're joking. In this place? One of her pals would see me and they'd be on the phone before I'd ordered a pint of heavy." He took his coat from behind the door. "Anyway," he continued as he pulled it on, "their tits'd be frozen solid in this weather. Knocking together like bowling balls."

"Jim," said Carston as his sergeant opened the office door, "you've got a lovely way with words."

"So they tell me," said Ross. He held up his notebook. "I'll type this up at home. Good excuse to use the new computer."

"Whatever suits you," said Carston.

"Night, sir."

"Night, Jim."

Ross went out, closing the door behind him. Carston lifted his coffee cup, thought better of it and put it back on the side of his desk. He admired the way Ross was so meticulous about keeping the job and his home life strictly apart. However interested he was in an investigation, Ross always let his wife know when he'd be home and he rarely let her down. He'd once told Carston that the minute there was any sign of the usual strain that police work injected into relationships, he'd be out of the force and into some private security outfit. Carston knew that it would be a pity if that happened. Ross was a clear thinker, had a knack of going directly to the point. Perhaps he was even a bit mechanical at times, but he was a good detective and Carston always knew where he was with him.

He hadn't always been as meticulous himself about warning Kath that he wouldn't be home. But Kath, or so he let himself think to rationalize his guilt, was a very capable woman, who often preferred being left to her own devices.

He looked at his watch. It was past ten. The possibilities that clustered around the Burnham case were tempting, but so was the thought of curling up beside Kath with some real coffee. He took his own coat, switched off the light and, as if on cue, the telephone rang. He thought momentarily of ignoring it but knew that he would regret it if he did, so he picked up the receiver.

"Carston."

"Yes. Thought you'd still be there."

It was Dr. McIntosh.

"I was just leaving, actually."

"Never mind. This won't keep you. I know how you like things to ponder on. Thought I'd let you know I took a blood sample from that woman, Burnham, this evening. Just to check, you know."

"Check what?" asked Carston.

"I thought she'd probably been drinking. I was right. Two hundred milligrams. More than enough for a lady in the middle of the day, don't you think?"

"Yes."

"Some of it could have come from bacterial activity, of course. They can produce alcohol as well as putrefaction as part of their normal metabolism."

"Thanks for sharing that with me," said Carston.

"Just thought you'd like to have something to think about in bed. If our friend wasn't sloshed when she died, she wasn't far from it."

"OK. Thanks very much Brian. Good of you to take the trouble."

"No trouble. I'll get the full story to you as soon as I can."

"Thanks again," said Carston.

He replaced the receiver, stood for a while, then left the office, rather cheered by the thought that there was at least the possibility of a little complication in what had been threatening to be tediously straightforward.

Michael Burnham was also speaking on the telephone. He was sitting on a bed in a hotel room. The police had asked him not to stay in his house until they'd made a thorough check of everything in it. They'd taken all the clothes he'd been wearing that day, including the jeans and sweaty shirt he'd had on while he was gardening. He'd been allowed to collect what he needed overnight, although to his annoyance each item he packed was noted by a constable who went with him to his bedroom. Now, in a soulless suite on the second floor of a place designed for business rather than pleasure, he had the bedside phone in his left hand and a glass of Chivas Regal in his right. He had showered and was wearing cream silk pajamas under a cotton dressing gown with a subdued, dark green tartan pattern.

"How did you hear about it?" he asked.

"On the news, of course. I'm surprised you haven't had them camping on your doorstep," said the woman he'd called.

Her voice was young, almost deliberately girlish, with a high, breathy register.

"I have. They arrived not long after the police."

"Well then."

"All the same, I'm surprised they've bothered reporting it. Hardly major news, is it?"

"What? A murder? Oh come on, darling. Anyway, it wasn't on the main news. It was BBC Scotland. The summary."

Burnham took a sip of his whisky.

"Yes. They'll be here again, I suppose," he said.

"Hasn't anybody offered to buy your story yet?" asked the woman, her voice teasing, smiling.

"Why should they?"

"You know, 'Gunshot Shatters Love Nest,' 'Local businessman tells of the agony of his tragic homecoming.'"

"Shut up, Barbara. It's not a joke."

There was a hiss of breath on the line. When the woman spoke again, the smile had gone and her voice was hard.

"Don't remind me, Michael. I've lived with it these last five weeks already. It hasn't been funny for me. Not a bit."

Burnham tried to placate her.

"I know, I know. I'm sorry. It's just ... Well, it's all a bit soon, isn't it?"

"What do you mean, soon?"

"Well, she only died today, for God's sake. She's still warm."

"She was never warm."

"Barbara, you can't ..."

"Oh no, I forgot. Not until she started playing mummy."

Burnham interrupted her with a shout.

"Barbara. For Christ's sake, shut up. It's over. She's dead. None of that has any ... relevance any more."

He breathed deeply to calm himself. When he spoke again, his tone was placatory.

"Look, darling. If we want to survive it all, we'll have to help each other. It's hard, I know, but the only good I can see in it is if you and I can ..."

He stopped, not knowing how to phrase his thoughts. The woman waited, trying to push aside her own anger, to gauge how to reassert her superiority over the dead wife.

"... well, you know what I mean," Burnham finished lamely.

"No. I'm not sure that I do," said the woman, her voice small again and back up in the girlish pitch. "Michael, two weeks ago, less, you said we'd probably have to stop seeing one another. Have you forgotten that already?"

"Of course not, darling, but ..."

"You meant it. You meant it. You explained it all. It was only reasonable, that's what you said. Bloody reasonable! Now you're talking about bloody relevance. God, Michael, you make it so hard."

Burnham's head tilted back onto the pillow. He opened his eyes and looked at the patterns the bedside lamp projected onto the ceiling.

"Darling," he said, as gently as he could, "it is hard. But just think for a minute, don't be so selective about what you remember. I also told you I loved you, right?"

There was no answer. He insisted.

"Right?"

"I know, but ..."

Burnham didn't want to lose the initiative. His voice cut across hers again.

"Right. And I meant it. You know I did. The other thing was getting in the way. I don't deny I reacted to it. I don't deny saying what I did, but it's all over, isn't it? This changes things. Drastically. In some ways, it's even better than it was before. I mean, I'm actually free, aren't I?"

He stopped, aware of the silence on the line.

"Barbara?" he said. "Barbara?"

The answer came in yet another change of pitch. The girlish edge had gone, the voice was rounded, concerned, somehow more mature.

"How do you feel about Stephanie now, Michael?"

The question came as a surprise.

"What do you mean?"

"Exactly what I say. How do you feel about her? Do you love her? Like her? Feel sorry for her? Miss her? What?"

Burnham had to consider the question. He knew there was an element of a trap about it.

"Barbara. I was married to her. I found her dead this afternoon. D'you think it's easy … d'you think it's possible for me to sum up any of it in the sort of formula you're asking for?"

"So you miss her," the woman insisted.

Briefly, Burnham's anger flashed in his reply.

"No, I don't bloody miss her. I wish I'd never met her, but that's not the same thing, is it?"

He calmed himself at once.

"Look, I've always told you I loved you. That hasn't changed. If that's not good enough, I … well, I don't know. Whatever I think or thought about Stephanie is gone. Permanently. The whole thing makes me sick."

After a pause, the woman's voice came back, beginning to climb into youth again.

"I suppose I won't be able to see you for a while?"

Weariness was creeping over Burnham. He closed his eyes. Negative images of the ceiling's patterns continued to move on his retina.

"Not for a while, no. Better for both of us. But one day, as soon as I can, I'll book that hotel in the Rue Cujas again. And we'll eat at the Polidor and pay outrageous amounts for coffee at the Deux Magots."

"Promise?" said the woman, her voice getting precariously close to the wrong side of adolescence.

"Promise," said Burnham.

"Darling."

"Mmm?"

"I'm sorry to pester you. You know why I do, don't you?"

"Of course. Don't worry, it'll be all right soon."

"I hope so. You'll ring me if there's anything I can do, won't you?"

Burnham had already disconnected mentally from the call.

"Of course," he said. "I'll talk to you as soon as I can. I love you."

"I love you too, *chéri*."

"Goodnight."

"'night, darling. Try to sleep well."

"I will," said Burnham.

He disconnected and let the phone fall onto the bed beside him. He was tired, too tired to deal with Barbara's demands and insistences. He'd already done so much for her.

Their affair had been going on for more than six months and there was still a sort of witchcraft about her. It had started when he and Stephanie were going through the motions of their stale, conventional, childless marriage. At a new product launch, he'd given a speech which had proved very successful. All the jokes he'd used were stolen but he'd chosen and delivered them well. Barbara was there representing a growing oil-related company who were potential customers. As the launch progressed from champagne through Chardonnay to single and double malt whiskies that were swilled down with little concern for the subtleties claimed by the distillers, Burnham noticed more and more often that she seemed to be studying him. Every time he looked across the room, she'd anticipated his glance and the green eyes were already locked on his.

She wasn't beautiful or even pretty but there was an attraction about her that came from something other than the physical. Slim, bright, elegant, and with a fall of auburn hair, she was the focus for many of the younger reps, especially as their alcohol intake made them less aware of the extent of their crassness. It was precisely the attentions of these incipient studs that stopped Burnham introducing himself to her and it was only when the party was beginning to break up that he'd turned and suddenly found her standing in front of him.

"Hullo," she'd said. "Barbara Stone, Dempster Associates. I liked your speech."

"Thank you," said Burnham, too surprised to say anything else.

The green eyes looked straight into him. They were smiling but her pale pink lips were serious and he could see her tongue moving slowly behind them. She let the pause hang.

"Very much," she added, her mouth now showing the same mischief she'd allowed into her eyes. Burnham was ashamed of himself. Whatever this woman had, he'd fallen for it like the pathetic creatures who'd fawned around her for most of the afternoon. He was angry with himself.

"Well, let's hope it's reflected in some closer co-operation with Dempster Associates," he said, realizing too late the ambiguity of what he had intended to be a businesslike reply.

Barbara Stone didn't let such chances pass.

"Forgive me, Mr. Burnham, but I've never believed in deception. I've spent most of this meeting listening to half-baked post-adolescents nudging me with innuendoes as subtle as six-inch nails. Business was the last thing on their minds. It's the same with me now. I'd like to spend some time in bed with you. If that offends you, I'm sorry. If not, I hope you'll get in touch."

Her eyes were still locked on his. She reached out a hand. Incapable of any coherent response, Burnham took it.

"It's a pleasure to have met you," she said. Then, with a formal shake and the lightest of pressures from her index finger in his palm, she turned and walked out of the room.

To a man of fifty-three, in whom passion was only ever aroused by the occasional visit to a racetrack and protracted meetings with accountants, such a melodramatic encounter was irresistible. It offered him youth, danger and a return to sexuality. The following day he'd phoned her at her office and, less than twenty-four hours after that, he'd been rejuvenated by an evening which had begun, continued and ended with sexual antics that tested his stamina and reawakened long-discarded fantasies. Inevitably, such a glorious validation of his virility had convinced him that he was in love and the contrast between his time with Barbara and the continuing tedium of his marriage made him impatient for a new beginning.

Their affair became an open secret and while from within it shone with the brilliance of elemental passion, to outsiders it was another tawdry middle-aged coupling.

Burnham roused himself, took another sip of the whisky and reached for his diary. For no reason that he could logically give, he'd been keeping a diary religiously since his fortieth birthday. At first, it had been intended to keep track of the changes in him, but every night as he scribbled in the bacon-and-eggs events of his days, he faced the truth that he was empty. There was no complex character evolving and building with the experiences it had, only a void where he looked for philosophy, meaning, significance.

He flicked back over the pages of the past few weeks, stopping now and again to browse. One of the things he read made him look deliberately for an entry he half-remembered making a month before. He found it, read it, then closed the book. He couldn't bring himself to write anything tonight. Maybe he wouldn't bother ever again. He lay back, the diary still in his hand, the whisky on the table beside him. For the first time in years and years, his eyes filled with tears which fell silently down his cheeks. He shook his head slowly.

"Murder was never the answer," he said.

Chapter Two

Aberdeen is known as the granite city, but the general availability of the material is obvious in most of the other towns in the north east of Scotland. Aberdeen's granite is either silver (if you're fond of the place) or gray (if you can't wait to get away from it). In West Aberdeenshire, however, one of the ways in which towns like Cairnburgh declared their independence of the oil giant on the coast was by choosing the gentler pink variety from around Peterhead. It was this which made the terrace along which Carston was walking look soft and warm in the morning sun. At regular intervals, flights of steps led up to big, solid doors with discreet plaques identifying insurance companies, lawyers, financial services and, incongruously, a video production company. The facades all proclaimed the success and reliability of what lay behind them.

Borney and Whitcombe were at number eleven. After the grandeur of the exterior, their reception area was unimaginative with the regulation Swiss Cheese plants, smoked-glass table tops, scattered financial magazines and a receptionist whose smile suggested that Carston was just the person she'd been waiting for years to meet. After the statutory interval, seven minutes on this occasion, he was directed up the stairs to the first floor, the receptionist's smile as she showed him the way seeming to suggest that his departure gave her as much pleasure as his arrival.

Matthew Borney, the senior partner, met him at the door of a meeting room. He was fiftyish, fattish, but disguised both these deficiencies with an immaculate dark blue suit, a blindingly white shirt and a tie that obviously proclaimed membership of somewhere exclusive. His handshake was firm but quick, his expression composed, and when he spoke it was clear that a lot of trouble had

26

gone into spreading an accent from the better areas of Edinburgh over his nasal north east tones. Coffee was ordered and Borney was quick to get down to business.

"It's a terrible loss for us. Stephanie was a very valuable colleague, a real asset. And to be … murdered. Such a waste!"

Carston noted with distaste that he made Stephanie Burnham sound like a ledger entry.

"How long had she been with you?" he asked.

"Almost three years. I remember, she came the week after her fortieth birthday."

"This was her first job in finance, wasn't it?"

"Yes, that's right."

"Rather a generous gesture on your part," said Carston.

"What d'you mean?" said Borney quickly, as if insulted by the accusation of generosity.

"Well, if you believe what you hear, being female and over forty doesn't look good on job applications."

Borney looked prim. His lips tightened into what must have been a smile.

"That sort of discrimination is anathema at Borney and Whitcombe. We appoint on merit, Inspector."

Carston's response was quick.

"How did you know she had any?"

The thin smile stretched further.

"One can never be sure, of course, but she was an impressive interviewee. We weren't disappointed."

There was a smugness about Borney that irritated Carston, but he needed the man's co-operation.

"So what sort of things did she do?"

"Well, how well acquainted are you with the workings of the world of finance, Inspector?"

"On my salary, only obliquely," said Carston, smiling but inwardly resentful of the insinuation of his ignorance.

"This year, Stephanie's been taking on more and more," said Borney. "She passed her Registered Representative exam fairly soon after joining us, then in July last year she got her Securities Industry Diploma."

"That's good, is it?" asked Carston, unable to resist the urge to imply that these arcane financial qualifications were the equivalent of scouts' badges.

"If a proven proficiency in private and institutional investment advice and management, expertise in Bond and Fixed Interest markets, fund management, financial futures and options and a thorough knowledge of the intricacies of Regulation and Compliance is good, yes, she was very good."

Carston pursed his lips and nodded. Despite his resistance to Borney's smugness, he had to admit that it did sound impressive.

"So good, in fact, that she was promoted quite quickly. Leap-frogged one or two of our younger men. Much to their disgust," added Borney with what he thought was a turn of wit.

"Really," said Carston. "Who would that be?"

Borney brought his hands up in front of his face and clasped them together.

"Let me see. There was young Ferguson and another chap. What was his name? ... Roach, I think. Yes, that's it, Paul Roach."

"D'you think I could have a word with them?" asked Carston.

"Oh, they're not here any more," said Borney, as if Carston should have known. "Ferguson's been in our Edinburgh office since last May and I've no idea what happened to Roach. He left in a bit of a huff. Just as well. Not our sort of material at all."

"When did he leave?" asked Carston.

"Oh I can't remember exactly. It'll all be on file if you want it."

"Please."

The coffee arrived and was duly poured by the young girl who'd brought it. Carston noticed that Borney's apparently enlightened attitude to equality still didn't allow him to pour coffee when there was a woman there to do it. He smiled at her as he took the cup.

"Was Mrs. Burnham working on anything in particular?" he asked.

Pointedly, Borney waited until the girl had left the room.

"Several things," he said at last. "You'd have to look through her portfolios, maybe talk to Mrs. Napier. She was her assistant. She could bring you up to date there."

"Yes, I'd appreciate that," said Carston. "What about relationships?" he asked as they settled back again. "How did Mrs. Burnham get on with people?"

There was the slightest of hesitations, barely perceptible, before Borney replied.

"Fine, as far as I know. We've never had any ... complaints from her clients. I always found her charming myself. What sort of thing did you have in mind?"

"Nothing specific. I just want to get some sort of idea of what she was like. Might be useful to the investigation."

Borney looked at him over his cup.

"No clues then?" he asked.

Carston took the chance to get his own back for the earlier lecture on financial affairs.

"I'm not sure what they are really."

Borney looked wary.

"I mean, all we do is accumulate information. If any of it's mutually inconsistent, it needs to be rationalized. In the end it's like sterilizing milk, you just get rid of the bits that don't belong. I suppose investigation just means homogenizing facts. I'm not sure where clues fit in to that lot. Now then, about Mrs. Napier ..."

Borney's expression was now one of frank suspicion. Carston knew he'd allowed himself to go too far. He hurried on.

"D'you think you could arrange for me to have a chat with her while I'm here?"

"Of course," said Borney, a new coldness obvious in his tone.

"Thank you," said Carston, before taking refuge in his coffee.

The rest of their conversation was characterized by the distance and dislike which Carston's aside had injected into it. There was, in fact, little more that Borney could offer. He reiterated his praise for Stephanie Burnham's work, knew nothing of her life outside the office and, for someone claiming that she was such a valued colleague, had very little awareness of anything other than the amounts by which her clients' commissions had swelled the company's accounts.

Mrs. Napier was altogether more productive. Carston guessed that she was in her late twenties. She was around five feet four, slimly built and had shiny dark hair cut neatly around very mobile features. She smiled easily, talked in short bursts, and had a way of annotating what she said as she went along. The only thing that prevented her being very attractive was the fact that her choice of outfit was better suited to a color-blind woman at least ten years older.

After a quick flick through various current portfolios, which revealed nothing of immediate interest, her replies to Carston's promptings painted a picture of Stephanie Burnham that was rather different from the one offered by Borney.

"She was a worrier, wasn't she?" she said. "Couldn't let a thing lie. Couldn't trust other people to do it."

"Is that what everybody thought?"

"You'll have to ask them. That's what I found. Always asking if this was ready, or if that had come back. Like I said, always worrying."

"Not easy to work for then, eh?" asked Carston.

"I've had better. Worse too, mind you. You're right, though, she wasn't easy. Between you and me, nobody here liked her much. Shame, really, but there you are."

"Why's that, d'you think?"

"Oh, all sorts of things. Never knew where you were with her for a start. Ambitious, see? One minute she'd be all smiles, the next you couldn't get a word out of her. Lonely, I suppose."

"What d'you mean, lonely? She was married."

Mrs. Napier's look was very expressive. Carston took it to convey either the infelicities of her own marriage, the desolations she'd seen in the marriages of her friends, or both. Whatever its source, it made her skepticism about the whole hallowed institution very clear. For a change, she said nothing. Carston had to press her.

"Did she ever say anything about her marriage, her home life?"

"Not to me."

She stopped, but Carston knew that there was more to come. He waited. Mrs. Napier toyed with a pencil on her desk, her eyes turned down and away from him.

"There's talk of course," she said.

Still Carston waited. Mrs. Napier looked around as if expecting witnesses.

"She was seeing a guy. Lorna saw her in town with him once.

30

Then he came here for her one evening. Younger than her. Nice looking too. It's not right to say it with her dead but he was too good for her."

Carston was amazed at the power of envy or whatever other emotion fueled her reactions to Stephanie Burnham.

"D'you know his name?" he asked.

"Yes. Sleeman. She was always on the phone to him. He rang her here a couple of times. Dr. Sleeman, he called himself."

"D'you know where he lives?"

Mrs. Napier shook her head then suddenly clicked her fingers.

"It might be in her book."

"Book?"

"Yes. She kept some of the numbers of what she called her private clients in her own book."

"And where would I find that?"

"Not sure really. I never saw it. It may be in her office. She could have kept it with her. I don't know."

"That's all right," said Carston. "We'll need to look through her things here anyway. I'll get someone to come round later on today. Now, what was that name you said? The man?"

"Oh, Dr. Sleeman," said Mrs. Napier.

Carston wrote the name in his book and leaned towards her again. He wanted to make the most of her confessional tendencies. She seemed to be enjoying this.

"So you don't think she was getting on too well at home?"

"I wouldn't know about that. She never said anything here. She couldn't've been happy though. Not the way she was."

"How d'you mean?"

Mrs. Napier suddenly leaned forward. The conversation had obviously become a full conspiracy.

"Look," she said, "I don't like talking behind people's backs, but there must have been something wrong there. Started a couple of months ago. All of a sudden she was different. Got worse. Moodier. I think it was the change."

"What change?" asked Carston.

Mrs. Napier looked at him with pity.

"The change. You know, the menopause."

31

Carston felt silly. He blushed.

"That's not her husband's fault though, is it?" he said, to cover his faux pas.

"No. They can help though. And the way she was, I don't think he did."

Carston noticed the generic "they" and felt his blush continue. Whenever the disparity between the sexes came up, he invariably felt guilty for being a man. He pressed on nonetheless.

"What makes you say that?"

"I told you, the way she was. All sort of inside herself. Not normal. Started drinking too."

"How d'you know?"

"You can smell it. Used to come back after lunch sometimes and I'd know she'd had more than a Perrier."

Carston sensed that information and speculation were beginning to get in one another's way. The more Mrs. Napier warmed to her subject, the more her own resentments or envies or whatever they were colored the picture she was painting. There was a light in her brown eyes now and her brows and lips were working even faster as she began to tell of one occasion on which she'd had to field a client's inquiries about a rights issue because Mrs. Burnham was in the lavatory being sick.

The interview was finally interrupted by Borney, who telephoned to ask for a portfolio he needed. It was, apparently, crucial for him to sell off a holding before some dividend or other was declared. The interview with Mrs. Napier had been too full and Carston was ready to leave.

"Well, I mustn't get in the way of high finance," he said.

"Nothing very high about it," said Mrs. Napier picking up some folders and cradling them in her left arm. "Not exactly Wall Street here, you know."

"Still, I won't hold you up."

A question suddenly occurred to him and he was surprised that he hadn't thought of it before.

"How come Mrs. Burnham wasn't at work yesterday?" he asked.

"She phoned in early on. Said she wasn't feeling too good."

"Did she often do that?"

"Now and again. She always took stuff home with her anyway. Usually got on with things. I was quite glad. Gave me a bit of peace and quiet."

Carston smiled, colluding with her, inviting more revelations. She hitched her thumb towards the ceiling.

"Of course, he didn't know about it."

"Who, Mr. Borney?"

"Yes. He'd have us clocking on and off if he could. Probably chain us to our desks."

"Kinky, is he?" said Carston. The woman giggled, producing a surprisingly attractive, musical sound. They were now allies.

Carston laughed with her. She paused in her work.

"Any idea who? You know ..." she asked.

Carston shook his head.

"We've only just started. It's early days yet. That's what all these questions are about."

She went back to her folder collecting.

"I'm sorry. I haven't been much help. Don't know what to say really."

Carston heard himself using the same old formula.

"You've been very helpful. I'm very grateful."

At last she was ready. Carston got up, moved to the door and waited there, holding it open for her. She came to where he was standing and he moved aside for her to pass. When they were in the corridor he closed the door. She stopped and looked up at him.

"If there's anything else I can do, I'd be happy to help."

"I'm sure there will be. I'll get in touch, I promise."

Mrs. Napier smiled and turned to go but then stopped and looked along the corridor, her eyes not focusing on anything in particular.

"Poor Mrs. Burnham," she said. "She wasn't bad really."

"I'll be in touch," said Carston, marveling that the demolition job she'd just done could be so quickly forgotten. He went down the stairs, through the warmth of the receptionist's delight at seeing him again and out to his car.

Driving back to the station, he smiled as he remembered his remarks to Borney about the process of matching information. On

33

this occasion that was already proving a rather elusive technique. According to people who seemed to know, Stephanie Burnham was pregnant, menopausal, and having an affair. Even to someone who had failed to pick up the significance of the expression "the change," it was clear that at least two of these conditions were mutually exclusive. And what was she? A charming colleague or a moody drunk?

He stopped at a red light and drummed his fingers on the steering wheel as he watched the pedestrians crossing ahead of him. The September sun was playing its tricks. Yesterday, the wind had been in the east. Today it had gone through 180 degrees and tempted the schoolgirls out of their cardigans and into white blouses under which theoretically untouched treasures swelled. Carston had once told Kath that he found girls in school uniforms infinitely more exciting than the glistening skin under the string vests favored by Tina Turner. Kath had laughed and, predictably, made comments about geriatric perversions ever since. But Carston knew that his feelings were nearer to love than lust and each time he saw schoolgirls in the sunshine he felt a gentle hunger and a sadness that it could never be satisfied.

Fortunately for him, his priapic meanderings weren't evident to his subordinates back at the station. In fact, only one of them was there. Carston's arrival in the office must have been a quiet one because Detective Constable Fraser, who was sitting at a desk with his back to the door, made no move. Carston stopped and watched him. He was holding the small tape recorder that Carston used to dictate notes into before writing up major reports. Modulating his voice with great care, Fraser said, "*Bonjour. Comment allez-vous?*"

Carston was taken completely by surprise. Fraser's voice went on.

"*Très bien merci. Et vous? ... Je m'appelle Mal Fraser. Comment vous appelez-vous?*"

"*Je m'appelle* Detective Chief Inspector Carston," said Carston, "and that's my tape recorder you've got there."

Fraser leapt out of his chair.

"Oh, sorry sir. I just ... er ... I was just ..."

His voice tailed off. Carston grinned.

"Relax, Fraser," he said. "I'm very impressed. What's it all in aid of?"

"Evening classes, sir. Me and Janice've decided to go to France next year. Thought I ought to learn a bit of the parlyvoo. Less chance o' gettin' ripped off."

Carston looked at the muscles which stretched the material of Fraser's shirt and wondered who'd be stupid enough to try to rip him off.

"Good idea. Not on the firm's time though, eh?"

"No, sir. Sorry, sir."

Carston went through to his own office.

"You're back early anyway," he called back through the door. Fraser came and stood just outside it.

"Aye sir. Waste of time really," he said. "Hardly anybody there."

He'd been doorstepping in Dyson Close and the streets around it with a constable in uniform, trying to find somebody who'd heard or seen anything around the time of the murder.

"No, they're all double earners up that way. Everybody out grafting," said Carston, looking through the papers on his desk.

"Aye. And them that was there didnae ken anything about anybody else. Keep theirselves to theirselves right enough."

"Nice little community, eh?"

"Aye, they wisnae even interested. Just embarrassed more than anything else. There was one thing, though."

Carston looked up. Fraser was waiting for encouragement to go on.

"Well?" said Carston, slightly irritated at having to prompt him.

"It was when I was speakin' to the guy that lives two doors down from the Burnhams' place. Flash bastard, he was. Hoped the murder wouldnae affect property values. Can you believe that?"

"Get on with it, Fraser."

"Aye sir, sorry sir. Anyway, when we was speakin', there was these shots."

Carston stopped riffling through the papers. Fraser had stopped again, pleased to have got his attention. Carston's irritation went up a notch.

35

"Well?" he said.

"Aye. He didnae even seem tae notice them. They was from the other side o' the canal. When I asked him about it, he said there was a clay pigeon place over past the trees."

Carston nodded.

"Yes, I knew there was something like that around there. Forgot all about it though."

"Funny thing was how he didna seem to hear it," said Fraser.

"You get used to anything in time," Carston observed.

"Aye, maybe," said Fraser. "Doesnae help us much though, does it? I mean, who's going to notice a single shot when there's volleys all the time?"

"Right," said Carston. "Is that it?"

"Aye, more or less sir."

"Did you go over to the clay pigeon place?"

"No sir. I came back here first. Told Sergeant Ross about it. He's awa' over there hisself."

"OK. So now you've got nothing to do then, eh?"

Fraser was caught. He began to turn away.

"Well, Ah've …"

Carston lobbed a clutch of folders at him. He just managed to catch them.

"Good. You can sort through these. Mostly stolen cars and petty break-ins. Get the paperwork going. And before that, you can nip down to Borney and Whitcombe's. Clear out Mrs. Burnham's office. Bring it all back here. You'd better get a uniformed boy to go with you again. Ask Sergeant Dwyer. Tell him I said it was OK."

"Right sir," said Fraser, starting to move away. Carston's voice stopped him.

"Fraser."

"Aye sir." The constable turned back again.

Carston's hand was held out.

"*Donnez-moi mon* tape recorder," he said.

Ross was holding a black disc, turning it over and feeling its weight.

"Doesn't look much like a pigeon to me," he said.

Forbes Grant, the owner of the clay pigeon range, was standing beside him. He'd obviously heard the same comment many many times before.

"Neither does a pigeon when it takes off hell for leather in front of you. It's the flight pattern that matters."

Ross just nodded.

"Coming out of the traps, these things are just like birds taking off. Range, angle of flight, everything."

Ross gave the disc back to him.

"Amazing," he said. "So the guns your members use would be the same they use for real birds, would they?"

"Mostly, yes," said Grant.

He was dressed for his part as an overseer of gun sports. Leather and tweed predominated and he had two satchels slung around him. The tight skin of his cheeks and neck was deeply tanned and his right eye was bloodshot.

"Only mostly?" asked Ross.

"Some of them have only got the one gun. Can't afford any more. So they use it for all sorts of things. Even deer sometimes. Astonishing really."

Ross pointed at the clay disc.

"Bit of a difference between that and the Monarch of the Glen," he said.

Grant didn't understand him. He began an explanation about how shot brought down a real bird but how the disc had to be spinning before it would shatter. As he spoke, Ross noted with a little distaste how the fact that he was talking about destruction didn't seem to occur to him. The animals that were his members' targets when they were in the field were just objects with different characteristics which required different cartridge sizes, shot types and loadings. Ross was no vegetarian, and some of the things he'd done in rugby scrums when he'd played lock for the East of Scotland police could almost qualify as carnivorous, but ever since the birth of his daughter Kirsty the previous year, he'd begun to value all forms of life very differently. As he'd stood in the delivery ward, trying to say the right things to Jean, he'd been overcome by a combination of fear and wonder. He could see the top of Kirsty's head held by an impossibly tight circle of skin between his wife's legs. Jean was yelling and swearing for it all to stop. Then suddenly, this tiny body was being hoisted, streaks of blood over its head and chest, and out of it came the scratchy little noise it needed to make to get its breathing mechanisms working. In that instant, for all his strength and size, he'd been suddenly aware of the fragility of everything.

"I've seen a deer," Grant was saying, using his squarish hands to underline the points he was making, "with hardly a mark on it. No blood, nothing at all. Just the impact, you see? Like hitting a brick wall."

Ross cut through his reminiscing.

"How long's Mr. Burnham been a member?"

Grant had to pause to orientate himself away from the hunting pictures in which he'd been indulging.

"Oh, best part of a year now. They joined when we had an open night in ..."

"They?" asked Ross.

Grant looked at him.

"Yes. He and his wife."

"She a member too?"

"Well ... not really. I mean, she's on the books but we rarely saw her after the first week or two. It was more ... social with her, I think." He stopped and sniffed before adding, in a lower, dismissive tone, "Not that she had many of the social graces."

"Oh?"

"No. I know she's dead and everything but I don't think many of our members will mourn her too long."

"Why's that?"

"Too sharp. Sarcastic. Especially for a woman. Didn't make any friends here that I know of."

"Enemies then?"

Grant shook his head.

"Wouldn't think so. She wasn't here often enough."

"When did you see her last?" asked Ross.

Grant thought a bit.

"It must've been sometime last month, I'd say. I'm not sure, but I think she bought him some kit for his birthday or something. I don't remember when she last did any shooting."

"How about Mr. Burnham? Did he have any particular friends among the other members?"

Once again, Grant took his time.

"Not that I've noticed. Bit of a snob in a strange sort of way."

"Oh?" said Ross.

"Yes. Not the normal sort of snob. Can't be, really, can he? Glorified salesman, that's all he is, for all his cash."

Ross made no response. Grant didn't seem to notice. He was intent on demolishing Burnham.

"No, more of what folks call an intellectual snob really. Liked to think so anyway. Didn't cut much ice around here."

Ross wasn't surprised.

"Have you seen much of them recently?" he asked.

"Not her. He was here, though. Usual session, Tuesday night."

"The day before yesterday?"

"That's right. He always comes on Tuesdays. Well, most weeks anyway. Actually, he's getting to be quite a good shot."

"Were there many others here that night?" asked Ross, flipping open his notebook.

Grant hunched his shoulders and lifted his two satchels higher around him.

"Look, I'm not sure I should be talking about our members like this. I mean, it's their business, isn't it? Shouldn't you be asking them yourself?"

"I would if I knew who they were and which ones were here," said Ross. "Got a membership list?"

Grant hesitated.

"Well?" insisted Ross, his impatience growing.

"Yes. In the clubhouse."

"Let's go then," said Ross, already on his way.

Grant tried to show some reluctance, but Ross was ignoring him. Grant hurried after him.

"Yes, I suppose that would probably be best," he said.

As they walked together, Grant rather huffily explained his reticence. As proprietor of a gun club, he was constantly having to deal with all sorts of people asking what he considered to be absurd questions. Ever since Michael Ryan had gone on his insane spree in

39

Hungerford, it seemed that anyone involved in shooting for sport had been suspect.

"You wouldn't believe the people I've had here, the questions they've asked," he said, his head shaking at his own disbelief in it.

"Like what?" asked Ross.

"Oh, all sorts of things. What do we wear? Are we all married? Have any of us been in the army? Or jail, for God's sake! They're looking for lunatics."

Ross reflected briefly that being able to talk about killing things as if they were just problems of trajectory and velocity to be solved wasn't exactly middle-of-the-road normal. He contented himself with a small taunt.

"You got any?"

"What?" asked Grant.

"Nutters."

Grant stopped.

"Lunatics," explained Ross, without breaking his stride. Grant started walking again but stayed a pace behind him. His silence showed that co-operation was over. Nothing more was said until they got to the building. As they went inside, Ross relented.

"Look, I wasn't meaning to be rude. But Mrs. Burnham's dead. Shot. When that sort of thing happens, we have to know about any folk who spend their time around guns. Have to check everything."

Grant was unlocking a small cupboard behind the shop counter.

"Yes, of course," he said, his voice still indicating his mistrust of the policeman. "We're all potential …"—he searched for Ross's word—"… nutters, aren't we?"

"Just the normal process of elimination, sir," said Ross.

"You think somebody in the club did it, then?" asked Grant, lifting an old-fashioned black ledger off a shelf.

"How do I know? That's what all the questions are for."

"A local … nutter … would be convenient, though, wouldn't he?"

"Only if he did it," said Ross.

"Well, I don't think you're going to get much luck with this particular line." Grant put the ledger on the counter. "All our people come here for sport."

"Right," said Ross, resisting the temptation to suggest that sport

40

and death were the same thing where guns were concerned. He picked up the ledger and flicked through the pages.

"How many members?" he asked.

"Seventy-two, theoretically," said Grant. "Only about twenty or thirty come regularly, though. Some of them we don't see from one year to the next."

"I'll take this, OK?" Ross indicated the ledger.

"For how long?"

"As long as it takes to get a photocopy. You'll get it back tomorrow."

"I suppose that's all right," said Grant, his reluctance very obvious.

Ross wrote a quick receipt and handed it over the counter.

"Was there anybody here yesterday afternoon?" he asked, as if as an afterthought.

Grant looked at him, his eyes narrow and suspicious.

"When she was killed, you mean? Can't say for sure."

"Why not?"

"Fifteen of us were at Gleneagles for a shoot. Jackie Stewart's place. The club was locked up, but members have got keys. They can come and go as they please. Sometimes a few get together for a wee competition," Grant said primly.

"What time did you all leave?"

"Leave where?"

"Here. To go to Gleneagles."

Grant's leathery features folded into a distinct smirk.

"It wasn't a coach trip, sergeant. Our members have got cars, you know. We met down there."

Ross wanted to reach over and squeeze his jaw to push the smirk up into his skull.

"How about yourself?" he asked, controlling his tone very carefully.

"I left at about half past eleven. Wanted to be there early. I'd arranged it all, you see?"

"Busy man, eh?" said Ross.

Grant looked at him sharply, aware of the aggression that was lying just under the words.

"That's right," he said.

41

"And there was nobody here shooting when you left?"

Grant paused only briefly to think before shaking his head.

Ross had had enough.

"Right then. Mustn't take up any more of your time for now," he said.

"Not at all. Glad to be able to help," said Grant with no attempt at sincerity.

Ross felt his dislike for the man's smugness pushing up in his throat. Grant lived in a little world of spinning clay discs and bleeding animals and gave the impression that little outside of it was of much significance. Ross sensed and resented the egocentricity of money and the confident superiority of class. As a boy in Perthshire, he'd been subjected to it far too often when he worked in his father's small grocer's shop. In the end, he'd preferred to do without the five pounds he'd earn for a Saturday morning behind the counter because he hated the women who'd come in with faces like magazine photographs and ridiculous posh voices and treat him like something they'd stepped in on the pavement.

Without a word, he picked up the ledger, turned his back on Grant and walked out of the door. He threw the book into the back seat of his car, climbed in and fastened his seat belt. As he let out the clutch, he looked through the window of the clubhouse and saw Grant take one of the guns from a rack behind him and break it open.

"Happy hunting," he muttered as his wheels spun in the gravel.

As usual, the prospect of reading through paperwork and filling in reports, requisitions and all the other forms that some administrator had designed to keep himself in a job left Carston looking for an alternative way to spend his time. Luckily, in an envelope on top of the pile, he found Ross's beautifully printed transcript of his interview with Burnham. Ross was always looking for ways to make the organization of his time more efficient. The latest angle was computerization. He'd bought himself a PC with all the recommended software and, the previous evening, he'd profited from his wife's absence and the fact that he had a real document to work on to start using the word-processing package. Since he was new to all the techniques involved, it had taken him longer to complete the transcript than if he'd written it in copperplate with a quill pen. But when it was finally printed out (just after two in the morning), on his new bubble jet printer, it looked very crisp and professional.

Carston read through it with something like enjoyment. Ross had already given him a précis of its more interesting aspects during their conversation in the office the night before and the formal signed statement was on file, but reading the actual words and sensing the changes in mood took Carston beyond the facts and into speculation about the person relating them. It was essentially a monologue. Ross had had to do very little in the way of prompting and, when Burnham did pause, his questions simply kept redirecting the flow into other areas of interest.

For all the stress that he must have been feeling, Burnham's character came off the page very strongly. He was clearly an educated, articulate man who reacted to the events and irritations of his day with apparent honesty. There was no attempt to play the grieving husband and yet, as well as the occasional barb directed at what he considered to be unreasonable behavior from his wife, there were, as Ross had suggested, scattered indications of his affection for her.

"I was hoping she'd help me with our half-yearly audit this month," read Carston. "She's learned a helluva lot from her dealings with Borney and his crowd. Flips figures around like bloody Pythagoras. Astonishing really. We could have cracked that over a weekend. Now it'll be bloody Patterson and his robots from accounts. God knows how I'll manage to deal with him and sort this out at the same time. Bloody nuisance, that is."

Carston turned to the next page. The word "marriage" caught his eye. Burnham had gone on talking about the audit at Calder and McStay and Ross had asked with apparent ingenuousness whether the pressures at work were particularly insistent at present.

"No," Burnham had replied. "Just the usual daily garbage. They bounce off me really. Can't afford to let them matter. You come home, take off your coat, dump the stresses of business in the hall and walk into the niggles of marriage, don't you?"

This provoked another question from Ross. Carston read on.

"Oh, don't get excited," was Burnham's reply. "We weren't at one another's throats. No more than you and your wife or any other poor sods. Anyway, none of it's important, is it? Not when this sort of thing happens. Gives it all a new angle."

Ross brought the interview back from philosophy to facts. Carston came to the passage that Ross had read to him the previous evening.

"... selfish bitch," he read. "I don't know what was the matter with her. She was ferocious. Shouting. Violent. The first time for six weeks and it was as if we were strangers. Of course, she was half-cut. Not the best condition to be in when you're trying to be sexy. Poor old Steph, she was never very clever at sorting that out. Eleven o'clock in the morning and she's slurring her words, stumbling about. God knows why."

Carston made a note on a pad at the side of his desk. Burnham had put McIntosh's finding from the blood sample in context. Evidently, there was nothing new about Stephanie Burnham's tendency to over-indulge. At least one of Mrs. Napier's slanders seemed to have some justification.

He heard the door to the outer office open and leaned over to see who it was. Ross was hanging his coat on one of the hooks on the wall beside the window. He called to him. Ross looked round and came through to the office. He put the ledger he'd collected from Grant on the desk. His movements were quick and Carston knew that he wasn't happy.

"What's this?" he asked.

"List of members of that gun club place."

"Sounds like you didn't enjoy the visit much."

"You could say that."

Carston waited for him to go on, his head tilted back.

"I had a word with his lordship, the prat who owns it or runs it or whatever. Stuck-up bastard!"

"That's your objective assessment, is it?" said Carston, trying to ease him out of his bad mood.

"He was a bloody good argument for police brutality," said Ross, sitting in a chair in the corner of the office and loosening his tie. "Running an exclusive little club for folk who like to kill things but don't want their privacy or their trips to Gleneagles fucked up just because another member gets herself totaled."

Carston was turning the pages of the ledger.

"Ah, so we won't be finding many social workers in here then?" he said.

Ross laughed without much humor.

"Not if they're all like dickhead Grant."

Carston was aware of Ross's sensitivity to class divisions. On one job they'd had down in Perth, Ross had pointed out the shop he'd grown up in and told him all about the Pekinese owners and Range Rover drivers who'd made his Saturday mornings so painful. Carston's own resentment of unearned privilege had never been very strong. His childhood had been in Devon, where most of his family had worked on trawlers or in the fish markets. All of their connections had been dictated by the sea and its demands so there was never much time for the distractions of class. It wasn't until he got a scholarship to the local direct grant school and found that, in a mock election they held, he was one of only four Labour voters in a class of thirty-two, that he noticed the strange separations that people seemed to need to make them feel secure. Nowadays, even though, politically, he was in an even smaller minority in the force, he was still slightly baffled by the urge people felt to establish and display an elevated social status.

He closed the ledger and held it up.

"Tell you what then," he said, "if this lot are as bad as you suspect they're going to be, we'll send Fraser along to talk to them, eh?"

Ross frowned his incomprehension. Carston put the book down and explained.

"I mean, if they're all members of the gentry, they'd only upset you. And I'd be too tempted to take the piss out of them. That wouldn't get us very far, so we send our resident man of the people, straight out of the bottom drawer. They'll hate it, but he'll do a bloody good job."

Ross grinned.

"Devious bugger," he said.

"Devious bugger, *sir*, if you don't mind," said Carston. "Now then, where do we go next?"

They talked through the information they'd already assembled. As yet, it didn't amount to very much. Until they received the full scene of crime and autopsy reports, they couldn't start directing specific questions at the people they talked to. For Ross, this was an inconvenience. He wanted to be definite, dispense with irrelevancies, collect facts that jigsawed together. Carston, on the other hand, was at home with a vagueness in which he could invent little scenarios, multiply motives and create connections that the facts might prohibit. He was a believer, for example, in the value of the newish tendency for psychological profiling of suspects, the process by which a picture of probable characteristics is built up in order to target a particular type of individual. In this case, it was the enigma of the victim's personality which fascinated him. At work she'd been admired, disliked and, ultimately, pitied. She seemed to have coped with the stresses and complications of financial transactions and yet was frequently drunk in the middle of the day. Less enigmatically, perhaps, she'd been sexless as far as her husband was concerned, but managed to interest a younger man who, according to Mrs. Napier, was too good for her. The mixture gave Carston endless permutations. Ross was less impressed.

"Aye, interesting all right," he said when Carston paused in his musings, "but not much use, is it?"

Carston was still thoughtful.

"Jim, she was sexy and sexless, pregnant and menopausal, drunk and competent ..."

"And now she's dead," said Ross.

"Yes, but this murder's specific. There's no robbery, no casual accident. This was intended. There was something about her that was ... definite enough to make somebody do away with her."

"So it's her fault then?"

"Who knows? Look, if she is all these things, she's a very complicated lady. And if she isn't, somebody's lying somewhere. Either way, we need to know her better if we're going to sort it out."

Ross sat back in his chair, clasping his hands behind his head. The gesture turned into a stretch which continued to develop into a full yawn.

"So you don't think we've got him," he said at last.

46

Carston looked a question at him.

"The husband," said Ross.

"Well, he's got to be favorite so far but we haven't exactly looked around much, have we?"

"No, but I wouldn't want you forgetting him while you're finding out who his wife was."

There was no insubordination in Ross's remark. Since they'd started working together, Carston had allowed him equal status in their investigations and encouraged complete openness. Ross knew that, in the end, decisions and the responsibilities that went with them belonged to his boss, but in the processes that led up to them his own contribution could be as free as he liked.

"Right," said Carston. "And who else have we got?"

"Nobody yet," said Ross. "I wouldn't mind locking that Forbes Grant guy up for a night or two, but that's personal."

Carston smiled.

"Well, there's this guy she was seeing. We'll need to find him."

"Do we know who he is?" asked Ross.

"Woman at her office mentioned him. Sleeman. A doctor, apparently."

"Got an address?"

"No. Fraser's down there looking through her stuff now. If there's nothing there, we'll have to run some checks."

"How about friends, neighbors?"

Carston shook his head.

"Nothing yet. Was there an address book amongst her things?"

"Haven't had time to get round to that yet."

"That's a nice little job for this afternoon then," said Carston.

"Right," said Ross.

He stood up and stretched again.

"Tired?" asked Carston.

"A bit." Ross pointed at the report on the desk. "I was up late printing out that stuff last night. Got a bit involved."

"Yes, I noticed how pretty it was," said Carston. "I thought computers were supposed to save time."

"It will when I've cracked it," said Ross. "It's a new operating system. More RAM than I'm used to."

"What's it like to be young and modern?"

"You'll never know."

"Cheeky bastard," said Carston.

Ross grinned and went into the outer office to start looking over the papers waiting for him.

Their relationship was good and Carston was grateful for it. When he'd arrived from England, he'd expected resistance from the people into whose territory he'd been drafted. Moves between forces were always difficult, except for members of the drug squad, and they always created suspicion in the new set of colleagues. On top of all that, Carston's unfamiliarity with Scottish law and procedures and the fact that he already held the rank of inspector only increased the mistrust. He'd known all this when he saw the advert in the *Police Gazette* for a post in Strathclyde. He knew his chances of being selected were better in such a large force but was still slightly surprised when he'd got the job. After an intensive study of Scottish law and an eight-week course near Alloa, he and Kath had moved to a police house in Glasgow while they began looking for a place of their own.

His surprise was much greater when, after only three months, the call came for him to transfer to a much smaller force in the east. The chief constable of West Grampian had apparently decided that his force needed an injection of new thinking and the things he had heard about Carston persuaded him that it was worth taking a chance with a foreigner. So far, the move had been inspired and Carston knew that a lot of the credit for that belonged to Ross. They'd formed an instant partnership of mutual respect, their attitudes and methods complemented one another and they'd even managed to become friends.

Carston was looking through the names in the black ledger when Ross called through to him.

"You said Sleeman, didn't you?"

Carston looked up.

"That's right. Why? You got something?"

Ross came back into his office and passed over an address book.

"It's hers," he said.

The book was open at "S." There were three entries. The bottom

48

one was in pencil. It simply gave the name, Bob Sleeman, and a telephone number.

"That'll do," said Carston, reaching for the phone. He dialed and waited.

"What code's this?" he asked.

Ross sat on the edge of the desk and looked at the number.

"Not sure," he said. "Morayshire somewhere, I think."

A voice on the phone proved him right. Unfortunately, it was an answering machine. Its message was something of a surprise.

"Hello. This is the Findhorn Yachting Association. I'm sorry there's no one here to take your call at present but if you'd like to leave your name and number, we'll get back to you as soon as we can. After the tone please."

Carston waited, then spoke.

"This is Detective Chief Inspector Carston of the West Grampian police. I'm trying to get in touch with a Dr. Bob Sleeman and I'd be grateful if he'd ring me back or if someone could help me locate him."

He gave his number and rang off.

"The Findhorn Yachting Association," he said, in disbelief. "What sort of phone number is that to give your girlfriend?"

"Maybe he works there," said Ross.

"As a doctor?"

"Or maybe he just didn't want to give her his home number. He's probably married."

"Yes, more than likely," said Carston. "Guns and yachts, eh? Just the sort of circles you love to move in, Jim."

Ross stood up, made a small V-sign, added "sir" to it and picked up the address book.

"Nothing much else here," he said, riffling through the pages. "Just the usual stuff. Business numbers, doctor, dentist, garage, insurance company. And there's a few down around Stratford. Family, I suppose, unless it's where they lived before."

"What's that number for Sleeman again?" asked Carston, pulling his notebook towards him.

Ross read the number. Carston made a note of it, then tapped the page in front of him.

49

"Oh yes," he said. "Here's another one. Somebody called Paul Roach. Used to work with her. See if you can find him. Have a chat if he's around."

"What's the angle?"

"She got promoted over him. Upset him a bit. He left the firm. Better check him out."

Ross was glad of something definite to do.

"D'you want to keep this?" he said, holding up the address book.

"No, put it back with the rest of the stuff. Get the names checked when you get a minute, just to see who they all are, how they're connected with her."

"Right," said Ross.

He took the book and went back out into the office.

Carston hummed a toneless little tune to himself as he reached for the papers he'd put aside earlier. There wasn't much more he could do with the Burnham business for the moment, and he knew that his tendency to put off routine things made them pile to near insurmountable proportions in a very short time. Making himself work through them was frustrating but led to an inordinate satisfaction when he finished.

He was interrupted by phone calls throughout the afternoon, of course. They were mostly welcome because they gave him a rest from the PF127s and the SO38s and 39s which he had to fill in, but none of them were of any consequence. The most interesting one came just before four o'clock. It was Kath.

"Hullo, love," he said, genuinely pleased.

"Hullo, Jack. Any idea what time you'll be home?"

"Not really. I won't be late, though, unless something comes up. Why?"

"Can you do me a favor?"

"Sure. What is it?"

"Got a pencil?"

"Yep," said Carston, reaching across for one.

"Right. Nip in to B and Q's and get me a piece of plywood or hardboard thirty-two inches by twenty-five."

"Eh? What for?" said Carston, scribbling the numbers.

"Never mind. It's my new hobby," said Kath.

"Interesting. Does it involve me at all?"

"It could do."

Carston lowered his voice.

"Will it hurt?" he asked.

"Not when it's all plumbed in."

"Christ," said Carston. "I'll be home early."

Burnham's XJS slid through the late afternoon towards Aberdeen. Although the police had rung to say that he could go back home any time he wanted, the night alone in the hotel had made him want to see Barbara. The thought of his house made him angry, nervous. He didn't understand the things that had gone on in the study. It was something he'd often wished for but he couldn't yet comprehend its reality. Now that he'd had a night to reflect on it all, the weary, supercilious pose he usually affected didn't seem to sit so easily on him. These were events that defied credibility. Stephanie's death was like a black incision in his life. All previous modes had to be revised, renegotiated. When the investigations were over, if he was still at liberty, everything had to start again, but without deceptions this time.

Instead of following the direct route, he'd cut across country to join the main road up from Dundee and was cruising along the dual carriageway at around eighty-five. His mind was numb, empty. He'd expected it to crowd with thoughts of Stephanie, questions, the turmoil that extreme distress generates. Instead, it had taken its usual leave and resurfaced only when, at fairly frequent intervals, some young, shirt-sleeved rep would feel the need to overtake him. The individual challenge implicit in their maneuvers brought him back to the insistence of the present. He became the achieving Michael Burnham again. He'd wait for the screaming, protesting SRi or Astra to come alongside and then ease away, effortlessly lifting the needle above the one hundred mark. It was childish, stupid, but it gave him the small satisfaction of affirming that while youth was definitely on their side, power was on his.

It was just after six when he came down the hill towards the River Dee. He crossed the bridge and drove up to Great Western Road. Turning left at the lights, he followed the North Deeside

Road until he came to the turning which led to a small development of five houses. The second house was a neat detached villa, set discreetly against a small copse of birch trees and partly hidden by a beech hedge. Its walls were faced with granite, except for the one which gave onto the Dee valley. There, the architect had managed to create what was effectively one giant window. Thanks to an absurdly generous divorce settlement, all this belonged to Barbara Stone.

He'd telephoned from the car to check that she was in and tell her he was on the way. As he lifted his key to the lock, he was surprised and mildly alarmed to find the front door slightly open. Recent events sent images of dozens of TV movies flashing in his mind—devastated rooms, the contents of drawers and cupboards strewn across them. He went inside carefully. There were no shocks. Everything was as it should be. He heard low music coming from the main bedroom.

"Barbara," he called softly. "Darling."

There was no reply. He shut the door, threw his coat over a chair and, calling her name again, went through to where the music was playing.

She was sitting in front of the mirror, a peach-colored silk dressing gown around her shoulders and a brandy glass beside her.

"Darling," said Burnham, "I thought you'd ..."

She looked at him in the mirror, raised her finger to her lips and said "Sssh."

He stopped as she turned slowly towards him.

"Take your clothes off," she said, her voice breathless again but this time with no girlishness in it, just woman. The sound was low and slow.

He smiled, tilted his head back and closed his eyes.

"Look, I don't think we're going to ..."

"Do as you're told," she insisted, with no change of inflexion.

Burnham was tired, still confused. He didn't want complications of any sort and with Barbara even small talk could get heated. He began to loosen his tie and unbutton his shirt. She nodded.

"That's better," she said, turning away and moving through to the bathroom. "And when you've finished, come in here."

As Burnham took the rest of his clothes off, he could see himself in the mirror. He was used to the face. He saw it every day, and wasn't aware of any aging process in it. Give or take a pouch or two, it was the face that had been with him since his teens. The forehead went back further than before, but the skin wasn't lined, the eyes were still clear and, in his opinion, the overall effect was attractive enough, maybe even handsome. It was the body underneath it that left no room for illusions.

The shoulders were OK but from a point some three or four inches below his pectoral muscles, things were beginning to sag. He wasn't fat, but a crescent of light shadow that hung from his hips down under his navel betrayed the fact that his stomach wasn't flat any more and when he turned sideways to check how bad the damage was, the image of youthful maturity was replaced irremediably with that of irrevocable middle age. He hated what he saw and he was unwilling to parade his decline in front of Barbara. On cue, her voice summoned him.

"What the hell are you doing, Michael?"

Suddenly, as he looked at the man in the mirror, the thought of Stephanie's body came to him, its arms twisted and the blood pooling out of its mouth, and another sort of disgust took over. What insensitivity made him able to be concerned about his waistline? What the hell did it matter? The real world was made of other things. He shook his head at his reflection, said "Bastard" to it and went quickly into the bathroom.

She'd taken off her dressing gown and the sight of her flowing, athletic body made the memory of Stephanie even more brutal. It was also a bitter reminder of the years between himself and this woman who claimed to love him. Her legs were long, her skin was pale with the sheen of mother of pearl and her movements were slow, simple and provocative. She was no female stereotype; her breasts were too small for that, her hips too slim. And yet, to Burnham, everything about her was utterly beautiful.

He was standing, just looking at her. She smiled, then, without a word, simply, gently, she took his hand and led him unresisting to the shower. As she turned the spray on and began the slow business of massaging lather into his shoulders, down his back and between his legs, he felt the weariness and strain drawn from him to be washed away with the foam and the water. Amazed, he noticed that he was crying again. But the quiet tears that came from his eyes this time were not for pity or sadness; they were simply an expression of his relief that, for the moment, things were being taken care of.

Chapter Three

At the same time that Burnham was relaxing in the shower, thirty miles further west Carston was solemnly handing Kath a piece of hardboard.

"Thanks," she said and took it to the cupboard along the hall.

"Well?" he said, still standing inside the front door. "Are you going to tell me what it's for?"

She simply beckoned him. He followed her and stuck his head round the cupboard door. It was more a small room than a cupboard and he saw that she'd been clearing it out.

"Come in," she said.

"Oh I see," said Carston. "It's like that, is it?"

She bundled him through the door and shut it. They stood close together in semi-darkness. Kath was still carrying the piece of hardboard.

"What now?" said Carston. "Don't tell me. You wobble that and we sing 'Tie me kangaroo down, sport.'"

Kath laughed.

"No, I'm not wobbling anything. Look," she said, turning and holding the hardboard over the small window which let light through from the hall. The darkness was suddenly total.

"See?" said Kath.

"No, not a thing," said Carston.

"Exactly," said Kath, taking the board away and opening the door again. "Total darkness."

They went back out into the hall.

"Well, that's very interesting," said Carston as he followed her through to the kitchen. "D'you want to go and have a rest while I call the doctor?"

55

Kath leaned the hardboard against the wall behind the door.

"I'm making a darkroom," she said.

"What for?"

"What do people usually do in darkrooms?"

As she said it, she knew what his response would be, so she answered her own question.

"Processing films, developing prints. I've enrolled at an evening class at the Technical College."

Carston was genuinely pleased at the news. When they'd been discussing the move to Scotland, he'd been concerned at the upheaval it meant for her. Unlike him, she had good friends down south and, without a job to come to, the potential for loneliness and disorientation was considerable. He had no fears about her being able to cope; she was stronger than he was when it came to dealing with change. Typically, she'd begun to make friends the moment they'd settled in Glasgow. Then, with the move across to the east, she'd formed new contacts just as quickly, despite the clannish reputation of the locals. This made it much easier for Carston to feel that the move had been right and that they belonged in their new surroundings. As well as still loving her, Carston admired this resilience and was grateful for the fact that her first impulse was always a positive one. Without Kath, he'd have succumbed to his own innate pessimism long ago.

After a meal of artichokes with garlic butter and pasta in a tomato and olive sauce, they sat in their living room, finishing the bottle of Cambon la Pelouse and, although not in the least hungry, picking at slivers of Brie. For Carston, this was contentment. However distorted his vision of things became as the result of dealing with the less appealing side of human behavior during working hours, the timelessness of sitting with Kath and washing his palate with a mellow wine was an experience that straightened things out, restored perspectives.

"Shall we watch the news?" she asked.

"If you like."

Carston sat forward, picked up the television's remote control and pressed a button. The news had already started. At first Carston listened to the patronizing evasions of rival politicians as they were asked about the latest economic forecasts, but their complacency irritated and insulted him and before long he let his eyes drift from the screen to the framed drawings of fishing boats and seascapes on the wall behind it. At the top of the wall, a piece of wallpaper was beginning to peel away. It had been like that ever since they'd moved in and they'd both stopped noticing it. It started him thinking of all the things he ought to be doing about the house. There were tiles off the roof, the gutters and pipes needed painting, the garden had been good during the summer but now its beds needed clearing out and the lawn ought to be cut and spiked.

"Good," said Kath, surprising him out of his dreaming.

"What is?" he said, looking back at the screen which she was still watching.

The fat little weatherman was waving an agitated hand over the south of England and pushing white clouds away towards Belgium.

"The weather," said Kath. "It's going to be fine for a while."

Carston looked at the sun over eastern Scotland and the predicted temperatures. She was right. It promised to be one of those Indian summers that Kath's friends in the neighborhood had claimed came frequently to the region but which he had yet to experience.

"Ideal for a trip to Loch Muick," she added.

He looked at her. She was looking steadfastly at the television screen.

"I'd love to, Kath, but this inquiry ..."

She turned and smiled.

"I know, love. Don't worry. I was just teasing."

Carston felt guilty. For ages, he'd been promising that they'd make a trip into the hills. They'd been told about the beauty of Deeside but as yet had only experienced it from the car. Loch Muick and Lochnagar, the mountain which rose to the north of it, were favorite walks for everybody within sixty miles of them.

"Tell you what," he said. "If we can make a bit of progress this week, I'll try to grab half a day at the weekend."

"Not enough," said Kath. "That'd only give us time to drive there, have a quick look and drive back. Never mind, it was a good idea."

There was no accusation in her tone but it made Carston feel worse.

"Right," he said. "A day. I'll make the time up in the evening, when we get back. Get more work done at night anyway."

Kath shook her head.

"Jack, it doesn't matter, really. I know that …"

"Sssh," said Carston. "It's settled. That's a promise. This weekend. Unless there's a massacre somewhere."

Kath pointed a threatening finger at him.

"If you let me down, there'll be one right here."

Carston smiled and sat back. The weatherman had disappeared and a smiling young man with sandy-colored hair and a silly mustache was saying enthusiastic things about Partick Thistle. Carston drifted off into thoughts of standing on a mountain top surrounded by people wearing special socks and shoes and humming folk music.

The phone made him jump.

"I bet that's a massacre," said Kath.

Carston smiled and went to answer the call.

"Carston," he said.

"Good. I hear you wanted me to get in touch."

The voice was a deep tenor with the rounded tones of the highlands. It wasn't one he knew.

"Bob Sleeman's the name," it went on. "Findhorn. You left a message."

"Ah yes. Dr. Sleeman. Thank you for calling."

As he spoke, Carston had time to wonder why Sleeman was phoning him at home. The number he'd left on the Findhorn answering machine was for the office and they wouldn't have passed on his home number to a stranger.

"So what can I do for you?" asked Sleeman.

"Well, I'd rather like to have a word with you."

"Yes, I wondered whether you would. Stephanie, I suppose, isn't it?"

"Mrs. Burnham, yes," said Carston.

"Thought so. Well, when d'you want to do it?"

"Whenever it's convenient." Carston pulled a diary out of his inside pocket.

"Do I have to come down to Cairnburgh?" asked Sleeman. "I could, but ..."

His hesitation showed that he wasn't keen on the idea. Recent memories of the weather forecast were still in Carston's mind and the thought of a drive up to the Moray Firth suddenly seemed very attractive.

"No, no, I'll come up to you," he said. "Is tomorrow too soon?"

"No. What time?"

Carston thought for a moment.

"About ten-thirty, eleven?"

"Fine," said Sleeman.

"D'you live in Findhorn itself?"

"Sort of, yes. D'you know it?"

"No."

"Tell you what, then. There's a stone jetty there. I'll meet you at the end of it and we'll go to my place if you like."

"Sounds good to me."

"Right," said Sleeman, and he hung up before Carston could thank him for calling.

"Findhorn?" said Kath, looking across the room at him.

"Yes. Mrs. Burnham's fancy man. He lives up there."

"At the foundation?"

"Don't think so," said Carston.

There was a little community living at the Findhorn Foundation, believers in the good life, organic foods, spiritual energies, all the sorts of things that Carston had grown impatient with around the age of thirty. He didn't know much about them and hoped very much that Sleeman wasn't connected with them. The prospect of being assured that the whole affair was explicable by bad karma didn't attract him. What he did like, though, was the thought of a solitary drive up to the coast in sunshine. As he poured another glass of wine for them both, he began to hum a tune which he thought was from Mozart but which was, in fact, so far out of pitch that it was nearer to Sid Vicious.

To be sure of getting to Findhorn by ten-thirty, Carston had to leave home straight after breakfast, which meant missing the usual morning's briefing. He phoned Ross at home, told him where he was going and they talked over the things that still needed doing, sorting out who should be assigned to what.

"What about that guy who left her firm?" asked Carston. "The one she got promoted over?"

"Roach. Yes, he's on my list," said Ross. "He's working for a building society in Jedd Street."

"OK. I should be back in the middle of the afternoon. I'll look over what we've got then. Don't forget to set Fraser on the shooters."

"You make him sound like a rottweiler."

"Well?"

"Aye, I see what you mean. Anything else?"

"Nothing I can think of. I want to talk to the husband myself as soon as I can. Find out if he's back at work, will you? Make an appointment for me. Soon as possible. Come to think of it, maybe we'd better both go."

"Right," said Ross. "Is that it?"

"I think so. Have a nice day."

"You're the one who's driving up to the coast."

"Privilege of rank," said Carston.

Ross smiled as he hung up. Beside him a complicated set of figures was spread across a computer screen. He pressed a button. The figures disappeared to be replaced by a graph consisting of a series of columns which got taller from left to right. He pressed another button and a cursor in the shape of a cross began flashing in the center of the screen. He moved it to a point above the graph, typed "AGE/WEIGHT" in capital letters and pressed the return key. The graph was reinstated with its new title attached.

He was trying to fathom the mysteries of spreadsheets and their uses and since he had no data of his own worth recording, he'd set up a table listing his daughter's weight at various stages of her development. He'd spent most of the previous evening manipulating the sparse set of figures until he'd created tables of variables which were intended to predict volumes for given weights, worked out parameters to measure surface areas for those weight/volume ratios and altogether elevated Kirsty's simple poundage to a complexity that wouldn't have been out of place in a statement from the Chancellor of the Exchequer. He looked once more at the results of his work, saved it all, switched off the machine and left for the station.

The team was already waiting for him. A busy set of rotas and the fact that West Grampian was still understaffed meant that only a small group could be spared for the case. As well as Carston and himself, there were just five constables. Two of them, Bellman and Thom, had been specially seconded.

The doorstepping in and around Dyson Close had been done without producing anything of obvious value. The next trawl would have to be through people whose names had come up in the course of the initial inquiries. Ross gave Stephanie Burnham's address book to Bellman and Thom and told them to phone every number in it to get whatever information they could about her. WDC McNeil's job was to get the names of the clients whose accounts Mrs. Burnham had handled in the previous two months and sound them out about their contacts with her. And DCs Fraser and Spurle had the list of names of the gun club members. As he briefed this last pair, Ross was very careful. He didn't want his own opinions coloring their investigations.

"Just find out where they were on Wednesday afternoon. Ask if they knew either of the Burnhams. Get them to talk about the club if you can. Nothing indiscreet, just their general thoughts about it. Is it any good? Are there any others around that are better? Stuff like that."

"Just socializin', like?" said Fraser.

Ross smiled at the thought of Fraser swilling back pints and playing darts with the likes of Colonel this and Mr. Hyphen-Hyphen that.

"Exactly," he said.

"OK," said Fraser. "Is that it?"

"That's it," said Ross.

"*Très bien*, sarge. *Au revoir.*" The constable stood up.

Ross stared at him without replying.

"It's French," said Fraser.

Ross's stare continued.

"Piss off," he said.

When they'd left, he looked through the papers on his desk, sorted them quickly into an order of priority and decided that none of them needed immediate action. He wanted to get out of the office before the phone started its daily pestering with tales of road accidents, pub fights and petty larcenies. Not that there was any sort of league table of preferred felonies in his mind, but he didn't like cluttering things up. His gut feeling told him that they needn't look too much further than Burnham for the perpetrator in this case and the sooner they'd brought all the evidence together, the sooner they'd be able to charge him. Unlike Carston, he didn't look for complications, but his application to details was just as thorough and, until the final proofs had been assembled, his mind was open.

It was this conscientiousness that, less than twenty minutes later, was making Paul Roach feel a little uncomfortable as Ross's questions drew him out. The two of them were sitting in a small office in the Grampian and Moray Building Society in Jedd Street. Ross's notebook was open on the desk in front of him and his dictaphone was recording their conversation.

Roach was in his mid-twenties. His dark blue, double-breasted suit, his well-cut hair and an air of scrubbed cleanness were all part of the confident exterior his job required him to present to the public, but the expression on his face showed exactly how wary this encounter was making him feel. He'd expressed surprise, although no regret, at the news of Stephanie Burnham's death and, as they talked about his work at the Grampian and Moray, he was trying to work out what Ross was after.

From what they'd said so far, it seemed to Ross that the biggest attraction of Roach's present job was the fact that he and the manager were the only men there. Ross played along with the nudging and innuendoes, causing Roach to become more expansive as he hinted at the sexual bonuses that were there to be enjoyed.

"Makes work a bit more bearable, doesn't it?" Roach was saying.

"I suppose it does," said Ross.

62

He left the slightest of pauses before continuing, his tone unchanged.

"Was there any of that with Mrs. Burnham?"

Roach's eyes dropped and started flicking about as they had at the beginning of the interview.

"What? Sex? You must be joking."

"What was she like to work with, though?"

The man was gathering his thoughts to deal with this new direction.

"OK, I suppose," he said. "I didn't do much with her myself. They thought she was shit hot, though."

"Who?"

"The bosses over there. Borney and Whitcombe. I reckon she must've been shagging one of them."

Ross looked up from his notebook.

"Why d'you say that?"

"Well, doesn't take much to work it out, does it? She'd been there, what …? Two, three years? Never worked in the business before, and she gets promotion. Two grand a year more."

"That's quite a bit of shagging," said Ross.

For the first time there was some aggression in Roach's tone as he replied.

"Look, I didn't like her, right? What's an old woman like that doing in amongst dealers? It's a young man's game. Everybody knows that."

Ross waited. Now that he'd started, Roach's memories of Borney and Whitcombe forced him on.

"I worked my arse off at that place. Made contacts. Chatted punters up at stupid bloody conferences. Just to end up getting stiffed by her. And what was she doing? Sitting around making phone calls. She had no idea."

"How d'you mean 'Stiffed by her'?"

Roach nodded his head.

"Done over. Stitched up. Set up. Call it what you bloody like. Made me look a right prat."

"Tell me about it," said Ross.

Roach shrugged, obviously unwilling to re-enter territory that had uncomfortable associations. Ross waited, his face composed in what he hoped was sympathetic interest. At last, Roach sat forward.

"It was about this unquoted company, Peridon."

"Unquoted?" said Ross.

"Yeah. Their shares don't have a full listing on the Stock Exchange. They're not dealt in on the first or second tiers."

Ross didn't have to pretend any more. He was lost.

"You'll have to help me out," he said blokishly.

Roach was pleased with his superiority.

"You get dealers off-market and they'll only operate a matched market."

"Give me a break," said Ross.

"Look, it's easy. They're the sort of shares dealers'll only sell if they can find somebody who wants to buy exactly the same amount, a matched order, see? It's rule 535.2. You can trade them through the Stock Exchange on a matched bargain basis."

"I'll take your word for it."

"There's not a lot of trading in them. The risk's too high. And the company may put restrictions on selling them, so they're not always easy to shift."

"Sounds a pretty crappy deal to me," said Ross. "You mean you can buy into these shares but it could be hard to get out of them?"

"That's it. Banks hate them. Never accept them as securities. Not just that, they're not even valued like ordinary shares; you get whatever the buyer's ready to pay."

"Why the hell do people bother with them?" asked Ross, genuinely puzzled.

"You can get great bargains. They're mostly smallish companies. Once they get going, lots of them are takeover prospects. If you can get in at the right time, you're on a potential biggie."

"So what's it all got to do with Mrs. Burnham?"

Roach's features darkened again.

"This Peridon lot, they made valves or something. She reckoned they were due for takeover. She'd heard something when she was in Edinburgh, she reckoned."

"She told you that?"

"No, it was in a report she wrote. She lost part of it and it turned up in one of my files."

"And you read it?"

Roach reddened.

"Course not. I sent it back to her. She came in to say thanks later on. Told me what it was about then. Said it was important because she knew someone who wanted to sell a stake in it."

He stopped. His eyes shifted over the various posters on the walls of the office.

"And?" said Ross.

"Well, I ... er ... I had a client. He was looking for a high-risk strategy. It was gambling money as far as he was concerned. I ... er ... I told him about it. He told me to go for it."

He was now very uncomfortable.

"And it didn't work out," said Ross. It wasn't a question.

"Too bloody right," said Roach. "Three weeks later, the receiver's called in. Peridon's accountant forgot the VAT, didn't he? The product was selling, the books looked good, the company was ripe for it, but ... well, that was it. Down the tubes."

"And your guy lost the lot?"

Roach nodded.

"Twelve grand," he said.

"But Mrs. Burnham's ... friend got out in time?"

"Too bloody right."

Ross whistled.

"D'you reckon that Mrs. Burnham knew Peridon was in trouble?"

"Of course she did."

"How d'you know?"

"I asked to see the report she'd written on it."

"And?"

"There wasn't one. She'd only written that one page. Left it in my file deliberately."

"Deliberately?"

Roach looked at him defiantly. His anger at his memories was hard to contain.

"Yes. I asked Sally Napier. All Burnham's stuff goes ... used to go through her. She'd never heard of Peridon."

"And you reckon she set you up?"

"What's it look like to you?"

It was Ross's turn to shrug. It was all a bit beyond him.

"Sounds like she was a pretty crafty operator," he said.

"She knew bugger all," said Roach. "Sometimes, Borney'd get us together to talk about any new ideas we had, any bits of business we'd heard of on the line. She hardly ever opened her mouth. She was bloody useless. One time I told them about a takeover I'd heard a whisper about. Nothing illegal, no insider stuff, but this mate'd said that Bessmar Offshore was a target. She rubbished the idea. Two days later, their shares were up forty-five pence. Some financial adviser, eh?"

"So how come she got that promotion?"

"I told you. Shagging. What else could it be?"

"But you thought she was an old woman."

"Well she was, wasn't she? But look at Borney. What else is he going to get?"

Ross noticed how Roach's animation had returned now that sex was back at the center of their conversation. He asked him about his other colleagues at Borney and Whitcombe and, once again, financial competence was of much less interest to him than breast sizes and the silhouettes their backsides presented as they consulted filing cabinets. Ross's initial dislike and mistrust of the man were comprehensively confirmed as they talked on and, when he eventually stood up and thanked him for his time, he was aware that he'd learned a little about Stephanie Burnham, but an awful lot more about Paul Roach.

"Just one other thing," he said as Roach moved towards the door to show him out. "Wednesday. You were at work, were you?"

"Of course," said Roach.

"D'you stay here for lunch?"

The blush that washed over Roach's face and neck was unmistakable.

"No ... I ... er ... usually go out for a sandwich."

"What time?"

"Varies. Sometimes twelve, sometimes one. Depends."

"And Wednesday?"

"I'd have to check. It was twelve, I think."

"And where'd you go?"

"I had some shopping to do. I was looking for a new pair of shoes … Trainers."

He was a very bad liar.

"Did you get them?" asked Ross.

Roach shook his head.

"Couldn't find the ones I was after."

"Shops are like that, aren't they?" said Ross. "Anybody with you?"

Roach shook his head again. He was refusing to meet Ross's eyes.

"What's up? Married, was she?" Ross asked.

The question brought Roach's head snapping up to look at him. His color deepened.

"You'd better have a good think about it," said Ross. "You might need her."

Roach pushed a hand through his hair, then smoothed the lapels of his jacket.

"I don't know what you're talking about."

Ross walked past him to the door.

"Think about it," he said, as he turned the handle.

They went into the front office together and, in view of the small queue of customers and the girls who were serving them, Roach's attitude changed utterly. The residue of his blushing was still there, but his face set into an official half-smile and he waved a gracious hand towards the front door to show Ross out. The message to everyone was clear; Roach was an important individual who had been helping Ross out of some difficulties. At the front door, he held out his hand. Ross ignored it.

"I'll be in touch," he said and turned away, leaving the watchers with the confused impression that they'd somehow got their signals all mixed up.

Carston's mood had got better and better as he'd driven north. There was very little traffic about and he'd cruised along the A96 at a steady fifty-five, looking about and enjoying the emptiness of the straw-colored countryside. This part of the north-east, between Aberdeen and the Moray Firth, was too functional to be beautiful.

It was all farming country, there were no stretches of water visible until you got nearer to Inverness, and the hills were low, rounded and undramatic. Compared with the valleys of the Dee, Spey and Don, this was relatively dull, but Carston had spent so much time in the south of England that the sight of a near-empty road reaching through a country uncluttered with houses made him sigh with pleasure and feel grateful that circumstances had given him the chance to move to Scotland.

Despite the dawdling drive, he got to Findhorn by ten-twenty. The tide was half in as he drove along the edge of the estuary. The boats inshore were still aground, some sitting squarely on their bilge keels, others leaning over on the sand. Further out, those that were afloat were pulling hard at their buoys under the pressure of the current that was pushing in from the open firth. The only persons in sight were an old man down on the beach who was dragging a long piece of flotsam up towards the high water mark and someone rowing a small dinghy between the boats out in the channel.

Carston parked at the side of the road and ambled slowly along towards where he guessed the center of the village would be. There were no radios blaring, no motor bikes or cars ripping the silence apart. The houses lined up along the road looked out across the estuary to the trees of Culbin forest and Carston felt comfortable with the peace of it all.

The jetty was obvious, the only structure breaking the sweep of the shoreline. As he neared it he saw that there was no one waiting to meet him and realized that he was a bit early. He was in no hurry though and was happy to stroll slowly along, breathing in the seaweed-scented air.

He watched the old man with his awkward load scrunch over the pebbles until he came to a pile of driftwood. He stopped there, dropped the piece of timber and took off his hat to wipe his forehead.

"Chief Inspector Carston?"

The voice made him start. He looked around to see that the man who'd been rowing the dinghy had come alongside the jetty, and climbed up onto it. The question that had been in his voice was still obvious on his lean, tanned face. He was maybe in his mid-thirties, wore a navy blue sweater and faded jeans and looked like the sort of male model who specialized in things rugged.

Carston was foolishly pleased. As a boy, he'd always been around people who spent most of their time on boats and used them with the same ease that motorists had nowadays with their cars. Sleeman's appearance from the water rather than the land was like a happy echo from a bit of his mind that he didn't use enough these days. He walked across to the man, stretching his hand out as he did so.

"Dr. Sleeman," he said.

Sleeman wiped his hand on his side before extending it.

"You took me by surprise," said Carston. "I was looking the wrong way."

Sleeman's lips moved towards a grin but didn't quite make it and there was a brief, slightly awkward silence before he gestured towards his dinghy.

"D'you want to come to my place?"

"Whatever suits you."

"Come on then." Sleeman started to get back down into his dinghy. There was no hesitation from Carston. It'd been far too long since he'd been out on the water in anything and this was a chance to add even more enjoyment to what had been a marvelous day right from the start. He settled in the stern of the dinghy and Sleeman immediately shoved off using one of the short oars. A couple of quick strokes got them going out towards the channel and, for a moment, Carston let memories of Brixham harbor come gently back. Shrimping along the quay walls, sitting on bollards to which lines of small motor boats were tied, living a perpetual summer in a lost reality where nobody got murdered.

Sleeman was strong and skilful and they were soon in the channel where he only had to dip the oars to steer. No force was needed because the current grabbed them and shoved them along at a surprising speed.

"Just as well the tide's flooding," said Carston.

Sleeman nodded. They slipped quickly past a buoy pulled tight in the water by the boat that was moored to it. Carston looked ahead. They were sliding towards a long white yacht. She was slim and sparkling in the hurrying water. Her mainsail was furled in a white canvas cover, her jib rolled tightly around the forestay and, as they curved round her stern, Carston saw the name "Raider" painted in turquoise across her transom. A rope ladder hung over the starboard quarter. Sleeman pulled hard on his port oar as they came level with the stern then he quickly turned and grabbed at the ladder before the tide could rush them past it. He took the dinghy's painter with his other hand, looped it round a small cleat on the edge of the deck a couple of times then let the dinghy turn with the tide and ride just off the ladder.

"This is it," he said.

"You actually live on board?" said Carston, unnecessarily.

"Yep," said Sleeman, stowing the oars.

Carston whistled.

"Very, very nice," he said, and he meant it.

They climbed aboard and Sleeman went below to brew some coffee. Carston's pleasure at being there grew as he looked around at the fittings and the condition of the boat. It was a Sadler 34, long and luxurious.

"She's beautiful," he said.

"Thanks," said Sleeman from the galley.

While they waited for the coffee they talked about the boat, the alterations that Sleeman had made to adapt her as his permanent home, the ease of sailing her and the sorts of trips he'd made. He was a marine biologist (the title "Doctor" indicating a PhD), so living on board was like having a flat over the office. As they talked, Carston thought how relaxing it would be to spend the morning chatting about things nautical. He had to shake away the temptation to indulge himself.

"Well," he said as Sleeman eventually brought two mugs up into the cockpit, "I mustn't waste your time. About Mrs. Burnham ..."

He left the name hanging like a question. Sleeman nodded, looking out at the other boats dipping against the current towards their buoys.

"Yes. Poor old Steph. What can I tell you?"

"Whatever you think's relevant. How you came to know her, what sort of person she was, anything ..."

Sleeman pointed across the water at the houses of Findhorn. "That's where I met her," he said. "That pub on the front. She was here seeing some guy about some oil shares. Came in there after she'd finished with him. Sat at the bar on her own. Caught me on a randy day. I chatted her up."

He looked at Carston. There was something of a challenge in his eyes. Carston was careful not to react.

"That easy, was it?" he said.

Sleeman shrugged.

"Seemed like it at the time. Anyway, women that age … Well, it's flattering for them, isn't it?" He paused thoughtfully, apparently unaware of the conceit his words betrayed, then continued, "Anybody would've done for her though."

"Why d'you say that?"

"She just wanted it. We were out here in the for'ard bunk in less than an hour."

"No hanging about then."

"Not with Steph. I'll give her that. You usually knew where you were with her."

"So you got to know her quite well then?" said Carston.

"Well enough."

The mood of relaxation was still there but Carston had quickly cleared the previous laziness out of his mind to concentrate on what Sleeman had to offer.

The affair with Mrs. Burnham had been sporadic. It had started in late spring and continued through the summer. For her it had meant the satisfaction of a strong sexual hunger. Neither of them had pretended that there was anything like love involved in their relationship; they'd simply used one another's bodies as playgrounds. When Carston tried to hint discreetly at the fact that her particular playground had been in use longer than his, Sleeman picked up the reference and, in a tone spread thick with smugness, told Carston that she knew games which younger women were either afraid of or hadn't yet learned. Then, with a coarseness that surprised Carston, he added that an old one closing was as good as a young one opening.

They'd sometimes met in Cairnburgh and Aberdeen but mostly

she'd driven up to Findhorn and he'd brought her out to *Raider*. The images of summer evenings sitting here drinking Chablis before going below to explore variations on erotic themes made Carston's groin grow warmer. His concentration was in danger again.

"When did you last see her?" he asked.

Sleeman thought for a moment.

"Last month. Couldn't tell you when exactly. It was all over, see?"

"Oh?" prompted Carston.

"Yeah. There's a limit, isn't there? I mean, she was getting to depend on it. Making demands. I just … well, told her that was it."

"And she went along with it?"

"No choice. She squeaked a bit. Even starting talking about her 'rights as an individual.' Imagine that. Sitting here, on my boat, claiming her bloody rights. When women start on that, it's time to wave goodbye. Anyway, that was it. Must've been about the middle of the month."

"And this happened here?"

"Yeah. Down below. We'd just finished and she was making plans to come for a weekend and I thought, No, that's it. She's getting too pushy. So I told her."

Carston looked around the bay to control his reaction. Sleeman's callousness didn't go with the scene. Most of the boats were now afloat, flicking their slender masts as the easing tide lifted them against the hold of their moorings. The September sun was warm and there was more activity along the shore.

"Did you know she was pregnant?" he asked.

Sleeman looked quickly at him, but his expression showed nothing.

"Stephanie? … Well, well, well," was all he said.

"Is that yes or no?"

"No. She didn't tell me."

"Don't suppose it would've made any difference, would it?"

"Why should it? Christ, she was a married woman. What were we going to do? Start a family out here on *Raider*? Not all that convenient for schools, is it?"

Carston's dislike of Sleeman was growing all the time.

"You don't seem particularly put out by her death, Dr. Sleeman."

"Don't be stupid. Of course I don't like the idea of her getting herself killed. But it's happened. No point in speaking in hushed tones and being respectful. That won't do her any bloody good, will it?"

He stood up, took Carston's empty cup and stepped down to the galley.

"More?" he asked.

"No thanks," said Carston.

Sleeman filled his own cup and came back up. The interval had calmed both of them.

"Did she talk about her marriage much?"

"Too bloody often. I told her I didn't want to know. Didn't want to be involved."

"What sort of things did she say?"

"What most women of her age do, I should think. Misunderstood. Not getting enough sex from her old man. Being treated like a servant … What bastards men are. The usual crap."

"Did she say she and her husband had rows?"

"Nothing serious, I don't think. As I said, I didn't really pay much attention when she was on about that. It was boring."

Suddenly, there was a small smile on his face and a softening of his voice.

"And old Steph wasn't really a boring person, you know. She wasn't thick. When she was talking about the deals she was doing, market movements, things like that, she could get quite excited. She was bright. It was only when she went on about home and him—whatshisname … her old man—that she seemed … I don't know, squashed, restricted somehow. Made her mind shrink. Like I said, made her boring."

He was obviously thinking fonder thoughts of her for a moment and Carston let the silence hang. The tide was slack now, the boats all faced in different directions and the rushing of the water past the buoys had steadied to restful laps and gurgles as it slapped against *Raider*'s hull.

"Did you hear from her at all after that last visit?" Carston asked finally.

Sleeman's voice was still quiet, preoccupied almost.

"She phoned a couple of times. Left messages at the association for me to call back. I did once. She wanted to come up. Wouldn't believe me when I said no. Wouldn't bloody accept it. Can't remember when the last call was. Some time ago. Thank God I didn't give her my mobile number."

He turned to look directly at Carston.

"Look, if I hadn't stuck to it, she'd've been up here every weekend. Why d'you think I choose to live on board? I like my own company. With two here it can get bloody crowded."

It wasn't a hint, but Carston took it as a cue. He stood up, thanked Sleeman for the coffee and suggested that they return to the jetty now that the tide had eased. The speed with which Sleeman responded to the suggestion showed that he, too, had had enough. As they rowed back, some boats were making their way out of the bay, pushed gently by a slight westerly breeze that was getting up. Carston exchanged waves with a couple in a dayboat as it moved past them; another memory of days on the water— greeting rather than ignoring other people.

"One more thing I have to ask. Where were you on Wednesday? The day she died."

Sleeman's rhythm didn't alter. His head nodded back towards *Raider*.

"On board. All day."

"Alone, I suppose?"

"Best way to be," said Sleeman. "I was working. Had some data faxed up from the marine lab in Aberdeen the previous evening. Stayed on board working on it with my laptop."

"And you didn't go ashore for food, newspapers?"

"Nope."

He looked directly at Carston.

"Not much of an alibi, is it?" he said.

Carston shrugged and turned to look at the dayboat which was gibing into the channel. Neither of them said anything else until the dinghy came alongside the jetty again.

"Thanks for the trip," said Carston as he hoisted himself ashore. "It's a beautiful boat."

"Thanks," said Sleeman.

"I'll probably be in touch again if that's OK."

Sleeman shrugged.

"You know where to find me," he said. "Better get me on the mobile."

He gave his number. Carston wrote it down, thanked him again and watched as he shoved off and began pulling back towards *Raider*. The little boat moved through the water quickly, the vee of its wake making the other dinghies bob as it passed. Carston walked back along the jetty and turned towards his car, looking across the water all the time. For all Sleeman's hard-bitten callousness, he could understand Stephanie Burnham's need to return here. Across the estuary, dark green trees lined up along the tan-colored beaches, the moored boats moved gently as the breeze caught them, the water sparkled under their dancing hulls and the whole scene was wide open and quiet. He could see Sleeman tying his dinghy at the stern of *Raider*.

"Lucky bastard," he said to himself. And his emphasis was very much on bastard.

Despite the warmth and the sunshine, Michael Burnham and Barbara Stone were spending the day in bed. They'd both rung in to their respective offices before breakfast, he giving bereavement as an excuse, she inventing a migraine. During the morning they'd had sex twice, dozed, done the *Telegraph* crossword and talked about anything but Stephanie, the murder and the consequences it might have for them. They both knew that, unless something nasty happened, when the fuss had died down he would be free. For her that meant a chance to realize some of the fantasies they'd concocted together: his clichéd preferences for skiing in Val d'Isère, navigating the Canal du Midi, spending autumn in New Hampshire and spring in Paris; and her own, wilder schemes of white water rafting in Zambia, trekking on Kilimanjaro and renting an entire château in the Loire valley for Christmas. And beneath it all, her present private hope that one of the options might turn out to be marriage.

She was a woman of weird fancies. In her early teens, she'd quickly become aware of her sex appeal. There were many girls in

75

her neighborhood with bigger breasts, thicker hair, fuller lips, but she was the one the boys wanted to touch and kiss in the parks and streets of Inverness where they hung out together. She had a way of moving her slim body and looking sideways with her green eyes that won her many concessions from them. They'd do anything, accept all sorts of semi-humiliations to go out with her, and, when any of them was granted the privilege, she'd invent tales about herself that bound them to her even more closely. They believed that she was sharing secrets with them, uncovering hidden pains and wonders as their hands pressed between her legs. For one, she'd been born in India in a monsoon, to another she confessed that she'd used a fence post to kill a sheep that she'd found severely injured on the roadside by Loch Ness, and as her encounters and experiences multiplied, the inventions became wilder and, to her contemptuous surprise, accepted and marveled at.

The tendencies had not only stayed with her in adulthood, they'd grown stronger. She craved intensity and couldn't bear the possibility that her life might be as narrow and empty as those of everyone around her. Her divorce had been the usual shabby business but she'd transformed it, for herself and others, into a fairy tale of brutality and stoicism. Her ex-husband, a production supervisor on a platform in the Brent field, had grown first angry, then weary of her playing around and of the fictions she'd offered him as cover stories. He'd started looking around himself and that was her excuse to switch to the role of abandoned wife. By the time her lawyers had finished, the hapless man had become, for everyone who listened to her version of events, a pedophile who made her watch bootlegged videos of rituals involving not only children, but cats, hamsters connected to the mains supply and a Shetland pony.

The multiplying lies had become essential to her; without them she would need to look at simple truths. She came to believe that she had indeed played tennis for Scotland, delivered a friend's baby in the back of a furniture van, been raped by a theology student and had two still lifes exhibited at the Royal Scottish Academy. Her present fantasy was of a new marriage, funded by Burnham's money and living in a Georgian apartment in Edinburgh during the week and, at weekends, in a house just outside Braemar from where they'd ride and hunt in summer and ski in winter.

Burnham knew about her imaginings. It was part of her wildness, her chemistry. She could never be predicted. His own plans were more guarded. She'd regenerated him and he owed all his new energy to her, but they lived on these pretences, always on the edge of some preposterous scheme or scenario which was fine while it remained as make-believe but which he knew would corrode the moment they tried to live it. In some ways, she was a witch. And magic didn't travel.

"I think Americans are built by dentists," she said suddenly, breaking into his thoughts.

"What?"

"Look at this."

She held a magazine for him to look at. A young couple stood on the steps of an aeroplane, waving and smiling perfect smiles.

"It's not just their teeth," she said. "Look at their jaws. Sort of engineered. Just right. Admit it, they couldn't be anything but Americans, could they?"

Burnham agreed. The pair did have the carved rightness of a quarterback and a cheerleader and yet, according to the accompanying story, they were just two students who'd come to see the Edinburgh Festival and joined one of the theater groups performing on the Fringe.

"They care about things like that, that's all," he said. "Self-image and so on."

She took a fold of his flesh between finger and thumb.

"How would you know?" she asked. "You don't have one."

He pushed her hand away and slapped it.

"Cheeky bitch," he said.

She went back to flicking through the magazine. When she spoke again, her tone was still light, playful.

"So, when can we get married?"

It shook him.

"I thought we were leaving that alone for a while," he said. He could see, in profile, the tightening of her mouth that showed her displeasure. The pages of the magazine made more noise as they were turned. She controlled her first response, then spoke with tension still in her.

"I'm not hanging around to mourn her, Michael. She's been a big enough drag on us all these months. She's gone. Fact. Time's a-wasting."

Burnham checked his own reaction to her words.

"I know," he managed. "Just … well, a month maybe. Till things settle."

"What 'things'?"

"I don't know. The police. The investigations. All that."

She turned quickly to look him full in the face.

"What sort of things have they been asking?"

He lay back on the pillow.

"Not much really. I've only talked to one of them. He asked the usual things. The sort they always say on telly. Did she have any enemies? Where was I when it happened? You know …"

She half-closed her eyes. It was a familiar gesture.

"Do they know about me?" she asked.

Burnham thought for a moment.

"I don't think so," he said. "I didn't mention you."

"Somebody's bound to, though, aren't they? All those creatures who live vicariously off us, the parasites who prowl around our passion."

She dwelt on the alliteration, enjoyed it. He knew the mood but when her eyes suddenly opened wide again, their wildness still excited him.

"Tell them," she said. "You tell them about me. Don't wait for them to find out from gossipers." Her head turned. She looked sideways from her green eyes. "Flaunt me."

It was another challenge, a dare.

"I don't know, darling. It could mean lots of trouble. We could …"

She turned suddenly in the bed, pushed herself onto her knees and sat astride him.

"We could die while we're waiting to start living," she said, her eyes shining. "Do it, Michael. Tell them. I want them to talk to me."

As usual, he avoided anything that might seem like a contradiction. For her he did things that he'd never done for women before,

78

accepted a subservience he'd never felt. Not because of what she was but because of what she could withhold. If she banished him from her games, stopped seeing him, deprived him of the pleasures that had woken up his body, he was afraid he'd sink further into middle age than he'd been when she rescued him. And the certainty that she'd not only do that, but twist the knife by letting him know that her affections and inventions had been transferred to someone else, made him accept propositions and compromises that bit deep into his self-esteem.

Her face was close to his, her lips were parted and shining. She moved closer still, her tongue delicate on his cheek.

"Tell them, *chéri*," she breathed. "Give them some work to do. Another trail to follow."

His own breathing was quicker. Her hands were cupped inside his thighs again and all other thoughts began to slide away as he felt himself respond. He smiled with an absurd pride that he was going to be ready again so soon.

"You will, won't you?" she whispered, her tongue now in his ear.

"Only if the price is right," he said, his eyes closing and everything but their contact already banished to another time and place.

Chapter Four

Later that afternoon, Carston was sitting in his office making notes for the evening's briefing session when Ross came in holding a large brown package.

"Autopsy and forensic reports," he said, handing them over.

"Christ," Carston said. "McIntosh's stock with Grampian must be high. They've shifted on this one, haven't they? He must be black-mailing one of them."

Ross was at the kettle. He lifted it and said, "Rat's piss?"

Carston nodded, already skimming through the first page of the reports.

As Ross plugged in the kettle and started spooning coffee into mugs, Carston began commenting on the findings.

"Confirms everything we've got."

"Oh?"

"Yep. Three months pregnant. General health good. Blood alcohol well over the top. Recent sexual intercourse accompanied with …" He paused and a change in tone showed that what he was reading was affecting him. "… very rough treatment. Lacerations inside her thighs, pre-mortem bruising around the vulva and anus. More bruises on her arms. Straight, regular, probably from banging against sharp edges. The bookshelves maybe. Fibers under her nails." He paused again and, to Ross's irritation, read silently. When he next spoke, his voice was quiet, reflective. "No marks on her neck or shoulders, though. And there ought to be bruising where he grabbed her arms or wrists."

"So?"

"If she was raped, how did he hold her down?"

Ross scratched patterns in the bottom of a mug with the spoon.

"Gunpoint. No need to hold her," he said.

"Why the banging about then? The bruises from the shelves?"

Ross shrugged.

"Could be just part of his pleasure. They're funny buggers, you know."

"Who?"

"Sex criminals."

"Maybe," said Carston and went back to the papers he was holding.

"Jesus, you could be right," he said, almost at once.

"What?" asked Ross.

"Three rows of pre-mortem stab wounds on the front of her left thigh. Two more on the inside of her right. Stabbed through her skirt. Small but quite deep. Maybe a kitchen fork, they reckon. What the hell is this? Torture, too?"

"Nasty bugger," said Ross. "Anything else?"

"Plenty," said Carston. "The gun's got prints all over it, nearly all the same. Same with the fork and the plunger. All the same. And there's blood and flesh tags along the gun barrel. Probably from being forced into her vagina. That plunger, too … He … Jesus Christ, Jim."

He stopped reading, looked at the ceiling, sighed and forced himself back to the file.

"He used that on her too. God, Jim, he gave her some abuse."

He shook his head and was silent yet again. Ross needed to shake him out of it.

"What about the wound?" he asked.

Carston read some more.

"Contact injuries from the barrel," he said, "bruising from the recoil. Entry wound's not big, ragged edges from the gases. Tattooing around it from unburnt powder, traces of soot. Quite a bit of charring and some local carboxyhemoglobin."

Ross was pouring water into the cups.

"It was fired at an angle across her chest. The entry wound's below the right shoulder blade but the charge went straight through her heart. There's a small exit wound beside her left breast. There's lots of shot dispersed in the chest cavity too."

He stopped as Ross handed him his coffee.

"Thanks," he said.

Ross pulled a chair round to sit beside him. The report lay on the desk between them. Carston sipped his coffee and was so absorbed by his thought processes that he didn't register how awful it tasted. He pointed to a paragraph halfway down the page.

"Look at that," he said.

Ross leaned forward and read that the autopsy had found more pellets than they'd have expected and that that fact, combined with the extensive charring and carbon dioxide coloring of the area around the wound, suggested that the cartridge used had probably been of the superspeed variety.

"So what?" said Ross.

"No idea," replied Carston. "Just something different."

The awfulness of the coffee got to him on his second sip. He was glad of the taste. It restored contact with some normality.

"Christ," he said, getting up and going to where the milk bottle was kept, "I didn't think this stuff could get any worse."

He topped up his mug with milk to dilute the taste and make it possible to drink it more quickly to get it over with. Ross was flicking through the pages. Suddenly, he stopped, read and nodded his head slightly.

"What is it?" asked Carston.

"I hate bloody guns," Ross said. "Especially shotguns. The way they spread out ..."

Carston looked out of the window.

"They used to fire them at repro furniture at the beginning of the century, you know," he said.

"What for?"

"Looked like woodworm. Instant aging. Authenticity."

Ross shook his head.

"They're so bloody mechanical."

"Yes," said Carston, "killing at a distance, by numbers."

"I read about this female terrorist in Malaya," said Ross. "She was hit in the ear by a single bullet from an FN rifle and her head just disintegrated. All to do with muzzle velocity and cartridge length, apparently. Who the bloody hell sits down and designs these things?"

Carston's thoughts had returned to Burnham.

"What sort of guns did you say our man had?" he asked.

Ross got up and went to his own desk. He took a notebook out of the top left hand drawer and flicked through its pages.

"A Tolley 3-inch Magnum Hammer with a 32-inch barrel. That's the one we found in the study. The other one's his best one, a 29.5-inch Beretta."

"Were they expensive?"

Ross looked for another page in his book.

"I wondered about that. I asked that prat at the club. He reckoned they'd be about twelve hundred quid. That's cheap, apparently."

"What's dear then?"

"Depends what you're after. A new top gun like a Boss costs twenty-five to thirty K. The cheapest second hand Purdey is between five and six thousand."

"So, relatively, Burnham didn't spend much on the sport?"

"I don't think he was serious about it. He could have afforded better gear if he wanted it."

They both turned back to the report, Carston's fingers running down the notes. They stopped at a description of the panties which had been found under the desk in the study.

"You see, that's weird too," he said.

"What is?"

"The knickers were torn off her, but there's semen on them. On the outside of them too."

"Why's that weird? I'd have thought it confirms what we've been saying about it all the time."

Carston shook his head.

"Surely if he's raping her," he said, "the semen doesn't arrive till he's stripped her and forced it in. I mean if he's ejaculated all over the knickers, why bother to take them off?"

Ross thought for a moment.

"Was there semen inside her, too?" he asked.

Carston picked up the file and skimmed through it.

"Yep. She was penetrated all right."

He put the file back on the table.

"You see, Jim, that's bloody strange, isn't it? I mean, what sort of state did he get in? Beats her around, stabs her with a fork, shoves his gun and that bloody plunger into her, comes all over her knickers, then manages to come again inside her. It's more like some sex thing than a domestic."

"You're determined to get him off, aren't you?" said Ross.

"No," Carston insisted. "But it's not gelling. I don't understand the guy."

"See this?" said Ross, pointing to another heading.

Carston read the note and nodded.

"That's more like it," he said.

It was about the material which had been clutched in the dead woman's right hand. It was made up of twisted strands of green and russet colored wool from some sort of garment. Apparently, they'd found the same material all over the study, snagged on the shelves, caught in the books, on the back of the chair and the desk.

"No chance there's anything like that among the clothes we took from him, is there?" asked Carston.

"Don't remember. I'll check it. We took everything he was wearing that day."

"Worth another look round, all the same. I s'pose there's still nothing from him?"

"No. I'll try his work again."

Carston got up and put his mug back on the side table with the kettle.

"One more thing," he said. "Before we go and see him, I'd like to have another look at the video of the study. Check it against these reports."

Ross handed his mug across to him, stood up and made for the door.

"Right, sir," he said. "I'll get it organized."

He went out. Carston went back to the desk, sat down again and picked up the report. He settled back in his chair, opened it at the first page and started reading it more thoroughly.

That evening's briefing session turned out to be quite productive. As well as giving them all the forensic details, Carston told them about his talk with Sleeman. Ross went quickly through his meeting with Roach and, although there was nothing tying either of them to the time and place of the murder, their connections with Mrs. Burnham were noted along with the possible complications their relationships with her might add to the investigation.

The rest of the team had been busy too. Bellman and Thom had religiously worked their way through Stephanie Burnham's address book. The routine trawl had been enlivened by two incidents. First of all, Bellman was mistaken for a heavy breather by a dentist's receptionist, who'd been having trouble with nuisance calls at home, and then Thom's rather direct style got him accused of being a *Sun* reporter by one of the older members of Mrs. Burnham's family. All of the Stratford numbers, which were answered by people with what the constables said were "posh voices," turned out to be family and long-standing friends, and the only ones that were out of the ordinary belonged to an estate agent in France, a travel agent in Nottingham and a local faith healer. All of these "weirdoes," as Bellman called them, had been left for Carston or his CID people to handle.

"Ah'll ring the frog estate agent if ye like, sir," said Fraser. "Try out my accent."

"Yeah, but we need to know more than his name and how he is," said Carston.

"Nae problem," said Fraser, "I could ask him how old he is, if he's got any brothers and sisters, where he bides …"

"Shut up, Fraser," said Carston.

"Yes sir."

Carston told Ross to make a note for them to phone the numbers Bellman and Thom hadn't tried, then turned to McNeil.

Mrs. Napier had been very co-operative about Stephanie Burnham's client list and McNeil had spoken to upwards of thirty people, all of whom had said how sorry they were to hear about the tragedy and were full of praise for the excellent service Mrs. Burnham had given them.

"Just being polite?" asked Carston.

"I don't think so," said McNeil. "Two or three of them told me about some very good deals she'd spotted for them. Made them some handy profits, apparently."

"Borney was right, then," said Carston, "she did know her stuff."

"Certainly managed to sort out Roach over that Peridon business," said Ross. "I can imagine how grateful that particular client was."

"Aye, but there's others not so pleased," said McNeil.

"Oh?" said Carston.

"Two of the clients' accounts were missing from her files. Mrs. Napier couldn't understand it. They'd been regulars with Mrs. Burnham for over a year. I asked Mr. Borney about them and he told me he'd taken them over himself. Said they had nothing to do with her any more."

"When did this happen?" asked Carston.

"What, him taking them over? Must've been within the last month according to Mrs. Napier. She didn't even know about it."

"Interesting," said Carston. "Who are they?"

McNeil glanced at her notebook.

"A Mr. Dunkley and ... er ... Dr. Strong."

"Any idea why they left her?" asked Carston.

McNeil shrugged her shoulders and raised her hands, palms upwards.

"Did you ask?" said Carston.

"Yes, sir. Mr. Borney said they weren't connected with her. I didn't try pushing him. Didn't know how sweet you wanted to keep him."

"McNeil, you can do what you like with the bugger as far as I'm concerned. Get back there tomorrow."

"Their office isn't open. It's Saturday," Ross reminded him.

"I don't care," said Carston. "You phone him and get him over there, McNeil. I want the files on those two customers and anything else you can find out about them. And if he causes trouble, get straight on to me."

"Right sir," said McNeil, her mouth lifting into its lopsided smile.

Carston turned to Fraser and Spurle.

"How about you two? Where've you been?" he asked.

"Speakin' to the gentry, sir," said Fraser.

"Aye, sir," said Spurle. "The members of yon club."

"And?"

Fraser grunted dismissively and Spurle flipped open his notebook.

"Half of them are in London. Only come up at weekends. We managed to speak to half a dozen directly."

"Aye. The rest was answerin' machines and butlers," said Fraser.

"None of them was there on Wednesday. Most of them were at Gleneagles. Four of them did see Mr. Burnham at the club on Tuesday night, though."

"Anybody say anything about him? Notice anything?"

Spurle shook his head.

"Nothing. We had to remind some of them who he was."

Carston sat back in his chair.

"What the hell does Burnham get out of spending time at a place like that?" he said.

Spurle looked at his notebook.

"There's a Major Lawrie who says he was getting to be a good shot. Reaching competitive standard, he said."

"Aye, but who'd want to compete with pricks like that?" said Fraser.

McNeil smiled along with the others. She preferred the fact that Fraser didn't feel obliged to tone down his style for her benefit. Carston noticed the smile but, despite himself, was still uneasy about the language. For all his desire to recognize and practice equality, his attitude to women was still very old-fashioned.

"Did this … major shoot with him then?" he asked.

"No chance," said Fraser, scornfully. "Burnham was always on his own there. None o' the others wants nothin' to do with him. I'll tell you, sir, if you've no got a silver spoon stickin' out yer arse, they're no wantin' to know ye."

"Fraser," said Carston.

"Sir?"

"When you're next learning your French vocabulary, have a look at some English too, will you?"

They all laughed, including Fraser.

"Just one more thing," said Spurle as the laughter died down. "Major Lawrie said he remembered talking to Stephanie Burnham in the clubhouse one evening a while back. Just polite chit-chat, he said."

"Oh? Well, it may be worth looking at, I suppose. Can I leave that to you, Jim?"

"I'll get on to it tomorrow, sir."

"OK. Anything else?" asked Carston.

They looked at each other and shook their heads.

"Right then, that'll do for now. I'll have a think about things and we'll see where we go next in the morning. Away you go."

They all filed out through the door. Only Ross dawdled around by his desk. Carston looked at his watch.

"Fancy a pint, Jim?" he said.

"Aye, great," said Ross.

They tidied their respective desks. For Carston, this meant a quick look at the papers on top of the single, scattering heap, for Ross a squaring off of the three very distinct piles and the jotting down of a note for himself.

The pub was less than five minutes' walk along the street. It was too early for it to be busy so they took their pints of lager to a table in one of the bay windows which looked out onto a surprisingly big garden.

"How's Jean enjoying Girvan?" asked Carston after their first sip. Ross smiled.

"Well, it was OK to begin with, but I think she's getting ready to come home," he said.

"Why's that?"

Ross wrinkled his nose.

"You know families. Great when you don't have to live with them. Her ma's already on about when we're planning to have a brother for Kirsty."

Carston laughed.

"I reckon she'll be home inside the week," Ross added.

"You glad?" asked Carston.

Ross looked at him, smiled and nodded briefly, a gesture too small to express the genuine pleasure the thought gave him.

"Yep," said Carston, "hard to beat, isn't it? Puts everything else into perspective."

"Pity Burnham didn't see it that way," said Ross, getting straight into the topic they both wanted to speak about. He sat forward, elbows on the table.

"Maybe he did," Carston said.

"Why get rid of her then?"

"Still think it was him?"

"Who else?"

Carston sat back in his chair and looked out at the leaves moving along in the wind.

"Yeah, you're right, but I wish we'd come up with something that confirmed it. The only things we're getting are just complicating it more."

"I don't see how," said Ross. "It's not a break-in, is it? Nothing's missing. So why did she get killed?"

"You tell me."

"She's got a bit on the side in Findhorn. That guy Roach said she was having it off with Borney. Maybe Burnham found out about it and lost the head. I mean, this pregnancy. He reckoned they haven't been having any sex for ages, so chances are it's somebody else's. That could've cracked him up."

Carston nodded.

"Yeah, fair enough," he said. "Doesn't strike me as the crime of passion type, though. Too bloody English altogether. I mean, you heard the way he talked about their marriage. And what about these customers that Borney's taken away from her? What's that all about?"

Ross sat back and thought for a moment.

"Could be to do with her drinking," he said at last. "Or maybe she fucked up on a couple of deals or something. Remember what Roach said about her missing out on some offshore shares or something."

"Yeah, but look at the way she shafted him. That was slick, Jim. And all her other customers are well pleased with her."

Ross shook his head.

"Well, I don't know why you always want to make things hard

for yourself," he said. "Everything we've got so far says Burnham did it. Motive, the gun, no real alibi ..." He let his voice tail off.

"Yeah, maybe," said Carston. He drank from his glass, then continued. "The trouble is, he's too bloody sharp for that. I mean, for somebody with his wits he's done a helluva botched-up job, hasn't he? Shoots her, leaves the gun lying there and I bet the prints on it are his. Doesn't get himself an alibi."

"No, like I said, he lost the head. There was no planning. They had a row. He knocked her about then shot her."

"And had sex with her too?"

"Why not? He said it was her idea but her knickers were dragged off, weren't they? Could've been rape. He could've been ... punishing her. And leaving the gun and stuff lying around ... could have been deliberate. Double bluff so that we'll think it can't be him."

Carston nodded.

"Yes, yes. You're right, Jim. It could've been like that."

"Well, we can ask him when we see him," said Ross. I tried his home number again and left a message on the answer phone for him to ring back. Nothing yet."

"He hasn't done a runner, has he?"

"What, just to make sure everybody knows he's guilty?"

"Lord Lucan did."

Ross smiled.

"Don't worry. I'll get him tomorrow," he said.

The barmaid came past them with a tray of drinks for people at another table. She wore a loose blouse in which her large breasts moved softly as she walked. The red material of her skirt clung around her thighs. Both of them watched her moving. Carston felt the warmth in his groin again.

"It worries me," he said.

"What?"

"Lust."

Ross looked at the barmaid again.

"Aye, I know what you mean," he said. "Jean's always coming home flaming mad at guys who've whistled at her."

"Oh, I'd never whistle, but you can't help thinking it, can you?"

The barmaid leaned over to pass the drinks across the table. She was facing away from them. It was too much for Carston.

"Jesus Christ," he whispered, turning deliberately away from the sight.

"You're as bad as that guy Roach," said Ross with a laugh. "He thinks the world's made of tits and bums."

"That's not the world, that's heaven," said Carston.

They drank again.

"What about him?" asked Carston. "He got the boot because of her."

"No chance," said Ross. "He's just a wanker. All wind and piss. I can't see him having the balls to argue with her, never mind kill her."

The talk of alternative suspects took them to Borney, Sleeman and the members of the gun club. But Burnham was so central to their thinking that all the speculating they did, although thorough, was unconvincing. Carston thought that Sleeman was certainly capable of murder and Ross had deep reservations about the moral and mental stability of people who killed for pleasure, but the talk was mostly self-indulgent and they knew that their next visit had to be to Burnham. It was just a question of finding out where the bugger was.

It was a quarter to midnight and Burnham's car was parked under trees some thirty yards down the road from Barbara Stone's gate. Burnham sat at the wheel, his head leaning back on the head rest but his eyes wide open, staring at the entrance to her small driveway.

He'd suggested having dinner at *Les Amis*, a small restaurant in Aberdeen where the food was usually cooked with care and invention and whose prices hadn't quite followed those of most of the city's other restaurants as they chased upwards after the oilmen's gold and platinum American Express cards. They'd been there many times before and always enjoyed it. To his surprise, she'd said no and claimed that she wanted to do some work because she had to go back in the morning. She'd said this just after their third bout of sex and he was drained enough not to argue, but there was something about her which seemed strange.

He left at seven, drove out onto the North Deeside road but then doubled back and parked under the trees, uncertain as to why he was doing so but ready to follow her if she went out that evening. Just before eight-thirty, a red Porsche had arrived and swished through her gate. Burnham didn't see the driver but his suspicions were confirmed.

He'd spent the whole evening waiting, hating himself for doing so, feeling his mind boiling with jealousies he hadn't felt for years, tormenting himself by imagining what was happening behind the beech hedge. Whoever it was, Barbara must have known all day that he was coming that evening. As she and Burnham had laughed and drunk and grappled on her bed, part of her harsh pleasures had come from the knowledge that she'd be coupling with somebody else in the same place almost as soon as he'd vacated it.

Twice he'd got out of the car and crept round to the house but he didn't see or hear anything. Lights were on everywhere but there was no music playing and no other sign that anyone was inside.

As the hands on the dashboard clock showed seven minutes to twelve, he thought he heard her door close. He turned down the heater control and listened. Almost immediately, he heard a car door slam and the cough of the Porsche as the driver switched on its ignition. He leaned forward, staring even harder at the gateway. The nose of the Porsche slid out. Burnham was looking from the passenger's side of it and, once again, as the car's body appeared, he couldn't make out the driver. The Porsche hesitated only briefly to check for traffic, then growled quickly away up towards the main road.

Burnham reached for the ignition and switched on. His first instinct was to follow the man and find out who he was dealing with, but, even as the Jag's engine caught, he changed his mind. It was nothing to do with the man. It was her.

He switched off again, got out and began walking to the house. After only a dozen paces, though, he found himself near to tears and running, swearing to himself and hot with anger. He dug out his key as he ran and when he got to the door scratched it all round the lock before his shaking hand managed to make it fit. He opened the door, slammed it behind him and started towards the stairs.

Her voice called from the bathroom.

"Steve?"

The smile and the mischief in her voice as she spoke the name slowed him. The last hope, that it had been some girlfriend or colleague who'd been visiting, was taken away. He went up the stairs and over to the bathroom door slowly, deliberately. Just as he got there, it opened and she looked out, a laugh on her face. She saw him and the laugh vanished. For once she was lost. She opened her mouth to speak but saw from his expression that this was trouble.

Burnham looked at her. She was wearing the peach-colored dressing gown and her eyes and skin were shining. He pushed at the door, grabbed her arm and pulled her towards him.

"Bitch," he said, surprised at the coldness of his own tone.

"Michael, what d'you mean?" she said, trying to pull her arm away.

They stood for a moment, staring hard into each other's eyes, before he released her. She rubbed her upper arm.

"That hurt," she said, conjuring up a pout and her little girl tone.

He punched her on the side of the head. She didn't have time to duck away from it and the skin on her left eyebrow broke.

"Fucking bitch," he said again, his anger excited by the blood which was starting to run down her cheek.

She turned to run but he had her arm again and this time he held her with his left hand while his right punched and slapped her head and shoulders. She raised her left arm to defend herself but his fist kept flailing at her until she fell away from him.

He let go. His fist hurt from the contact he'd made with her skull and he was breathing very hard. He looked down at her. She was cowering, crawling away, but not crying. Her eyes were half shut with fear of him. He wanted to hurt her some more, wanted her to die. But as well as that, he wanted to be in bed again with her, wanted her to kiss him, wanted them to be happy.

She'd reached the corner between the washbasin and the bath. She curled up into it.

"What?" she said. "What?"

"Fucking bitch," said Burnham in a very quiet voice.

Saturday morning offered a typical example of meteorological Calvinism. On Scotland's east coast, a spell of warm weather always carries a penalty. The warm September sun had had a couple of days to suck up vapors from the North Sea and, as the light arrived, a heavy mist, the haar, rolled in to remind the locals that every pleasure has its price. Normally, its effects were restricted to the coast itself and the river valleys, but this time it even reached as far as Cairnburgh.

As Kath opened the curtains in the bedroom her reaction to the dull gray light was surprising.

"Right," she said. "Perfect. Don't bother with any tea for me. I'm off."

Carston pulled the duvet down from his face.

"What?" he said, his face screwed up against the light.

"I'm going down to the river to take some photographs."

She was already pulling on a pair of tights.

"What of?" asked Carston.

"I don't know. Whatever's there. Trees, shrubs, cows."

Carston watched as she stood and stretched her legs and wriggled her bum to get comfortable.

"You're round the bend."

"You wouldn't understand," she said, "it's art."

She stepped into a pair of black jeans, put on a vest and two sweaters and sat on the edge of the bed to tie the laces of a pair of gray and white trainers. When she was ready, she leaned over and kissed Carston on the forehead.

"Get up, you lazy bugger."

Carston reached his arms towards her.

"Come back to bed and talk dirty."

She laughed, avoided his grasp and went out. He lay back briefly, then threw the duvet aside and went over to the window. Outside, everything was muted, there were no contours, no lines. The edges of the houses across the street blended into the paler spaces that separated them from one another, trees were shapes that looked as if they were probing the unaccustomed gray light that hung from them, even the parked cars were muffled by the mist.

He washed, shaved and went down to make breakfast, aware as

he was most mornings of the irritation caused by the fact that the papers didn't arrive until after eight o'clock. In England, he'd always had one propped in front of him as he ate his toast and it was the ritual that he missed. Magazines, books and yesterday's unread bits were no use. Breakfast was the time for new news. It started the day slowly, with a scattering of subjects that got your mind going. The fact that they were all forgotten the minute you folded the thing up again was irrelevant.

He half-listened to the "Today" program on Radio 4, only switching it off when they got to Thought for the Day. Kath still wasn't back so he decided to get in to work early to clear away some of the paper on his desk before pinning down Burnham. He was in his office by eight-fifteen, drinking awful coffee.

As he flicked through the forms and memos, he toyed, not for the first time, with the idea of having a rubber stamp made which said "Considered, Reviewed, Acknowledged, Processed" on it with each initial letter a bold capital. He knew that most of the stuff was circulated to convince certain individuals of their own worth and was a waste of time, resources and mental energy. The implementation path of most of his circulars ran straight from his in-tray to the wastepaper basket. This had been his system ever since he'd been made an inspector and there had never been any comebacks, but whenever he saw programs on television about destroying rain forests, he invariably felt personally responsible for several acres.

The severity of his screening process helped him to get through it all very quickly and, by the time Ross arrived, his desk was clear and he was looking through the batch of reports on the various injustices that some of West Grampian's residents had perpetrated on others in the past couple of days. Amongst the usual thefts and brawls there was one rape that looked particularly unpleasant and a case of indecent exposure at the Technical College.

"Has McNeil been on the rape counseling course?" he asked.

Ross was hanging his coat behind the door.

"Think so," he said.

"Right," said Carston, picking the rape file out of the bundle and holding it up. "When she's finished checking those two clients that

95

changed accounts to Borney, we'll make her available to whoever's looking after this one. Find out who it is, will you?"

As Ross reached for the phone, Carston stood up.

"I'll get 'em briefed and on their way," he said. "See you there."

As he left, he heard Ross begin speaking to Sandy Dwyer.

The team was waiting for him, McNeil and Spurle involved in a discussion about the value of women in the force, Bellman and Thom listening and chipping in with predictable reservations about having to defend female colleagues when things got heavy on Friday and Saturday nights. Fraser, to everyone's amazement, was reading. The briefing itself was straightforward, since most of the work had already been allocated. Within ten minutes they'd been sent on their various errands and only McNeil and Ross remained. Carston flicked through the file he was holding.

"You have been on the rape counseling course, haven't you, McNeil?" he asked.

"Yes, sir."

"Got a case for you here. Whose is it, Jim?"

"DCI Baxter, sir," said Ross.

"Right," said Carston to McNeil. "As soon as you've sorted those two clients out at Borney and Whitcombe, get on to DCI Baxter. I can't really spare you but I think you'd probably be useful to him for this. It's not very nice. I think the woman's going to need a bit of looking after."

"Right, sir."

"Away you go, then."

"I had a thought," said Ross as he and Carston went back into the office.

"Congratulations," said Carston.

"Before we go and see Burnham, I'd like to just check out some of those phone numbers. In case there's anything there to ask him about."

Carston looked at his watch.

"Yes, OK. Get on to him first, though. Just in case he's there. Tell him we want to see him today. I'll take a look at that video."

Ross went back to use a phone in the squad room and managed to get Burnham right away. He told him that they'd be calling within the hour. To his surprise, Burnham said nothing and just hung up. He sounded passive, subdued, and Ross was confident that he'd be there waiting when they arrived. Without putting down the phone, he pressed a button, read out the number of the estate agent in Gourdon and asked the switchboard to get it for him.

His French, although infinitely more competent than that of Fraser, was still less than rudimentary and he wasn't looking forward to a protracted conversation with a fast-talking salesperson who would no doubt try to make him buy a converted Perigordian pigeon loft while prices were low. Just as it occurred to him that the estate agency might well be closed on a Saturday morning anyway, making his anxiety academic, a woman's voice in his ear said "*Allo, oui?*" with a question mark at the end of it. Ross went straight into plan A.

"*Parlez-vous anglais?*" he said and was flooded with relief when the woman replied, in an American accent, "Of course. How can I help you?"

He explained the reason for his call and waited while the woman fetched files to consult. She was back on the line almost immediately.

"Yes. Mrs. Burnham's an active client ... I'm sorry, I mean, she was. Asked me to look for a particular type of property for her and her husband."

"What sort of place?" asked Ross.

"They wanted somewhere detached, with some ground, on the edge of a small town. In fact, I have three schedules I was about to send her. One of them would have been perfect, I just know it."

"Have you spoken to Mr. Burnham at all?"

"Just one time, I think. The rest of the time it was always Mrs. Burnham."

"Did you talk to her often, then?"

"Not recently. But up to about a month ago, yes, quite often. She was very keen."

"When was the last time she called?"

"As I said, last month some time."

"What did she talk about then?"

"Well, I can't remember anything special, but it must have been the same as always. Did I have anything yet? That's all we ever spoke about."

Ross asked if she would mind sending him anything she had from Mrs. Burnham and, after an embarrassing attempt to lighten the call by congratulating her on her English and promptly being told she was from Massachusetts, he rang off.

Next came the travel agent in Nottingham. Ross was impressed: another office open early on a Saturday, but she had no idea what he was talking about and there was no trace of anyone called Burnham in her files. The nearest she'd ever come to anyone from Cairnburgh was when she'd booked flights for an oilman from Aberdeen to Houston via London, Boston and Chicago.

The local faith healer was interesting. Her name was Joyce Creedle and her husband was the manager of one of the branches of the Clydesdale bank. She remembered meeting Mrs. Burnham at a lunch he'd organized for a charity fund-raising in the summer. Her memory had been jogged by reading about the death, of course, but Mrs. Burnham's seemingly genuine interest in faith healing had also made the meeting stick in her mind. She'd asked lots of questions and seemed interested in how healing worked on the mind, rather than on the body. When Ross asked the woman if she could remember anything a bit more specific, she only said that the impression she'd got was that Mrs. Burnham wasn't just interested in the theory of faith healing or the belief systems behind it, but in whether or not it actually worked, and particularly whether it worked for mental illnesses.

"Did she mean herself, d'you think?" asked Ross.

"Oh no, I don't think so," replied Mrs. Creedle in a voice that made Ross think of cardigans and afternoon tea. "She seemed ... very lively, bright, very interested. Her aura was very positive."

The word aura made Ross hesitate a little.

"So who d'you think she was thinking of then?" he asked.

"Thinking of?"

"The person who needed healing. The person with mental problems."

"Oh, I'm not sure there was anybody in particular. I couldn't be certain, of course, but I don't think so ..."

Her voice tailed off as she tried to focus on her recollections. Ross was irritated by her. First she was convinced that Mrs. Burnham was making a genuine inquiry, then she backed off and said that it wasn't specific and with the whole thing being illuminated by auras, he didn't see her contribution being worth much. As he pressed her further for more precise details, she became more and more defensive and less and less certain about what had been said. After a while Ross was fully expecting that she'd suddenly reveal that she'd been contacted by Stephanie Burnham from the other side. To have the murderer identified by the victim would save lots of time and trouble but would be hard to incorporate into a prosecution case. In the end, as Mrs. Creedle began to react to his skepticism and lecture him on negative attitudes and auras, he cut his losses, thanked her and rang off. He made the sign of the cross over the phone and immediately felt guilty for doing so.

Barbara Stone drove a dazzling white Honda CRX. It was over a year old now and she'd have preferred a Porsche or the new Toyota Turbo but the Italian restaurateur who'd bought it for her had become a rich man by knowing when to draw the line. She'd been with him for seven months the previous year and, after only two weeks, had convinced him that his penis was to sex what Pavarotti's voice was to opera; huge and masterly in its application. If she'd taken her time and simulated more orgasms, the Toyota might have been forthcoming, but when the Honda had been offered as a gesture of post-coital largesse, she'd wisely decided to accept the bird in the hand.

She usually enjoyed the effect she always had when driving it but this morning the stares of the men she passed didn't register. Her mind was elsewhere. Burnham had phoned her repeatedly when he'd got home, leaving ever more desperate, pleading messages on her answering machine. She didn't know yet whether she'd ever get in touch with him and renew their affair but, while she was deciding, she needed to know that he was suffering. And she wanted to talk to the police while her bruises were still ripe.

She swept into a parking space outside the station and got out,

99

pushing her dark glasses higher on her nose and pulling the turquoise silk scarf further forward over her head. At the desk, she asked the uniformed constable who was in charge of the Burnham investigation. She managed to make the young man feel that she'd come specially to ask him that and he was on the point of showing her straight through to Carston's room when Sandy Dwyer, the desk sergeant, wanting his share of the contact, eased him aside and asked Stone if he could be of any assistance. After a short conversation, in which she'd suggested that she had information relevant to the case and also managed to convey the pleasure she was getting from their chat, he picked up the phone, punched up Carston's number and announced her presence.

In his office, Carston answered the phone absent-mindedly.

"Who?" he said.

He listened for a while.

"Look, Sergeant Ross and I are about to go and interview Burnham."

He listened again.

"Well, what's she supposed to know?" he asked eventually.

The answer still didn't satisfy him.

"Can't she tell you about it? Make a statement or something?"

He listened again.

"Well, Spurle or Fraser then."

The incoherence of the answer surprised him.

"Is there something the matter with you, Sandy?" he asked. "She's not holding a gun in your face, is she?"

He looked at his watch as he listened to the desk sergeant's renewed encouragements to talk to the woman.

"OK, OK," he said. "Send her up. But if she's wasting my time, it's your balls, Sandy."

He was surprised to get the reply "you don't know how right you are, sir," and continued to scan the open file on his desk until there was a knock and the door opened. Sandy looked round it.

"Mrs. Stone, sir," he said as he stood aside.

Carston didn't understand this. Sandy was acting like a bellboy in a bloody hotel. Stone walked in, her hand outstretched, and her attention directed exclusively at Carston. He stood up, accepted the handshake, motioned to the chair beside the desk and looked at Sandy, who was still at the door.

"Thanks, Sandy. I'll see you get your tip," he said.

The sergeant left with a final smile at Stone and Carston sat down again.

"Thank you very much for seeing me," said Stone, her voice throaty, small. "I know you're busy but I wanted to get in touch before the poisoned tongues did. A sort of pre-emptive strike."

Carston noted that her clothes were expensive, classy and calculated. She wore a dark, wine-colored suit that had the sheen of cashmere. The silk scarf was still pulled forward on her head and her face was shadowed by it. The effect was the same as that created by film stars who try to avoid being recognized by wearing a disguise which screams out that there's somebody special underneath it.

"The sergeant said you had some information," said Carston.

Her voice dropped lower still.

"That was a small lie. I don't really have anything definite …"

She saw annoyance begin in his face and hurried on.

"… but I am connected with it all. In a way. I think it's relevant. I promise you I'm not wasting your time."

Carston was annoyed not only by the fact that she was there under false pretences but by the blatant way in which she was trying to woo him. He felt her attraction, knew the appeal she'd worked on Sandy Dwyer, but was secure enough in himself not to need the flattery her attention seemed to offer. The sexual sub-text of their contact was of no interest to him.

"I really am very busy, Mrs. … Stone," he said, making a point of referring to the scrap of paper on which he'd written her name. "Usually, my team filters out interviews before they get passed on to me." He was aware of how pompous he sounded but, instinctively, he disliked the woman and wanted her to know that she was wasting her sexual energy. "Perhaps you could speak to one of my …"

"I'm Michael Burnham's lover. We've been having an affair since February." The voice had changed completely. It was clear, businesslike, direct. Carston stopped. This was interesting. But he still wasn't hooked.

"And you think that has some direct relevance to his wife's murder?" he asked.

Stone shrugged.

"You're the detective."

Carston grudgingly recognized her confidence. He'd prefer someone like this as a friend rather than an enemy. There was also the fact that if he passed her on to Spurle, Fraser or the others, she'd probably end up getting them to confess that they'd committed the murder themselves. McNeil would be able to handle her, but she'd already left. He leaned forward on his desk, inviting confidences.

"Right," he said. "What d'you think we should know?"

Stone smiled.

"I'm not making it that easy for you, Inspector."

He resisted the temptation to remind her of his correct rank.

"OK," he said. "Let's start with the day of the murder."

"Ah, I can't help you much there, I'm afraid. I was at home in Aberdeen. Working, actually."

"Alone, I suppose?"

Again the smile.

"That's right. And I didn't even speak to anyone on the telephone. It's a project I'm presenting to an offshore conference in Birmingham next month. I need to get it finalized. So no interruptions. I had the answering machine on."

"Handy things, aren't they?" said Carston.

"Very," she replied. "In fact, I was surprised Michael didn't call."

"Why? Does he usually?"

"No, not necessarily. But he was supposed to be looking by for a spot of lunch that day and he didn't show. He usually calls if he can't make it."

Carston allowed a space for himself to absorb this news and for her to add to it. She certainly wasn't naïve. She knew exactly what damage she might be causing her lover. Her glasses and the shadows on her face made it difficult to see any expression but her tone was all innocence.

"How often do you see him?" he asked, very interested now.

"Two or three times a week. Sometimes more."

"Have you seen him recently?"

Her hand lifted as if to adjust her glasses but stopped and fell back in her lap. It was a gesture he was supposed to notice.

"Oh yes," she said. "Yesterday evening. His wife dying didn't change anything." She paused before adding, "D'you want the truth?"

"Nothing but," said Carston.

Stone leaned forward in her chair, matching Carston's own attitude.

"He was insatiable. He phoned me the evening of the murder. Wanted to stay with me then. Imagine."

"No accounting for taste," said Carston, pleased with the ambiguity. Stone picked it up and her smile was fuller, more generous.

"Are you taking me seriously, Inspector?"

Carston sat back. Despite his dislike of her and the seriousness of her information, it was true that he'd been drawn into a sort of banter. This bloody woman was making him act very unprofessionally.

"I'm sorry, Mrs. Stone. Of course I am. As you said at the start, this could be very important. Perhaps if we go back a little and you tell me how your relationship with Mr. Burnham started."

"Certainly. What would you like to know?" asked Stone, settling back.

They talked about the beginnings of the affair, Burnham's infatuation with her, the weekends they'd grabbed in North Wales at a hotel near Beaumaris Castle, short trips to Paris which rushed through business to make as much time as possible for pleasure, and a summer which sounded more like a teenager's dream than the journal of a man on the edge of middle age.

"Was it all good?" asked Carston, when she described the last weekend they'd spent away, at a hotel in West Linton, just south of Edinburgh.

"Yes. Mostly," she said without hesitation. "He'd get a bit morose sometimes, sort of gooey. He'd talk about leaving his wife and start regretting that we couldn't be together more, but there was no point in all that and mostly we just had a good time. No responsibilities. Just … you know."

"He was serious about leaving his wife, was he?"

"Oh yes. No doubt about that. They'd grown out of each other

103

really. I don't think she had much to offer him. You're married, are you?"

Carston nodded.

"Well, you know what it's like then."

Carston was surprised by this blind spot. Could she really not conceive of a relationship that might last? He decided against getting into a discussion about it and just nodded. His expression must have betrayed him, though, because she immediately covered her tracks.

"Oh, I know some people are content. But they're the happy few, aren't they? None of the problems of passion, just videos and TV suppers."

Carston flushed as he recognized the precise description of a typical Wednesday evening with Kath.

"Maybe they have both," he said, defensively.

"Yes, maybe," she replied, meaning "No chance!" "But that wasn't what Michael wanted. He's a passionate man, Inspector."

"Why didn't he leave, then?"

"Oh he was going to. I tried to talk him out of it but he was all ready to move out in the summer."

"But he didn't."

Her smile had gone and Carston knew that she was controlling her voice very carefully. The words were slower.

"No. She was pregnant. He couldn't leave her, could he? That would have been cruel. I told him so."

"So he was still ready to? Even with her pregnancy?"

"No. I don't think so. Hard to say, but I don't think he would have. I certainly couldn't have lived with him, knowing that."

Everything she said about Burnham was pushing him deeper and deeper into trouble and, for all the apparent innocence of the woman, Carston knew that she knew it. He couldn't work out why she would do such a thing to a man she'd been having such a good time with. In all her tales of their summer wanderings, it had seemed that her enjoyment had been as great as Burnham's and yet she'd conned her way into the office and not only made his alibi even shakier but given him a very strong motive to get rid of his wife. Carston wanted to know more about her.

"What did you feel when he told you about the pregnancy?" he asked.

"Honestly?" she said.

"Of course."

"I was jealous."

She said it as a challenge. Carston was careful not to react, but Stone was continuing.

"Not of her having a kid. I've never felt the need to go through all that disgusting rigmarole, thank God. No, I was jealous that Michael had fucked her. Sorry if that shocks but why bother with euphemisms?"

"It affected you quite a lot, then?"

"Oh no. That was just my first reaction. He and I were having a good time. I was just … well, maybe a bit disappointed to find that he'd been lying to me."

"Lying?"

"Yes. He said he and Stephanie slept in separate rooms. Said they hadn't … made love for ages. Of course, maybe he didn't do it. Maybe it was somebody else's kid. Who knows nowadays?"

"Was Mrs. Burnham seeing someone else, then?"

Stone drew her head back.

"Inspector," she said. "Now how am I supposed to know that? I've never even met the woman. From Michael's description of her, her lover would have to have a white stick and a guide dog, but his view's a bit jaundiced, isn't it?"

Carston felt another pang of sympathy for the dead woman. Her life had been surrounded by venom. Even people who hadn't met her dismissed her with some ferocity.

"Mrs. Stone. Her murder was brutal, remember," he said.

"Yes, I do remember. And that's why I'm here. Voluntarily. To try to help you with it if I can. But don't expect me to pretend anything. I didn't know the woman. Everything I say about her I've heard from Michael."

It almost amounted to an outburst. Carston waited but she had composed herself again.

"So where has all that left your relationship?" he asked.

Her hesitation was calculated.

"I don't know," she said, her voice soft now, perhaps a little hurt. "I haven't spoken to him since he ... It's hardly the time to talk about us, is it?"

"I thought he'd managed to come to terms with his grief. Insatiable was the word you used, I think."

His provocation was deliberate. She didn't bite.

"I'm sure that was just shock. Since then ..."

She stopped, shrugged, and Carston saw her hand move again to adjust her glasses. This time she went through with the movement and her fingers brushed briefly at her left temple. He'd already noticed the darker patches of bruised flesh, especially on that side of her face. She picked up his stare and her hand went back up to cover her cheek.

"You noticed," she said. "That's what all the Garbo gear is for."

"What happened?" asked Carston, knowing that he was supposed to.

She took off her glasses and held back the scarf to show the black eye, the cuts on her eyebrow and the purple stains on her face and neck.

"Pretty, isn't it?" she said. "That's what you get when you pull out a drawer that's stuck. My own fault. Stupid. Reaching up, yanking at the thing. It just came away. Fell right on top of me, the drawer and everything in it."

The lie was totally unconvincing and they both knew it. In any case, Carston had seen enough beatings to know almost exactly what had happened to her. It was her business, but it was very intriguing.

"Maybe you need a man about the house," he said.

She put the glasses on, pulled the scarf back again and smiled with admiration at him.

"No. I don't think so."

Rather than ending, their conversation had come to an impasse. Each had a different opinion of the other than when it had started. Stone found Carston's imperviousness to her appeal both challenging and exciting, and for him, her obvious sexual charisma had been supplemented by a mysteriousness which was much more compelling.

Carston broke the silence. "Look, I'm afraid I really do have to leave."

Stone stood up immediately.

"Of course. I don't want to take up your time."

"On the contrary," said Carston, coming round the desk to her. "You've been most helpful and I'm glad you came."

She smiled a wider, different smile from the ones she'd used earlier. This was a dangerous woman. He opened the door and walked her down the stairs and out to the front door. There, they shook hands again.

"I'd like to talk to you again later, if I may," said Carston. "Can I get in touch?"

She took a card from her bag and handed it to him.

"That's got both my numbers, business and home."

"What if you've got the answering machine on?" he asked, flirting in spite of himself.

"For you, I'll answer," she said.

Carston couldn't stop his smile.

"Thank you for coming, Mrs. Stone."

"Thank you for having me, Chief Inspector."

Apart from the blatant innuendo, she'd also stressed the "chief" just enough to let him know she'd been teasing him earlier. He pointed a finger at her and she blew him a kiss. He forced himself not to watch her walk to her car and turned back to find Sandy looking at him.

"Your balls too, sir, isn't it?" said the sergeant.

In the squad room everyone knew that Julie McNeil was tough. She'd worked at her resilience and developed a capacity to keep silent when the remarks of colleagues like Fraser and Spurle needled into her exasperation. She could distinguish between their deliberate provocations and the unconscious sexism that showed through so much of their banter and responded to each with a quiet strength that denied them the satisfaction they were looking for. Suppressing her reactions to the sort of condescension with which Borney was treating her as she sat in his office, however, was much more difficult. Fraser and Spurle at least recognized that she was part of their team; Borney hardly acknowledged that she belonged to the same species.

She'd explained that it was necessary for the police to look at every aspect of Mrs. Burnham's activities in the weeks before her death and that any unusual events, like the sudden reallocation of clients' accounts, were of particular interest. After making it very clear to her that, for those who worked in finance, Saturday was a rest day, he'd begun to lecture her about client confidentiality and the need to guard against betrayals of trust. What had irritated her more than anything else was the "I-wouldn't-expect-you-to-understand" manner in which it had all been offered.

"Well, I'm afraid DCI Carston insisted, sir. You see, we do need to get access to those two files," she said at last, breaking in on his lecture on financial morality.

"Out of the question, my dear … constable," he replied, hesitating over her rank as if he found it mildly amusing. "You see, they're both active. I couldn't possibly let them out of the office at any time. An active file means exactly that, and it could hardly be active if it's sitting on your inspector's desk, could it?"

His eyes held hers briefly then flicked down to her breasts. McNeil had become used to this division in his attention and it added to the irritation she felt.

"Right, sir. I'll have to clear it with Mr. Dunkley and Dr. Strong themselves then, won't I?"

Borney's smile almost broadened to a laugh.

"Oh my goodness me, no. I couldn't possibly allow that. I think they'd be quite shocked to find their financial affairs being investigated by the police, however attractive the investigating officer."

"It's not about financial affairs. It's about murder," said McNeil.

"No, you're wrong," said Borney, as if he were explaining something to a simpleton. "As far as we and our clients are concerned, it's about financial security, the faith that makes them entrust us with their affairs. It's a sacred bond which I will not jeopardize."

He was obviously pleased with the stance he was taking. McNeil snapped her notebook shut and put it away.

"Right," she said, "maybe I'd be better contacting DCI Carston now to get him to come along and explain your rights and duties to you."

Borney was about to reply when she went on.

"I ought to tell you, though, that he's quite busy and that he's delegated the job to me, so if I have to report back and tell him ye're no co-operating, he'll give me a rollocking, but he'll be bloody sharp wi' you, too."

She'd deliberately allowed her accent to thicken, wanting to shake his smugness, to provoke something other than his tolerance. He looked at her with a question on his face, his eyes staying on hers this time.

"You're surely not threatening me, Miss ...?"

McNeil's gaze held his.

"Detective Constable McNeil. No sir, it's not a threat. It's a fact. You've got your client's interests to look after, we've got the public to protect. It's not easy."

Her eyes were harder, stronger than his and he was forced to look away.

"We seem to be in something of an impasse then, don't we?" he said.

"No sir," said McNeil, giving no ground. "We need to see those two files. You've got them. Simple as that. They're an important part of our inquiries. If we don't get them, you could be charged as an accessory."

"What?" he said, sitting upright in his chair.

McNeil had no idea of whether what she was saying was true or not but she'd had enough of his superiority. She stood up to indicate that their interview was over.

"So what do I tell DCI Carston?" she asked, looking down on him.

Fortunately for her, Borney was even less sure of his legal position than she was. He shook his head.

"This is all most regrettable," he said, then he bent down, unlocked the bottom drawer of his desk and took out several folders from which he selected two.

"Now listen," he said, trying to re-establish himself. "I can't let you see these until I've informed our clients of the circumstances. Thereafter, if, and only if, they give us permission, I'll arrange for copies of all relevant documents to be made available to your chief inspector."

"And how long will that take?" asked McNeil, still standing.

"It depends where they are. Certainly by the end of the day, I should think."

McNeil sat down again but perched forward in the chair, not wanting to lose the dominance she'd established.

"Right, by this evening then. Now, why the change?"

"What?" said Borney, for whom she was now moving too quickly.

"Why the change from Mrs. Burnham to you?"

Borney tapped on the top file with his fingers, disorientated by her aggression, looking to reinstate himself. Eventually, he shrugged slightly.

"I suppose you could call it incompatibility of interests."

"And, if you did, what would it mean?"

"They were looking in different directions."

McNeil was exasperated by the man's refusal (or inability) to speak directly to her.

"Mr. Borney," she said, "I'm not a financial adviser. I'm a simple policewoman. Now do me a favor and tell me what you mean."

It gave him back a little security. Her admission of ignorance made her vulnerable again. He sat back further in his chair.

"It was about five weeks ago. Dr. Strong and Mr. Dunkley had both phoned in and asked about the same thing. Some traded options in Dexters, a food processing company. Apparently Mrs. Burnham thought it was an unwise investment and advised against it. They insisted and ..."

He stopped.

"And?" McNeil prompted.

Borney began looking through one of the files.

"Well, there was ... an altercation. The more they tried to press her, the less co-operative she became. Here ..."

He pushed a piece of paper which he'd taken from the file across the desk to her. She picked it up. It was a letter from Stephanie Burnham to Mr. Dunkley and although it began and ended with the usual polite epistolary formulae, there was no semblance of business etiquette in its substance.

"Your persistence in pursuing the acquisition of these options," McNeil read, "is tantamount to a declaration of incompetence on my part and as well as compromising your financial position and deflecting the main thrust of your portfolio, it calls into question the professionalism of your adviser. Such a serious demonstration of a crisis in confidence on your part makes my position as manager of your portfolio completely untenable. I shall continue to oppose your desire to take option contracts on Dexters shares and, if your determination to buy continues, I shall recommend to my superiors that your account be transferred elsewhere."

"Strong stuff," said McNeil, handing the letter back to him.

"Yes. Completely out of character, too. She wrote exactly the same letter to Dr. Strong. They were on the phone to me as soon as they received them."

"What happened?"

"I had to pacify them, naturally. They were furious. Well, for God's sake, it's like some sort of personal attack on them."

"So you transferred their accounts to yourself?"

"Of course. Couldn't risk any more of that sort of nonsense."

"And did you buy the things they wanted?"

"The Dexters options? Well, yes, of course. It was their money after all."

"And?"

"What?"

"Well, was Mrs. Burnham right or not? Was it a good idea?"

Borney shook his head.

"Neither good nor bad. Nothing's happened to them. They've stayed where they were. Still got seven weeks to run, so anything could happen."

"Any idea why Mrs. Burnham was so against buying them?" she asked after a pause.

"None at all. Just a straightforward deal. Nothing to get het up about."

His memories of the events had opened him up a little. McNeil gently pressed on with her advantage.

"Did she often get things wrong like that?"

Borney shook his head again.

"No. She was very good, really she was." He tapped the files on his desk. "If you look through these, you'll see that she's been very shrewd. Dunkley and Strong actually did very well out of her until this blew up. Perhaps it was just options she didn't like. She wasn't a gambler, you see."

"No, tell me," said McNeil.

Borney was slipping back into the comfort of his role. He looked at her, smiled a smile of superior knowledge, let his eyes fall to her breasts again and condescended once more. He explained that options were a way of gambling on shares going up or down without having to lay out the full share price. It was a more risky type of investment but offered potentially greater rewards.

"So Mrs. Burnham really was trying to protect their interests?" she said when he'd finished.

"Well, yes. But if an investor wants to go for high risk strategies, we have to provide the same level of service. As I said, in the end it's their money that's being invested."

McNeil nodded.

"Can I ask you just one more question?" she said.

Borney was now fully reinstated into his sense of security.

"Of course," he said, both hands offering magnanimity.

"Can you think of any other times when she reacted like this, or was this a one-off?"

Borney put his head back, looked at the ceiling and appeared to be considering her question.

"I can't remember anything like this before."

He made a noise that sounded like a chuckle.

"If there had been, we'd hardly have promoted her, would we?"

"Probably not," said McNeil with a smile. She wanted to ask about Stephanie Burnham's drinking but wasn't sure how much of that had come out in the conversation that Carston had already had with him. It was also outside her brief and she couldn't afford any mistakes. Mistakes by male colleagues were the source of jokes and backchat, by her they were confirmations that women in the force were a waste of space.

She got up again and thanked Borney for his time. He stood up, tugged at his waistcoat and pulled in his stomach before saying that it had been a pleasure. She reminded him about the files and quickly made her way down the stairs and out into the street.

The mist was still hanging around and she pulled her collar up as she walked to her car. On the passenger seat was the file on the alleged rape that would preoccupy her for the rest of the day. The conversation with Borney had been a strain but she knew that the one she was about to have with the woman who'd been subjected to the rapist's appetites would be agonizing.

Chapter Five

When Ross went back into Carston's office, ready for the trip to Dyson Close, Carston was peering at the buttons on the remote control. He'd used the video recorder many times before but had a pathological distrust of things electronic and never remembered how to operate them. He found the play button and pressed it just as Ross came in. Ross looked at the color bars on the screen. They watched the color bars fade to be replaced by a wide shot of the study with its overturned chair, the skirt, gun, scattered books and dark huddle of Stephanie Burnham's body. Carston looked at the remote control again, found the pause button and pressed it. The picture rewound fast and the color bars were back.

"Shit!" said Carston. "I never get used to these bloody things."

Ross came to stand beside him.

"I've phoned those numbers," he said. "One or two interesting things. I'll tell you all about them in the car."

"Right," said Carston, still peering down.

Ross reached across and pressed a button. The bars steadied, then disappeared. The study materialized again. Ross touched another button. The picture rolled, then the frame froze.

"Bloody clever," said Carston. "Misspent youth, that's all that proves."

Ross grinned and went out, leaving Carston looking at the screen. He pressed the play button again. From the wide shot, the picture suddenly cut to one in which the body filled the screen. Slowly, the camera moved around, lingering obscenely on the woman in her terminal helplessness. As her face appeared in close-up, Carston paused the tape again.

The glazed appearance of the half-closed eyes left no doubts that this was a corpse. No actor in any of the films or television plays he'd seen could ever simulate that total lack of light. But the roundness of the flesh of her cheeks and the tumble of dark hair across her unlined neck were tantalizing. Carston had learned so much about this person and her contradictions and here she was, two feet from the lens, her individuality still functioning and yet locked in stillness. He pressed the play button, and the camera panned along her body, dwelling on the folds of her blouse, catching the swell of a breast pushed up by the arm under her chest, following the twisted line of her bare legs, picking up the detail of her clenched fist with its fibers and finally closing in on the hole in her back.

Carston paused the tape again and sat for a while before restarting it. When he did, the shot pulled wide and showed the body in relation to the overturned chair. Next came the skirt, then the gun, the books and finally, the desk and the things lying near and under it. Each item was located in relation to the other things around it before being scrutinized more closely. In the darkness under the desk were her knickers, a crumpled shape which only became recognizable when the camera's light was angled directly at them.

Each of these objects was studied by Carston along with the forensic notes on the desk beside him. He was looking for events, trying to create a sequence that had placed these things in their final locations and led up to the murder and, as Ross had said when they first speculated about it, it was all too obvious. She'd tried to stop her attacker, grabbing at books and scrabbling at the shelves, door and walls as he'd pulled her down. Her skirt and knickers had been pulled off, tearing in the process, and been flung aside, the knickers ending up under the desk. So how come they had semen on them? And the only bruises on her arms came from her banging against the shelves. Why were there no other more generalized bruises apart from those on and around her vagina and anus? Why were there no other marks where she'd been held and dragged down? The autopsy report noted small bruises and abrasions on her buttocks consistent with her being pushed against the floor by someone on top of her. There were also the sickening details of how she'd been forcibly penetrated with the gun and the plunger.

It all added up to a particularly savage rape and yet she carried so few signs of having resisted it all. Perhaps, then, she'd not been forced at all and the chaos of the books and all the rest was the result of violent, consensual sex. But did that include sticking a fork into her, for Christ's sake? Three times in one leg, twice in the other. What was that for? OK, say she went along with it. Then they'd had sex. But why was the gun there? Was that always a part of their weird games? Surely she'd never have just sat there and let him put it against her back and fire. She'd have tried to run away. But it was a contact wound. OK then, maybe she thought it was a game. Maybe they had done this sort of thing before. Carston had seen the bodies of women with all sorts of objects broken off inside them; it wouldn't come as a great surprise to learn that, with or without her consent, Burnham now and again rested his own erectile tissues and substituted for them a broom handle, or even the barrel of a shotgun. Like everything else about Stephanie Burnham, her death was cluttered with inconsistencies.

Carston rewound the tape, ejected it (at the third attempt) and switched off the machine. He'd learned little from it and yet lurking amongst all these details was an explanation, a reconstruction which would account for every distinct thing, every spatial relationship. It would accurately describe the single set of circumstances that had actually happened. It would be the only way in which all these features could be accommodated but Carston had no idea what the hell it was.

In the car, on the way to Dyson Close, Carston went back over the interview he'd had with Barbara Stone and summarized the information for Ross. When he'd finished, Ross whistled.

"Motive, opportunity, no alibi. Don't need much else, do we?"

"I suppose not," said Carston.

They were driving along a row of large semis, built by money from agriculture and fishing and valued ever upwards since the early Seventies by oil. Each house had a broad front garden and the predominating flowers were roses, big hybrid teas, Peace, Pink

Peace, Just Joey. Even this late in the year, there were still plenty of blooms, brazen and exciting against the granite. They were the only outward show of joy. The houses behind them were solid, closed against the elements and the curiosity of strangers. Carston was quiet for a while as he looked at them.

"I wonder if we can trust her, though," he said at last.

Ross flipped the indicator upwards, ready to turn right.

"Why shouldn't we?" he asked.

"Dunno. It's all … calculated. She uses that sexiness of hers like a sort of screen. I'm bloody sure that half the time she's talking to men they're not listening to what she's saying. They're mentally up her skirt or down her jumper."

"Prick teaser, eh?"

"Seems like it. One of the best, though. She could get away with murder."

"Literally?"

Carston thought for a moment.

"Why not?" he said. "She wouldn't have to do it herself. She'd get some sex-slave to do it."

Ross's wife had been away for more than a week and brief fantasies about sex-slavery kept him quiet for a while. Carston indulged in some more silent thinking about the enigmatic Barbara Stone.

They turned into another row of expensive middle-class barracks and eventually Carston forced himself out of his reverie and asked about the phone calls that Ross had been making. Ross told him first about France, then the faith healer.

"Bloody hell," said Carston. "Frank Creedle's wife? A faith healer. No wonder he keeps quiet about her."

"You know her then?"

"Not her, no. But Frank was at those golf lessons I went to in the summer. You know, the evening classes. It was talking to him that made me change from the Royal Bank to the Clydesdale."

For some reason, the thought that Creedle's wife was nutty enough to be a faith healer made him feel more pleased with himself.

"That Major Lawrie's not much use, either," said Ross.

"Oh yes," said Carston, remembering. "The guy at the gun club who spoke to Mrs. Burnham. What did he have to say?"

"Nothing much. Just like Fraser said. She was there with her husband one evening. He was out with that pillock who runs the place. She and Lawrie were in the clubhouse. He'd just finished shooting. They got talking. She tried to sell him some shares apparently."

"Eh?" Carston was genuinely surprised. "I didn't think she was that pushy."

"No. Took Lawrie by surprise. 'Not the sort of thing you expect from a filly.' That's the way he put it. He wasn't interested anyway. They talked about guns, gear, the club. He can't remember much else about her, he says. Didn't know why she was there. She obviously didn't know anything about sport."

"Well, fillies don't, do they?" said Carston.

They were pulling into Dyson Close. It was quiet, untroubled, the fronts of its houses newer than those they'd been driving past but equally closed. Most of them had an alarm box jutting prominently over the front door. They parked, walked up to the door and rang the bell. Carston was irritated by the predictable double chime. They always sounded so bloody cheerful.

"How d'you want to play it?" asked Ross.

"By ear," said Carston. "I'll start it off. Chip in if you like."

They heard Burnham's footsteps and Ross nodded briefly just as the door opened. Burnham said nothing. He simply held the door wide, stood back and waited for them to come in. He was wearing dark blue trousers, a stone-colored linen shirt and a tie with claret and blue stripes. Today, he looked his age. Carston and Ross stopped in the hall.

"Straight through and second left. You know your way," said Burnham, his tone betraying that their presence was an irritant.

They followed his directions and went into a room that Carston only vaguely remembered from his first visit. It was large and somehow clinical. The sofa and two chairs were of soft dark brown leather, the walls were covered in a textured oatmeal paper and the carpet was rust colored, deep and expensive. The tones in the two prints on the longer wall opposite the fireplace were muted and presumably intended to be restful. Everything was exactly right, mathematically proportioned and completely cold. The only unpremeditated element of the whole scene was the dark blue jacket draped over the arm of one of the chairs.

A drinks cabinet was open in the corner beside the window. Burnham followed them into the room, waved them towards chairs and went across to it to add more whisky to the tumbler from which he'd been drinking before their arrival. He held the bottle towards them, his gesture and expression asking if they'd join him. Ross held up a hand, the palm facing Burnham. Carston wondered if the whole interview was going to be conducted in mime, decided that would make his job much harder and said, "Not while we're on duty, sir." Burnham and Ross both looked at him, suspicious of the cliché. Carston's face was innocent but he enjoyed the effect. He waited for Burnham to sit down and let the silence last. It was Burnham who broke it.

"Well? It seems you're desperate to see me."

Carston looked at Ross then back at Burnham.

"Desperate?" he said. "I wouldn't say that. Just that a few things have come up and we'd like to check over them with you."

He could see the strain in Burnham's face. He guessed that the man hadn't been sleeping very well.

Burnham took another sip of his drink.

"OK, but I'd rather we got through whatever it is as quickly as possible."

"Of course," said Carston, making a show of becoming businesslike. "First of all, would you mind if Sergeant Ross took your fingerprints?"

Burnham looked up quickly. Carston smiled reassurance.

"For elimination purposes as much as anything else. All the prints in the study. Yours are bound to be there, aren't they? We need to find out who else has been there … If anybody."

His pause before the last two words was beautifully timed. Both Burnham and Ross reacted to it. As Carston settled back in his chair, Ross busied himself with the kit he'd brought from the station. He opened an ink pad and spread a strip of paper on the coffee table.

"Well," said Carston brightly as Ross rolled the first of Burnham's fingers across the pad before transferring it to the paper, "let's start with France, shall we?"

Burnham frowned.

"France?" he said. "What do you mean, France?"

"Your house there. Well, no. The one you're going to buy. Unless you've changed your mind since the … since last Wednesday."

Burnham was completely thrown.

"What on earth are you talking about?"

"Sergeant?" said Carston.

Ross continued the fingerprinting as he spoke.

"*Agence Voisins*," he said in bad French. "Estate agent in Gourdon. Says you and Mrs. Burnham were looking for a place in their area."

Burnham's confusion continued.

"I've never heard of them," he said. "What nonsense is this?"

Ross paused for a moment and looked at him.

"They've heard of you, sir," he said. "Found just the place you were after, too. That's what the person I spoke to said."

"She must have mixed me up with somebody else, then," said Burnham. "Why would I want to live in France? What am I supposed to do, commute to Grampian?"

"She?" asked Carston.

"What?" said Burnham.

"You said 'She.'"

"I don't know. He, then. What's it matter? I've got no idea what you're talking about."

"It's just odd that you should know the estate agent was a woman," said Carston.

"Oh, come on," said Burnham. "What's that, a clue? I just assumed, that's all. Don't you read *The Sunday Times*? They've got ads in every week for that sort of thing. The agents are nearly all women."

"So you've been looking at the ads then?"

Burnham sighed and controlled the irritation that had been evident in his reactions.

"OK. This sounds like question time. This is me 'helping you with your inquiries,' is it? I'm being accused, right?"

"If that were the case, I'd have cautioned you," said Carston.

"Yes, but this is no quiet little chat between blokes. This finger-printing stuff. No apologies for intruding on my bereavement. You've got something on your mind, haven't you?"

"What I've got on my mind, Mr. Burnham, is the murder of your wife and the need to solve it," said Carston, slowly and quietly.

"Don't you think I have?" said Burnham, his voice rising. "Christ, a few days ago I was a married man expecting my first child, now I'm busy trying to arrange my wife's funeral. D'you think that's easy?"

"Of course not," went on Carston. "But, as I said, some things have come up, like the French estate agent, and I need to know more about them."

Ross had finished and he handed Burnham a tissue. Burnham took it, wiped the stains from his fingertips then drank more from his glass. It wasn't a sip this time. Soon he'd need another refill.

"OK," he said. "I've answered that one. I don't know anything about houses in France. That one must be down to Stephanie. She never said anything to me about it, but it's just the sort of stupid thing she'd get up to. Next?"

"The estate agent seems to think you spoke to her, certainly on one occasion," said Ross.

"Not me, sergeant," said Burnham. "Mistaken identity."

His slight loss of control hadn't lasted long. He even looked less tired. Carston realized to his disgust that they'd only succeeded in putting him on his guard. They needed to find some vulnerability. When Carston spoke again, his voice was light and casual.

"Tell me a bit about Mrs. Stone," he said.

It was unsubtle but starkly effective. Burnham's glass had been on its way to his lips. It stopped, held ready, as he looked straight at Carston. His brows drew together in a small frown. He was puzzled, interested even, and certainly disconcerted. Slowly, he took a sip of whisky and put down his glass. He got up, walked to the window and looked briefly out at the garden before pulling a drawstring to bring the floor-length curtains together. Carston wondered about the symbolic value of the gesture.

"I don't see what that relationship has to do with anything," said Burnham at last.

"I'd rather decide that for myself," said Carston.

121

Burnham considered this, walked back to his chair, sat down and said, "OK. We … we're lovers." The word came quietly.

"I see. And you met fairly regularly, did you?" asked Carston.

Burnham nodded.

"When, evenings? Weekends?"

"All sorts of times," said Burnham.

"Lunchtimes too?"

"Yes, sometimes. Why? What's all the …?"

Carston interrupted him.

"How about last Wednesday lunchtime when your wife died?"

Burnham reacted quickly.

"Of course not. Where'd you get that idea?"

"Mrs. Stone, actually. I had a chat with her this morning. She seemed to think you had a lunch date last Wednesday."

The answer came at Burnham from a completely unexpected direction. His lips parted but at first he had no idea what to say. He was too surprised even to take refuge in his glass. He shook his head.

"Why?"

"Why what?"

"Why did you speak to her? Who told you about us?"

"Nobody. She came in of her own accord. Thought she might be of some help in our inquiries."

Both Ross and Carston were fascinated by the depth of the impression the news made on Burnham. He sat forward in his chair, elbows on knees and his head slumped forward. Carston signaled to Ross not to speak and waited for Burnham to say something. It was almost a minute before he did.

"Chief Inspector, I don't know what her game is, what she's after." He stopped again, his head shaking.

"There's no way I can …"

His fingers were clasped together, rubbing at one another.

"There was no lunch date. I can't prove it. Barbara's a born liar. She … dreams her life, makes things up. And then she believes them. I don't know where she's got this one from though." He stopped, then added, "Vindictive bitch!"

"Vindictive?" asked Carston, quietly, inviting the confidence.

Burnham nodded, then looked up at Carston, a challenge in his expression, his voice bitter as he spoke.

"I ... I saw her last night ... We ... I ..."

He stopped.

"Yes," said Carston.

Burnham's head dropped again.

"I hit her. I'm not proud of it, but she deserved it. She was ... Anyway, that's why she came to see you. She's trying to make things ... difficult for me. It's just spite."

He seemed to have no idea how deep a hole he might be digging for himself but his anger at Stone's betrayal, fueled by a resurgence of his jealousy, made him oblivious to anything except the need to justify what he'd done to her.

With Ross taking copious notes, Carston drew Burnham back through the previous twelve months and especially the affair with Stone. Most of the details he gave matched those which Stone had offered him earlier. Having met the woman, Carston could easily understand the infatuation, but he was nonetheless surprised by the degree of blindness it had caused in Burnham. In most ways, he seemed to be an achiever, still ambitious for power at work and proud of policies he'd introduced. He described the lean period he'd had to put up with as Calder and McStay had just managed to crawl out of a bad patch. For a while, his own job had been on the line, but he'd survived, mainly by reducing staffing in his department by over 20 percent and simultaneously increasing productivity by 32.6 percent. He described graphically a board meeting at which his strategic plan for the coming financial year had led to the resignation of two departmental heads. When the activities he was speaking of didn't involve Stone, the picture conveyed was of a hard, successful individual in charge of his own destiny.

Stone's lover, however, was a different creature: immature, unworldly, ready to jeopardize everything else to inhabit any fictions she offered. Indeed, it was the subject of Stone that made him so garrulous. Carston guessed that if the talk had simply been of work or his marriage, he would have been far less amenable; the impetus to open himself to them came from the need to re-enter the elusive magic she'd wrapped him in, to advertise his association with such a woman. In a way, thought Carston, Stone had brought some humanity back to him. Living with the single-minded achiever must have been hard; lovesickness might at least provide an interesting counterpoint.

Burnham was at the cabinet, pouring another drink.

"How much did your wife know about all this?" Carston asked.

Burnham shrugged.

"Nothing. She was … She usually had other things on her mind."

"Like what?"

Burnham's confessional urge, bolstered by the drink, continued.

"Babies," he said, taking another swig.

He left the word for them to pick up. Carston and Ross looked at each other. Carston flicked his head at Ross, inviting him to take over.

"Ah yes, sir. The pregnancy," said Ross. "D'you mind if we talk about that?"

Burnham made an expansive gesture with the hand holding the glass.

"Well, your wife was past the normal child-bearing age, wasn't she?"

"I think 'elderly prim' is the expression, sergeant."

"Yes, sir. And what was your reaction to the news?"

Burnham considered the question. His answer was a sort of confession.

"Confused," he said. "Very mixed. First of all, you think of how you have to give up your freedom. But then … It's different, isn't it? It's a future. All this stuff …" He waved his free hand to encompass the room, the house, the garden. "So what? You buy it. Set up a home. What for? There's nobody in."

Carston listened hard. There was contradiction but there was also an exposure of something that hadn't appeared before, even in his ramblings about Stone. Ross, too, knew that this was different.

"So the pregnancy wasn't planned then?" he asked.

Burnham gave a small, humorless laugh and shook his head. He put the glass down on the small table beside his chair.

"No. We didn't have sex often enough for that. That's what I thought, anyway. Then, suddenly, well …"

He stopped, remembering things. Carston suspected that he was investigating the experience again, perhaps for the first time since his wife's death. Neither of the policemen spoke as Burnham went on to tell how, to his surprise, the news had even made him stay away from Stone for a while. Not completely, but enough for her to ask questions. She'd forced the news from him and was furious, demanding choices, insisting that his talk of leaving home had to become reality. But the prospect of the baby and a renewal of his life, a regeneration of feelings he was afraid had atrophied, drew him back towards his marriage. Stone's magic was still hypnotic but, away from her, he could tease open his own dreams, independent of sex, built on simple instinctive truths.

"Look at this," he said suddenly, holding his left wrist towards Carston. He tapped the watch on it with his forefinger.

"I was looking at this one night in bed. That second hand sweeping round like that. D'you know what it's doing?"

Carston didn't know where this was heading. He waited, making no signs.

"It struck me ... That watch face, it's like the top of a great long column. And that hand's going round, slicing little thin bits off the top. And one day, there's going to be no column left. And that's me. Gone."

He let them think about the image for a while. When he went on, he looked straight at Carston.

"There was a chance to forget about that. Do something. Get another future. Not just sit watching it get ... sliced away."

For the first time, Ross had doubts about Burnham's guilt. His investment in the baby was obviously greater than he'd even admitted to himself before. What could have driven him to kill the wife who was carrying it? Whatever his motive, surely this passion was greater?

Carston was even more troubled by the new individual Burnham's words had uncovered. This troubled, expectant father, seeing meaning and purpose in a child he hadn't originally wanted, was a stranger who'd suddenly loomed up between them and the cases they were building.

Then, with equal suddenness, the paternal regret faded, the man preoccupied with the flight of time vanished. Once again, the calculating egocentric of the earlier exchanges returned. His voice dragged them both back from the beginnings of sympathy to their previous mistrust.

"And then, what does my darling Stephanie do? She wants to have an abortion."

In his earlier days, Carston had enjoyed complications. He'd never liked the idea of walking into a room, finding a knife-wielding individual drenched in gore standing astride a freshly butchered corpse, muttering, "It's a fair cop, guv." Traffic wardens could handle that sort of thing. For him, criminal investigation had always been a creative pursuit; fingerprints and forensics accumulated the data but it was imagination which recreated the event. Yet the present affair was already obscured by too many tangential things which failed to connect. Burnham's latest revelation shook the tangle once again. Carston could do without it.

Burnham loosened his tie with fumbling fingers before going on.

"It's a hellish business," he said. "I can't explain it to you. It was my child. Me ..." He looked up, his eyes moving from Carston to Ross and back again. "We've made it too easy, see? Hidden it behind words. Termination sounds harmless, even abortion's a sort of legal term nowadays. The real word's murder."

Even though the words had been spoken with a deliberateness that betrayed how much the whisky had to do with them, Ross was enough of a believer to appreciate and share their significance. He let none of his feelings show but, once again, found himself re-evaluating the man. Carston's own attitude to abortion was less rigid, but he was impressed by the obvious strength of Burnham's conviction.

"It must have been the source of some friction, I imagine," he said, aware that the question was petty and absurd in the context but needing to keep the interview moving. Burnham laughed.

"Friction? Good word. Yes, you could say that," he said. "Plenty of friction. Friction in abundance. Nothing but rows and silences from then on. Pulling each other's faces off, then walking about this place like two strangers. She was so wrapped up in her own ... Couldn't see past it. I was ... furious."

126

He was controlling his impulses, but the venom in them was obvious. As well as being a defender of the unborn, Burnham was also an angry man quite capable of striking out at the source of his annoyance. He was on his feet again and standing at the cabinet. The measures he was pouring were bigger every time.

"This stuff didn't help," he said, waving the whisky bottle. "She got a taste for it. Not whisky. Wine, martini ... I don't know, all sorts of stuff. Half the time you couldn't get any sense out of her."

He sat down again, bumping against the side of his chair as he did so.

"Great mother she'd have made," he said, before taking another mouthful.

Carston realized that, for all the poise Burnham was managing to sustain, returns would soon start to diminish very rapidly as the booze took over. In a way, though, he was talking as much for himself now as for them.

"She was mad, you know. That day. When she died. Wanting sex like that. What for? We had nothing to say to each other. But I came in and she was all over me."

Carston and Ross were very attentive. Burnham went on without a pause.

"Can you believe that? I was sweating, covered in filth from the garden, and she came on like I was Richard bloody Gere or something. I didn't understand her. If women can rape men, that's what she was doing to me."

He stopped, remembering the morning his wife died. Carston was reluctant to break the spell but he wanted more.

"So she was violent, then?" he suggested.

Burnham looked at him and nodded.

"I told you. Rape, it was. Pulling my shirt up, grabbing at me."

"And you were wearing your gardening clothes?"

Burnham stopped, aware once more that he was being questioned rather than chatting over a drink with friends.

"I told you that before. Yes. I was gardening."

"Just a shirt and trousers."

"Yes."

"No jumper or anything? It was chilly, wasn't it?"

"No, no jumper." Suddenly he stopped. Carston and Ross looked at each other.

"You're sure, sir?" asked Ross.

"No. I'm … I'm not. I think … I may have had one on. May have taken it off. When I was mowing the lawn."

"You didn't tell us that on Wednesday."

"No. I … I only found it this morning. It was soaking wet."

Ross looked at Carston.

"You found it this morning?" he said.

"Yes. I do it all the time. I take it off and just chuck it over a bush, or on the hedge or something. I'm always coming across stuff I've left out there. Is it important?"

The question was naïve but he seemed unaware of the fact.

"I don't suppose you could let us have a look at it, could you?" asked Carston.

Burnham hauled himself up.

"Of course," he said.

Suddenly, at the door of the room, he stopped.

"What d'you want it for?" he asked.

Carston controlled a small surge of irritation.

"We took all your other things, if you remember. We ought to have that too if you had it on that morning."

"Yes, of course. Sorry," said Burnham. He went out and they heard him banging his way up the stairs.

"What d'you reckon?" asked Carston. "Is this an act or what?"

"What, the drink?" said Ross.

"All of it."

Ross looked at his notes.

"Hard to say," he said. "He's not thick, is he?"

"No," agreed Carston. "It could all be a set-up."

"And he's lying about the jumper."

"Oh?"

"Aye. The lads had a look over the garden on Wednesday. Didn't find anything."

"Well, well," said Carston. He looked at the glass which Burnham had left on the arm of his chair.

"Can't see us getting much more sense out of him today, though. Not with the amount he's put away," said Ross.

Carston nodded.

"Just what I was thinking. All the same, we'll have to get him to go through all this again. We need it on tape. I think we ought to get him down to the station. At least there's no booze there."

"Are we charging him then?"

"What do you think?" asked Carston.

Ross made a so-so gesture with his right hand. Carston nodded.

"Yes. The more he says, the muckier it all gets. I don't know where the hell we are now. It's another motive, though. Get rid of her because she wants an abortion."

"Bit cock-eyed. Either way he loses the kiddie."

Carston shrugged.

"D'you think that'd occur to him? He's not normal," he said. "Maybe he just lost his temper in one of their rows. If they were both drunk …"

He stopped as they heard Burnham returning. He came back into the room and handed Carston a jumper. As soon as he saw it, Carston looked across at Ross. The sergeant nodded. It was a thick, woolen turtleneck which, according to the label, had been hand-loomed in Ireland. The autumn colors which predominated in its pattern were just like those of the strands they'd found clenched in Stephanie Burnham's right hand and spread all over the murder scene.

"And you found this today?" asked Carston.

"Yes."

"Where exactly?"

Burnham sat down and reached for his glass again.

"Down at the bottom by the shed. There are some cotoneasters there. I must've thrown it on them and it just fell over the back."

Carston turned the sweater over and looked at it more closely. There were holes in the elbows and the hem at the front was frayed and ragged. The way in which some of the smaller pieces of ribbing were snagged and puckered higher up suggested that the stitches had been pulled at from below. Carston didn't believe it. Maybe they only looked that way because he wanted them to. Maybe the colors were completely different. If they weren't, it was like suspending a big neon arrow over Burnham's head and flashing the word "guilty" on and off. With a sign to Ross, he stood up, folding the jumper under his arm.

"I think we've taken up enough of your time for today, Mr. Burnham."

"Oh. Right. Yes," said Burnham.

"But I'd like to arrange for you to come to the station to make a formal statement."

Burnham stopped at the door and turned back to them.

"So I am being charged then?" he said.

"I'd just like a formal statement, sir," said Carston again. "I'll give you a ring. Fix a time." He sounded as if he were suggesting a game of golf.

Burnham considered his words, then nodded and led them through to the front door and out onto the pavement. There, he held out a hand. Each of them shook it, formally. When Carston tried to let go, Burnham hung on.

"Barbara just wants attention," he said. "She wants to be part of it. It's exciting for her, you see? She's … she's …"

Carston was embarrassed. It was as if Burnham was near to tears. Fortunately, they didn't materialize. Instead, Burnham's grip was suddenly released and, without another word, he went back inside and shut the door.

Back at the station, as they went along the corridor towards the squad room, they were surprised to hear McNeil's voice yelling "Fuck off, Spurle." Carston opened the door and the scene in the room froze for both of them. McNeil was standing beside the photocopier, Spurle was facing her, Fraser was sitting on the edge of one of the desks and Bellman was behind another desk in a corner. A sudden silence had fallen over it all.

"What the bloody hell's going on?" said Carston.

"Nothing sir," said McNeil, her white face making it very clear that something was.

Carston looked at Ross, motioned with his head for him to come into his office, turned back to the others and said, "Right. Spurle, McNeil, in here."

He went back inside. Without looking at one another, the two constables followed him, McNeil moving quickly, the anger that had made her shout still evident, and Spurle affecting an air of troubled innocence. With a look at Fraser and Bellman, Ross went in after them, closed the door and stood beside it.

Carston sat at his desk, gave each of the two constables standing in front of it a long look, then asked quietly, "Right. What's it all about?"

McNeil stared ahead of her and said, "I lost my temper, sir. Sorry."

Spurle was looking at Carston.

"My fault, sir," he said.

Carston waited. There was silence.

"Look, stop pissing me about," he said. "I want to know what was going on. There's too much work to do to waste time with playground games."

Spurle shook his head slowly to suggest that this was all a fuss about nothing and said, "It was about Fraser's French, sir. I made a wee joke."

"It wasnae a joke," snapped McNeil.

"Let me decide that," said Carston, his tone as sharp as hers. He nodded his head at Spurle for him to go on. Spurle looked embarrassed.

"Just eel's for men and elle's for women, sir."

Carston looked at him, waiting for more. Spurle's embarrassment thickened. His voice dropped as he explained his feeble joke.

"Fraser was telling us that and I said, right enough, women was hellish." He stopped, shrugged.

"And that was it?" said Carston. Spurle shrugged again.

"Well, Julie got a wee bit …"

"Who's Julie?" interrupted Carston.

Spurle hesitated, looked at him.

"McNeil, sir," he said.

"Say so then," snapped Carston.

"Yes, sir," said Spurle, still with no idea of what Carston was getting at. "Well, sir, McNeil was a wee bit upset, and I just … well, I was taking the mickey, sir. I was out of order."

Carston looked at McNeil.

"What's your story?" he said.

"That's it, sir," she said. "Just like Spurle said. I lost the head."

Fleetingly, Carston wondered if this was a time-of-the-month reaction, then realized that that was probably exactly the sort of thing that Spurle had said. He knew that he wouldn't get any more out of them and recognized that, in the face of his authority, they'd at least managed to team up on the same story. For the time being, their solidarity before him had overcome their differences.

"Right," he said. "Spurle, no more of this crap. I don't care how bloody macho you are, don't bring it in here with you."

"No, sir," said Spurle.

"And you, McNeil. You knew what it was like when you joined. If you can't stand the smell of the bread, get out of the bakehouse."

"Sir," said McNeil.

"Now get on with some bloody work," said Carston.

The two constables scuttled out, relief having taken over momentarily from their other impulses.

Ross closed the door again when they'd gone and looked at Carston. Carston returned his silent gaze.

"What?" he said.

"'If you can't stand the smell of the bread, get out of the bakehouse'?" said Ross in a way that suggested he didn't believe what he'd just heard.

"My auntie used to say it to me. She had a chip shop in Brixham," said Carston, his tone defensive. Ross smiled, not sure of the connection. Carston put Burnham's sweater on the desk and picked up an envelope that was lying there.

"What d'you make of it?" he asked as he began to open it.

"What, McNeil and Spurle?"

Carston nodded.

"Ah, they're always at it."

"I know, but she lost it there, didn't she? Never heard her swear like that before."

Ross admitted that it was unusual. She was tough, but she was usually quiet with it.

Carston had taken two files from the envelope. "Think I'd better

132

have a word. Just in case," he said. "Send her back in, will you? I need to talk to her about this, anyway."

"What is it?" asked Ross.

"Couple of files," said Carston, looking at the envelope. "Delivered by courier from Borney and Whitcombe. The two accounts that were transferred from Mrs. Burnham."

"Right," said Ross. "I'll go and get these prints checked, too."

He went out. Carston sat down and began leafing through the first file as he waited for McNeil's knock. When it came, it was loud.

"Come in," said Carston, becoming even busier with the file. McNeil came in, still tense, still ready to fight, and stood in the doorway.

"Shut the door," said Carston. "These files, from Borney and Whitcombe's. Quick work. What happened there?"

McNeil was relieved that it was business as usual. She recounted her visit, sticking to the facts about how the accounts had come to be transferred. She was more businesslike than Borney, selected only the essentials and called Carston's attention to the tone of the letters Burnham had sent. Together, they read not only the ones that Borney had shown her, but a selection of the others. Apart from the ones that had caused the trouble, the rest were models of politeness, efficiency and charm.

"What d'you make of it?" he asked.

"Hard to say," said McNeil. "One minute she's making money for them, the next it's as if they've got the plague."

"And he reckons it was just because she wasn't a gambler?"

"Yes, sir. Seems a bit thin to me, though. It's ..."

She hesitated. Carston looked at her.

"Well?"

"Well, it's more personal than that, isn't it? It's as if they'd sort of ... insulted her."

Carston nodded. "But there's no suggestion that they did? Borney didn't say anything else?"

"No, sir," said McNeil.

"OK. Nice job, McNeil," he said, closing the files again. "I'll go through them later. What about the other business?"

Their concentration on the letters had taken some of the tension out of her. The glance she gave him in reply to his question told him that it was back.

"With DCI Baxter?"

"Yes."

Her lips tightened.

"Not good, sir. She'll take a while to get over all that. And I can't see her being much good as a witness."

"Have they picked up her fella, then?"

"Not yet, but they know where he hangs out. It's only a matter of time."

"Where's she staying?"

"The hostel. She can't be on her own. She'll crack up."

Carston shook his head.

"Yes, I saw the first report. Nasty."

"Yes sir," said McNeil.

She knew that Carston was genuine in his response and that he was by far the most sympathetic of the people she worked with, but even his reaction was totally inadequate. She'd talked for the best part of four hours with the woman who'd been raped. She'd been grabbed in her own house, tied face down on her bed, raped and buggered. She'd then been violated again and again with various objects her assailant had picked up around the house. She lived alone. Her common-law husband had been served with a court order to stay away from her only three weeks before. He was the one who'd raped her.

McNeil's training along with her genuine compassion had eventually opened up a channel of trust and the woman had gratefully unloaded not just the tortures of the rape but the years of indignities that had preceded it. It wasn't the first time the man had tied her up. It wasn't the first time he'd taken bottles, vegetables, rolled up newspapers, pencils and other things that were handy and forced them up into her. But only a month before, she'd managed to bring herself to file a complaint about him and he'd been ordered out of her house. His present assault was no more brutal than before but her belief that she was free from his appetites was shattered. There really was no escape.

McNeil had listened and willed herself to stay calm as the

woman described the nights when he brought his mates home with him, made her crawl on hands and knees like a dog, forced her to lick and suck them all. The stories she told were not just accounts of isolated, drunken abuse, but a catalogue of systematic, progressive degradation. She'd met him just three years ago on a shining beach in Spain. She still had photographs of the two of them as smiling young lovers. Since then, he'd stolen her humanity from her, reduced her to a thing.

Carston's voice brought McNeil out of her recollections.

"Are you seeing her again?"

"Yes, sir. She'll need a lot of time."

Carston nodded, sensing how much was unspoken.

"Give it priority. There's not much more you can do on the Burnham case at the moment."

"Right, sir," said McNeil.

Carston looked at her. He wanted to say something, comfort her, let her know he was on her side, but he knew that even that was a patronizing impulse which he'd never think of offering the others. Nobody could win, the conditioning was too deep.

"Listen," he said. "If DCI Baxter doesn't need you tomorrow, take some time for yourself. There are one or two things I'll need, but not till Monday."

McNeil looked at him, unsure of how she was expected to react. Carston waved his hand towards the door.

"Thank you, sir," said McNeil as she went out.

Chapter Six

Two hours later, Carston and Ross were sitting in the Pizzarama in Glasgow Road eating rubbery slabs of pastry spread with red stuff that was supposed to be tomato sauce and topped with unbreakable ropes of cheese and minute, forlorn pieces of olive. Carston was taking advantage of the fact that Kath had gone with friends to the theater in Aberdeen. Meals with her were so good and so healthy that, on the rare occasions that she was away, he actually enjoyed eating unspeakable garbage.

Inevitably, they'd been talking about Burnham. Although it was difficult to assess how much of what they'd heard from him had been true, they both felt that they knew him better. On balance, Ross's persuasion of his guilt was now stronger. Carston was still uncertain.

"If the prints on the gun match, and the fibers," said Ross, "we've got to bring him in."

Carston nodded.

"Trouble is," he said, "we can't really do that till Monday. The lab's already been quicker than we could've hoped. We can't push our luck by asking them to do tests on a Sunday."

They munched on.

"Anyway," said Carston, wiping grease from his chin, "there's still plenty of stuff that needs clearing up."

Ross shook his head.

"Here we go," he said.

Carston insisted.

"No. What about the information McNeil brought back? Why did Mrs. Burnham fall out with her clients? And her and Sleeman, what were they up to?"

"Guess."

"And what about Barbara Stone? What's her game?"

"Ask her."

It was exactly what Carston wanted to do. He sensed that there was more to come from Sleeman and Stone, especially Stone. The Burnham ménage seemed to be the center of a tiny web of relationships driven by self-interest and deceit. Any of the individuals involved could have set up the vibrations that led to Stephanie's death.

"There's the neighbors too," Ross went on. "We haven't got much from them yet, have we?"

"No. Good idea. We'll get Fraser and Spurle onto them tomorrow. They're bound to catch somebody in then."

"Another thing that struck me when I was looking through what we've got so far," said Ross. "Burnham's diary. He took it with him when he went to the hotel last Wednesday. Why haven't we looked at that yet?"

"Haven't had time to. Been moving too bloody fast," said Carston, but acknowledging at the same time that it was a surprising omission. "That's maybe a job for McNeil. Tell you something else," he went on. "I'd like to find out whose baby she was carrying. Burnham says it's his, but who knows?"

Ross pushed his plate away and wiped his fingers.

"I don't know what's going through your mind, but for me Burnham's still favorite by a long way. For the kiddie and the murder."

"Maybe, Jim. But we're stuck now till Monday. I don't want him in until we've done the check on those fibers."

"So what do we do tomorrow?"

A guilty little thought had been lurking in the back of Carston's mind all day. It centered on the promise he'd made to Kath to take a trip to Deeside. Ross's question brought it into focus.

"We take a day off."

Ross was surprised.

"In the middle of an inquiry?"

The guilt resurfaced and Carston was anxious to suppress it.

"Look, you're the logical one. What can we do? We need the lab report, we need the prints, the fibers. I'd like to talk to Sleeman and Stone again. We can't do any of that till Monday. And if we're getting him in and charging him, we're not going to have much time off next week, are we?"

Ross was quick to agree. A whole day free would mean he could drive down to spend time with Jean and Kirsty. He was missing them badly.

"Right then," said Carston, standing up. "I'll go in in the morning and get Fraser and Spurle organized to do a bit more doorstepping."

He belched and rubbed his stomach.

"That bloody pizza's only managed to get halfway down."

"You could refloat it with some lager," said Ross.

The thought was disgusting but the idea was good and they set off to toast the unexpected bonus of the free time they were about to snatch.

When he eventually got home, Ross checked his watch. It was just past ten-thirty. Kirsty would be in bed and Jean's parents would be creeping about starting their pre-bed rituals. He decided to wait another half hour before ringing her and, almost at once, the phone rang and it was Jean. This sort of coincidence had happened too often for Ross to be surprised by it. His religion aside, he had no time for mysticism and accepted that there was a type of telepathy which occurred when people's lives became so closely interlocked that they naturally tended to think of the same things at the same time.

Jean was ready to come home. She and Kirsty were both missing him and her parents' attentions were becoming intrusive and irritating. It was as if she had simply been a means by which they could acquire a grandchild. There was a strange generation leap. To her disgust, they'd dubbed themselves "Grammy" and "Grampy," and, at least in their eyes, they'd forged some secret bond of understanding with Kirsty which bypassed their own daughter. Jean was disappointed to find her own folks stained with the egocentricity of age. She wanted to be back in charge, back in a home which didn't continually echo with "I remember when ..." The phone call, in fact, was a direct plea to be rescued. The day off was beautifully timed. He told Jean to be ready by midday and he'd be there to fetch her. It was past eleven when they eventually said goodnight and each was feeling much happier that within twenty-four hours they'd be home together again.

On Sunday morning, Carston woke Kath at seven-thirty with a cup of Earl Grey tea.

"I want you to drink this," he said. "I've just got to nip in to the office but I'll be back by half past eight. I want to see you in your equipment then."

She screwed her eyes up and looked at him.

"No bondage, Jack. It's the Sabbath."

"Don't be disgusting," he said. "I'm talking about your walking gear. We're going up Deeside, remember?"

He drove in to find Fraser and Spurle already there. He looked quickly through the Burnham file, selected a folder and handed it to Spurle.

"This is for you," he said. "Bellman and Thom are back with their lot. Not a lot for them to do. I want you two to get back to Dyson Close. We've got bugger all from there. It's like a bloody ghost street. Ask around again. See if any of the neighbors are back. Have a look at this lot before you go but leave it on my desk. OK?"

"Right, sir," said Fraser and Spurle together.

"I'm off for the day. So's Sergeant Ross."

They made no attempt to hide their reactions.

"I know, I know," he said. "You're due some too. We'll see what we can do next week. But for now, it means that you're in charge. Don't fuck up."

He drove home to Kath, leaving them with a confused feeling that they were both underprivileged and important.

He and Kath had a quick breakfast and, by a quarter to nine, were driving south to pick up the road between Aboyne and Ballater. The fat weatherman had been right. The sky was the sort of blue that painters never manage to reproduce, the hills on either side of the road bulged with all the colors of autumn and the breeze that came through the sun roof was as warm as a July wind. At Ballater, they forked left onto the South Deeside Road and then left again into the narrow road that led up through copses of birch into Glen Muick. It wound up clear of the trees, into the great scoop of the glen and on towards the mountains of the Lochnagar range which enclosed it at its western end.

They were surprised to find that the car park was already fairly full, even though they'd seen no signs of other people around and met very few cars on the road. They sorted out their packs and set out down towards the wooden bridge over the stream, savoring the huge silence around them and the taste of the highland air.

At one o'clock, they stopped for lunch in a birch copse right down at the water's edge. When they'd finished, Carston's mind, briefly, drifted back to thoughts of the Burnhams.

"D'you ever think about kids?" he asked.

Kath watched the breeze scatter dark points over the surface of the loch.

"Not really," she said. "Why?"

"Nothing really. This'd be a nice place to bring them, that's all."

"Thinking of starting a nursery, then?"

"No, I mean our kids. If we'd had any."

She turned to look at him.

"You're not getting broody, Jack, are you?"

He smiled.

"No. Just wonder what we've missed by not having any."

Kath didn't like this turn of the conversation. When children hadn't come in the early days of their marriage, she'd been relieved because she wasn't ready for the sacrifices they'd have needed to make. As she and Jack had grown beyond the jealousies and irrational angers of their early twenties into a security she hadn't really had in her own family, the idea of intruders into it all was less and less appealing. Eventually, by the time she turned thirty, they'd both accepted that their life was good and that starting a family might make it better but could easily make it worse. Whenever they'd spoken about it, they'd admitted that their attitude was selfish and timid, but they nonetheless felt grateful for the comfort of their cocoon. It was a long time since the subject had come up and Kath was curious.

"What's brought this on?"

Carston shook his head, looking out across the shivering water.

"Nothing really. That woman, the one who was murdered, she was pregnant. Our sort of age. I just wondered."

Kath stretched out on the grass, closed her eyes and rested her hands on her stomach.

"I don't want a body as perfect as this one pulled out of shape," she said.

Carston looked at her. It had been a joke, but she was still a good-looking woman with a body younger than her years. He watched her breasts rising against her shirt and was surprised to feel a warmth in his groin that was usually the prelude to an erection. He turned towards her, trailed his fingers down her neck and over her right breast, then bent to kiss her. Her lips were smiling as she responded. The sun was warm on them and, naturally, slowly, simply, they made love by the loch in full view of any walkers who might have been strolling along the path on the other side of the glen.

When they'd finished and rearranged their clothing, Kath suddenly started laughing.

"What?" said Carston.

"It's disgusting," said Kath, still picking pieces of grass out of her hair. "You're supposed to be a pillar of the community, a mature, no, almost senile individual, your erections are an endangered species and here you are you flinging me to the ground and having your way with me in public."

"You needn't think I enjoyed it," said Carston. "I only did it as a favor."

They laughed together and the mood stayed with them so effectively for the rest of the afternoon and evening that just after ten o'clock, in the privacy of their own home, and to the surprise of both of them, they made love again.

Fraser and Spurle were getting little pleasure from their visit to Dyson Close. It certainly felt as if they were prowling along a ghost street. The residents must all be either heavy sleepers or dead. Whatever the reason, very few of them answered their doorbells. The gardens all lay neatly along the houses, cropped, clipped, regularized. No dogs wandered along to foul up the even pavements or stain the gateposts. No postmen, milkmen or paper boys whistled their way around. There weren't even any cars parked. If anything was alive here, it was walled up inside the neat, expensive structures and having nothing to do with the rest of Cairnburgh.

By nine-thirty, they'd tried every door and managed to speak to only one man and two women at the far end of the street from Burnham's place. The women had been on holiday with their husbands the previous week, golfing in Portugal, and, although they'd heard all about the murder, they had nothing to contribute except small nods of the head that suggested that it came as no surprise to them. The man was in a hurry to get to his riding lesson and offered even less help.

In such a context, the arrival of the green van was an event. It stopped outside number twenty-seven and disgorged a short, fat man in baggy brown trousers, a blue collarless shirt and a Fair Isle pullover. He looked to be in his sixties and moved very deliberately as he opened the back of the van and took out a bundle of gardening tools. He laid them against the front wall of the garden, shut the van door and began a slow wander around the rose bushes and heather beds of numbers twenty-seven and twenty-nine. Spurle and Fraser came up to him just as he got back to his tools and was picking up a hoe.

"Morning," said Fraser.

"Aye," said the man.

"Wonder if ye could help us," Fraser went on. "We're police officers …"

"Ah knew that," said the man. "Naebody else goes round in twos and wears that sort of suit, 'cept mebbe Jehovah's Witnesses. But you dinna look very religious."

Fraser took that as a compliment and smiled.

"It's about yon murder. Ye heard about it, did ye?"

"Aye. Mucky business," said the man, shaking his head.

"Aye," said Fraser. "Did you know her?"

The man shook his head.

"Na. He always did his own garden. Never spoke tae me. I saw 'em, o' course, now and then, but never to speak to, like." He waved his hand round at all the houses in the street. "None o' this lot ever speaks to folk like us, do they? Nae to gardeners."

Spurle was ready to react to the suggestion that gardeners and policemen were at the same debased social level, but Fraser hurried on.

"Ah don't suppose you was here last Wednesday, was ye?"

The man nodded his head. His wispy hair blew about.

"Aye. Every Wednesday morning. Ah never miss." He pointed at the two houses in front of which they were standing. "Ah tidy up for these two. And two more down at the other end, like."

"What time were you here then?" asked Spurle, wanting to get down to business and knowing that the old bugger would stand yapping for ages to them if they let him.

"Same as every week, ten till two."

"Did you see anything ... unusual?"

"Like what?"

"I don't know. Whatever."

The man folded his arms and leaned on his hoe.

"I dinna think so. Nothin ever happens here, like. I never usually sees a soul. They're all away when Ah gets here. Ah just gits on wi' ma gardenin'."

"What about number thirty-six?" asked Fraser. "Anything happen down there? Did ye see anything? Hear anything?"

Suddenly, the man wagged his finger at Fraser.

"That's funny. Aye, I did. It was him, what's 'is name? Him that bides there."

"Mr. Burnham?"

"Aye, that's him. He went out just after twelve."

Fraser and Spurle looked at each other.

"You sure it was that time?" asked Spurle.

"Aye. It struck me, see? I'd just took out mah piece. Ah'm regular as clockwork wi' mah food. Always eats at twelve. Anyway, Ah'd just started eatin' when Ah sees him come out."

"How was he acting?" asked Spurle.

The man looked at him.

"How d'you mean?" he asked.

"Well, was he looking strange, hurrying, looking around?"

The man shook his head, trying to remember.

"Aye, he was in a hurry all right. Chucked his coat in the car. Made a helluva racket drivin' awa'."

"Are ye sure?"

The man looked at him again, unimpressed by the hurry he seemed to be in. He turned and looked down the street.

"Have a look round here. Nae exactly crowded, is it? Ah ken everybody that lives here but Ah never sees nobody durin' the week. Ah was surprised tae see somebody, that's all."

Fraser was writing in his notebook.

"And how about after that? Anything else? Did anybody else go in or come out?"

The man shook his head. His hair waved about again.

"Nah," he said.

"You sure?" asked Spurle.

"Pretty sure, aye. I think I'd've noticed."

"And ye were here till two o'clock?"

"That's right. I work till two, then pack up mah gear. I'm usually awa' by ten past."

"So did ye hear any shooting?"

The man raised his chin, looking up as if his memories were written on the clouds. He scratched his neck and let his hand run up over his cheek and mouth.

"Ah canna mind. Ah might have."

"Oh, come on," said Spurle. "Ye remember a guy comin' out of a house but nae somebody shooting off a twelve bore?"

"There's shootin' here ever week," said the man. "Yon club round the back there. Ah canna mind if Ah heard any or nae last week."

Spurle made a gesture of impatience but Fraser silenced him with a look. He remembered his own experience of hearing shooting when he was doing the first round of inquiries and how the neighbor he'd been interviewing had hardly noticed it.

"Why don't ye go down tae number thirteen? See if she's back yet," he said to Spurle. "I'll take all this down."

"Aye. Rather you than me," said Spurle, still impatient at the old man's lack of urgency.

He set off along the pavement as Fraser turned back to the gardener with a smile.

"Dinna mind him," he said, sitting down on the wall and turning to a fresh page in his notebook. "He's from Kilmarnock."

The man eased himself down beside him, nodding his head slowly, accepting this explanation for Spurle's curtness.

"Aye, Ah kent he wasnae quite all there," he said.

On Monday morning, Ross was in early. It wasn't that he was desperate to get away from his family now that he'd at last got them back, but he'd been awake since well before six. Kirsty had made sure of that. There was no crying, there were no demands, but Ross and Jean couldn't help but hear her. She was excited to be back in her own room and it was her singing that had woken them. They'd listened for a while, broken one of their rules by letting her come into their bed and compounded it by all having breakfast there together. The result of all this was a very contented threesome and an increased load of laundry. In spite of such a happy start to the day, there was no temptation for Ross to linger at home. Being a Catholic, guilt came easily to him and even though he'd been given permission to take the previous day off, he felt that he owed his employers an extra effort to compensate them for his dereliction of duty. By the time Carston arrived, he'd started to work through the papers that had been dumped in the tray on his desk. There was a fax from the estate agent in France. It contained copies of the correspondence she'd had with Mrs. Burnham. It was all as she'd indicated on the phone and there were no traces of any contacts with Burnham himself. The letters referred frequently to "my husband and I" and gave the impression that the hunt for a property was a joint venture but the man was only a shadowy anonymous presence in their dialogue.

Just before eight-thirty, voices in the squad room told him that the day was beginning.

"No, you prick. It's vooly-voo, not vowliz-vows," said Fraser, shaking his head at Spurle's ignorance.

"Says vowliz-vows here," said Spurle, pointing at the book he was holding.

"Didn't you do no French at school?" asked Fraser, grabbing the book from him.

"Nah," said Spurle. "What's the use o' that crap? Everybody speaks

English abroad. It's a well-known fact. What do you think, Julie? You're the intelligent one."

McNeil didn't even bother to look up from the typewriter she was using.

"Ignore him, Fraser. He's pulling your leg," she said.

"*Oui. Il est stupide,*" said Fraser, managing to make the words sound like pure Cairnburgh.

Spurle slumped down into a chair beside the window.

"As long as you ken the words for beer, fuck and how much, what else d'you need?" he asked.

"In your case, a brain transplant," said McNeil.

"Bollocks," said Spurle, and was looking for another witticism to follow it up with when Carston and Ross came in.

Carston's manner was unusually brisk and McNeil noticed that he seemed to have taken more trouble with his appearance. He was wearing a new-looking charcoal gray suit, a pale gray shirt and what appeared to be a silk tie. It seemed to change him from a relaxed, comfortable presence into someone more dynamic, more authoritative. The way he conducted the briefing confirmed the impression. He started speaking the instant he arrived.

"Right. Sergeant Ross will be co-coordinating things today because I'm off to Aberdeen. Things are shifting with Burnham. McNeil, DCI Baxter wants you again but he's going to have to wait. There are a couple of jobs I've got for you first. We need to get hold of Burnham's diary. Get in touch with him, see if he'll hand it over. Use some of your counseling tact. Works with fellas, too, does it?"

"I'll try, sir," said McNeil.

"If not, we'll have to get a warrant. I really would like to have a look at the thing. Sergeant Ross and I had a long chat with him Saturday night and we'll be getting him in to make a statement later on today."

"Something new, sir?" asked Spurle.

"Dunno yet. I'm taking a jumper of his to the Aberdeen lab. See if we can get a match. So, first the diary, McNeil, right?"

"Right sir," said McNeil.

"Then," went on Carston, almost without waiting for her reply, "see what you can dig up on a Barbara Stone. Works for Dempster

146

Associates. She's been seeing a lot of Burnham. Reckons they were supposed to have a date the day of the murder. You'll probably have to go into Aberdeen, too. Quick as you like."

"What about us, sir?" asked Fraser.

Carston was already on his way out of the room again.

"You'll be with Sergeant Ross getting all the paperwork ready for when we bring Burnham in."

Fraser and Spurle looked at each other. Paperwork was one of their many weak points. Carston stopped at the door.

"As soon as you've finished that," he said, "get lost. Take as much of the day off as you can. There won't be any leave once we've got Burnham in."

He disappeared before they could respond. McNeil picked up a phone book and started looking for Dempster Associates. Ross beckoned to Spurle and Fraser and they got up to follow him out. At the door, Fraser stopped.

"Wait a minute," he said. "Ah just thought o' something."

"What?" asked Spurle.

"It's nae enough just to know the words for beer, fuck and how much."

Spurle and McNeil both looked at him.

"What're you on about?" asked Spurle.

Fraser smiled.

"What's the point of askin' how much somethin' is if you don't know what their answer means?" he said. "They could be saying anything from fifty pee to fifty pound."

"Nae in France. It's francs there," said Spurle.

"Ignorant bastard," said Fraser, opening the folder again.

McNeil made a note of the number and address she was looking for, got up and took down her coat. At the door she pushed past the two men, who were still arguing about the price of sex in France.

"Could be écus soon," she said, before going out and letting the door swing shut behind her.

"You know her trouble, don't you?" said Spurle. "She wants a good fuck."

Since the talk they'd had with Burnham, Carston had begun to feel a new momentum growing. The whole investigation had already moved very quickly, but suddenly fresh contours were forming, shadows were darker and highlights more evident. It was hard for him to get out of the habit of relishing uncertainties. Conclusions quickly arrived at made him nervous because he was always so intent on keeping his mind open. But Burnham's guilt, which had been probable from the start, had continued to insist and press more closely round him. There was no point in denying the obvious any more.

He drove back to pick up Kath. Cairnburgh's photographic supplies were limited to the films and processing services offered by Boots and the other chemists. Kath's needs were a little more sophisticated and she'd been planning a visit to Jessops in Aberdeen to get various bits of equipment for her darkroom. When she'd heard that he was driving in, she'd grabbed at the chance of going with him.

He dropped her in Union Street, arranging to meet her at Marischal College at one o'clock, then went on to Grampian Police headquarters. There, he identified himself and asked to see Superintendent Nichol, with whom he had a ten o'clock appointment and for whose benefit he had put on the suit. Brian McIntosh had briefed him on how to get access to the forensic lab which had analyzed the fibers from Stephanie Burnham's hand and warned him that it entailed being nice to Nichol. He had a reputation for being a cross between a filing cabinet and a fossil. In his world, nothing existed if it wasn't on a list, preferably one associated with budgetary considerations. Apparently, he had absolutely no sense of humor, no conversation, and no conception of there being opinions other than his own. He was neat, correct and always punctual.

Carston was chatting to the desk sergeant when he heard a clock striking outside. At the tenth stroke precisely, the phone beside the sergeant rang and Carston was summoned to room S14.

Nichol was behind his desk as Carston went in. He remained seated, ignoring his visitor while he continued to read a document on the desk before him. Just over a minute was obviously enough to make his point, then he pushed the paper away, sat back and said, "Detective Chief Inspector Carston."

It wasn't a question. Carston felt like telling him that he hadn't driven from Cairnburgh to find out who he was. Instead, he said, "Yes sir. It's very good of you to spare me the time."

"What do you want?" asked Nichol.

Once again, outrageous alternative responses flashed into Carston's mind but he kept his shoulders hunched submissively, his gaze never higher than Nichol's chin as he outlined the relevant features of the Burnham case and explained his need to test Burnham's jumper against the fibers that had already been analyzed. As a coda, he added that the request was relatively urgent. His brief, polite explanation provoked a mini-lecture on the assumptions of everyone who came to see Nichol that their errands merited special priority. Carston was ready for this and managed, apologetically, to make the point that, if the examination of the garment could be expedited, the specific investigation might be rendered more cost-effective. As McIntosh had promised, the fiscal terminology had its effect. It provoked a conversational turn which, again thanks to McIntosh's advance warnings, didn't take Carston by surprise. He was able to tell the superintendent exactly what his staffing levels were and how he was about to adjust them downwards by assisting the process of natural wastage and obliging cleaners and janitors to make up any resultant slack by working longer hours. As a clincher, and with his fingers crossed, he repeated a formula which McIntosh had forced him to learn.

"I'm trying to institute a new hierarchy of accountability in my squad. Devolutionary dispersion of funds. A quantifiable product."

The look which Nichol flashed at him was brief and suspicious but seemed to satisfy him that Carston was the sort of man he wanted in his force. He scribbled his name on a form which had already been filled in.

"Give this to the lab supervisor," he said, handing it over.

Carston took the paper and hovered, wondering what else was needed. Nichol, however, was back at his reading. He looked up once, his face expressionless, his eyes lingering on Carston.

"Well?" he said.

"Thank you very much, sir," said Carston, noting that Nichol was already bent over his desk again. He went quickly to the door, turned and said, "I appreciate your time and help." Nichol made no reaction. Carston risked a small V-sign before opening the door and leaving.

McNeil had had no luck with her efforts to get hold of Burnham's diary. She'd tried his home number without success and eventually, when she'd managed to get through to him at Calder and McStay's, he'd snapped a blunt refusal. She should have taken the hint offered by his secretary that his mood was foul but she'd hoped that an oblique approach might be productive. Unfortunately for her, Burnham connected the extent of his hangover with Carston and Ross's visit and wasn't predisposed to co-operate with the police any further. When she'd suggested that the next step was for them to get the diary by having a warrant issued and that that was a far less pleasant alternative than having her pop round to fetch it, his reply had been defiant, angry, and surprisingly coarse. She was rather anxious that her approach might have alerted him to the diary's importance and that he might therefore be minded to destroy it (if he hadn't already done so). When she broached the subject, with all the tact and deviousness she could find, he saw her coming a mile off, called her a small-minded bitch and rang off.

Her inquiries about Stone, however, were proving much more interesting. Stone was away at a meeting so McNeil was able to talk to several of her colleagues at Dempster Associates instead. She made it clear that Stone had done nothing wrong and that her inquiries were aimed at protecting rather than accusing her. The flimsiness of such an excuse didn't seem to bother anyone because everybody she spoke to, male and female, had an opinion about Stone which they were eager to express.

To the two secretaries who handled her appointments and typed up her accounts, reports, projections and so on, she was a glamorous, exciting boss who always remembered their birthdays and was generous in recognizing when they'd earned time off by putting in extra hours on a project. They were all on first-name terms and the two women clearly felt that their working relation-ship with her lifted them into the firm's central hierarchy and brought them away from coffee machines and close to decision makers. Indeed, the older of the two, Doris Blenning, spoke as if she were a partner in some of the deals Stone was negotiating rather than a convenient means of servicing them.

"We've almost sealed the contract with Texaco," she said at one point and, less than a minute later, "Our bid's on the table at Shell Expro."

McNeil's technique of exploiting her own ignorance of the affairs they were referring to and seeming genuinely impressed at the dynamics of the oil contracts market place drew everyone out. It meant that men and women alike felt they could patronize her which, in turn, made the information they offered more expansive. She was most interested by the contrasting responses of the two men who were closest in status to Stone. Dirk Harfield was a new-comer. He'd only been in Scotland for ten months, had come from a plastics manufacturer in Liverpool and was clearly born to sell. He was in his early thirties, had thick, fair hair, a health club tan, a cream-colored shirt with sleeves rolled halfway up his forearms, a silk tie in dark chestnut and well-cut tan chinos. McNeil recognized that he was good looking but she also thought that he looked like a Milky Way bar. His initial responses to her questions about Stone were expansive but considered, managing to praise her skills while suggesting that they needed to be applied with a little more care. As McNeil smiled an encouraging wide-eyed interest at him, the expansiveness took over.

"D'you want me to be completely frank with you?" he asked, leaning back and clasping his hands behind his head.

"It would help," said McNeil.

"Sex, that's Barbara's trouble," he said, holding her eyes with a steady, challenging stare.

"In what way?" asked McNeil, holding his look, meeting his challenge.

"She's quick, got a good grasp of the game, but she relies a bit too much on lip gloss and Chanel Number 5. Fine when she's dealing with guys who like playing away, but can get in the way if they're just up for business."

McNeil looked puzzled, both because she wanted him to say more and because she was.

He leaned forward.

"It's a stock technique with her. She reckons to get them thinking about taking her out to dinner, slipping between the sheets. That way they want to get the deal tied up and get on with the extramurals. Trouble is, she gets too much of a buzz from it herself. Gets in the way sometimes. She's so busy coming on to them, her mind's only half on the job. I reckon it's lost us a couple of contracts."

"Mixing business and pleasure, is that the problem?" asked McNeil, still playing out her ignorance.

To her surprise, his expression hardened a little and his tone changed.

"Depends what sort of pleasure you're talking about. For her it's not the sex. More the power thing. Wants to be in charge. Wants to ..."

He stopped, looked at her, wondering whether to go on. A good five seconds went by before he finished his sentence.

"... crush balls."

It was a deliberate provocation. McNeil felt herself respond but didn't let it show.

"Speaking from experience?" she asked.

Harfield's reaction was instantaneous. He leaned back again, a practiced smile showing well-polished enamel, his left eyebrow lifted in a gesture designed to entrance her, and he pointed an index finger at her.

"On my own doorstep? What a naughty suggestion, Constable," he said, following it with a barely perceptible chuckle.

The act was good, but precisely for that reason, McNeil knew she'd got to him. She pressed her point.

"Well, I just thought, if she turns on the charm for clients, why not for colleagues?"

The eyebrow was lowered, the smile narrowed.

"Elementary. Unprofessional, isn't it? Office parties are one thing but ... dalliance on the firm's time?" He tutted an apparent disapproval. "That's not Barbara's style. Ask Phil Pickard, down in Finance. He'll tell you what she thinks of in-house frolics."

McNeil tried to draw him further but soon realized that she'd touched on something even less pleasant for him than she'd suspected. He seemed suddenly to tire of the interview and become aware of the important affairs from which she was keeping him. His sex appeal and charm were switched off as if in acknowledgment that they were wasted on her and, although his politeness didn't waver, she was obviously being dismissed.

Donald Bellamy, in an office on the other side of the corridor, was everything that Harfield wasn't, or, rather, wasn't everything that Harfield was. He and his clothes smelled of stale cigarette smoke. He was at least fifty, well below medium height, bald and wore bifocals. His white shirt was clean but a size too small and the condition of his cheeks, jaw and neck suggested that he'd shaved with a liquidizer. For all his disadvantages, however, he greeted McNeil with a nice smile, which spread to unqualified delight when she told him what she wanted to speak about.

"Oh, Barbara. Yes. Wonderful person. Pleasure to work with. How can I help you?" he beamed, waving her into a chair.

McNeil just switched him on with an innocuous generalized question and he immediately responded with a rambling description of all the positive attributes Stone had brought to the firm: her generosity to colleagues and clients alike; her willingness to take on any clients that were assigned to her without querying the probability of success; and the sheer joy it was to be able to confer with someone of such grace, conscientiousness and, yes, he had to confess it, beauty. There were no vestiges of the sexual combat that had marked Harfield's answers and yet there was little doubt that Stone's gender was a major factor in Bellamy's pleasure. His remarks were all directed at her commercial and professional qualities and yet they were full of words like freshness, charm and elegance. McNeil decided that a reference to Harfield's reservations was legitimate.

"Yes. It's strange, isn't it?" she suggested. "Some people seem to think Mrs. Stone uses her charms deliberately."

Bellamy stopped, seemingly confused.

"For business purposes, I mean," said McNeil. "Flatters her clients, that sort of thing."

"Oh no," said Bellamy. "No, no, no. That's not like Barbara at all.

You see, people always do that, don't they? It's jealousy really, isn't it? I mean, she's attractive, she takes trouble with her appearance, she creates a good impression. And so some people see that as being sinister, talk about her, say she's … I don't know … fast or something. It's jealousy. Pure and simple. Barbara's a very beautiful woman, it's true. And she has far too much self-respect to take advantage of the fact."

"I was told to ask a Mr. Pickard about that. It seems …"

A snort from Bellamy interrupted her.

"Exactly. Just what I was saying. It was disgusting. I've no idea what went on but Barbara told me how much it upset her. She was very, very angry about it. Quite right, too."

"But what was it about?"

"I've no idea. Ask the man. My own suspicion is that he made some sort of lewd suggestion to her. That's the only thing that could have made her do that."

"Do what?"

Whatever it was, Bellamy didn't like to be reminded of it. He dismissed it with an impatient wave of his hand.

"Oh, she hit him. With … I don't know, something in his office. Broke his arm. But it served him right. He was trying to take advantage of her. Some of these men, you know, do that sort of thing."

McNeil watched him carefully as he went on. It seemed bizarre to her that someone his age should subscribe to attitudes that belonged to the nineteenth century. His conviction that Stone was some sort of fragile innocent beset by the satyrs of Dempster Associates didn't sit easily with his job of hard-nosed negotiator with representatives of the major oil companies. And the more he defended Stone, the less convinced she was of his naïveté.

"Did you ever have much to do with Mrs. Stone socially?" she asked, out of the blue.

It was enough to stop Bellamy's protests. To her surprise, he took it as some sort of accusation.

"What are you suggesting?" he said, the scraped patches on his cheeks and chin turning redder.

"Nothing at all, I promise you. I just wondered what sort of things she was interested in, that's all."

His eagerness to protect Stone suddenly became a desire to protest at the nature of whatever it was that she was implying.

"Just what sort of investigations are these?" he said. "It seems curious to me that Mrs. Stone's not suspected of anything and yet here you are asking all sorts of personal things about her as if she's done something wrong."

"Not at all, Mr. Bellamy. I only …"

He wouldn't let her finish. Where before he had been accommodating and open, he now seemed all at once hostile and secretive.

"I think I've said enough about her. I have nothing but respect for her as a colleague and I don't think there's anything I can usefully add. So …"

He stood up and his posture indicated that McNeil was dismissed. She thanked him and tried to reassure him that there were no ulterior motives behind her questions. He made a perceptible effort to adjust his attitude back to extreme civility but the freedom of their early exchanges had gone. His smile as he shook her hand at the office door was formal, guarded.

On her way back down to reception, McNeil heard a bucket clang as she passed the door to the ladies. She'd been given a surprising degree of access to Stone's colleagues but their co-operation had left her wanting more. The solidarity of the professional classes could do with being diluted with some old-fashioned hearsay. She pushed open the door and saw a woman wiping the wash basin with a blue cloth. She smiled at her.

"Mornin' love," said the woman. "New girl, are ye?"

"No, I don't work here," said McNeil, turning on a tap and beginning to wash her hands. "I'm a policewoman."

The woman's interest was instantaneous. She carried on wiping the cloth around the basin but was desperate to know what the police wanted in the office and very ready to stop for a chat. So was McNeil. By the time she'd started drying her hands, they were already well into a conversation. McNeil spoke about being in the force, what the training involved, how she coped with drunks, how many arrests she'd made. The woman listened, asked questions, and, to the amusement of both of them, told her about a cousin of hers who was in prison for doing something or other with two jars of peanut butter and a cat. She didn't exactly know what it was but she knew that it was to do with sex and that the cat hadn't suffered. At last, she got round to the question that McNeil wanted to hear.

"So what're ye doin' here, then?"

McNeil grinned.

"Wastin' my time," she said. "I was wanting to talk to Mrs. Stone, that's all. But she's no here."

"Ah," said the woman, triumphantly. "Bonkin' Barbara. Ah'm nae surprised it's her."

"You ken her, do ye?" asked McNeil, letting her accent broaden.

"Everyb'dy kens her," said the woman. "Intimately," she added, stressing each syllable and accompanying the word with a wink so huge that it must have burned up several calories.

"*News o' the World* stuff, eh?" said McNeil.

She saw the woman suddenly check her laugh and knew that it had occurred to her that she was not just involved in blether but in "helping the police with their inquiries." It happened all the time, in the most innocent of contexts, and McNeil knew how to deal with it. She was fortunate in that she genuinely did relate more easily to the woman than to the likes of Bellamy and Harfield and there was no trace of condescension in her attitude.

Gradually, she regained the woman's confidence and teased and joked out of her some of the gossip about Stone. There was plenty of it. It was true, for instance, that she'd broken Pickard's arm. She slammed a filing cabinet drawer shut on it while he was taking something from it. But that was after she'd worn the edge of his desk smooth by bracing herself against it to receive his attentions. Depending on which story you believed, the bone breaking was the result of her anger at being rejected by him, his over-enthusiasm during a particularly acrobatic session or her refusal to submit to his advances. Margaret (the cleaner), was inclined to believe that it was Stone's fault because she'd actually witnessed her temper at first hand. One day she'd emptied a wastepaper bin from Stone's office earlier than usual and it had apparently had something in it which Stone was anxious to retrieve. When Margaret told her it had been incinerated, she all but strangled her and called her names that Margaret usually only heard from her old man on Fridays and Saturdays.

The speculation about why Stone had broken Pickard's arm extended to which of the office personnel she'd really had affairs with. On this score, though, Margaret seemed charitable.

"See, the trouble is, they'd all like to. That Dirk Harfield (Dick Harfield, if ye ask me), he was tryin' fer ages tae get into her knickers. But she wouldnae have him."

"How about Mr. Bellamy?" asked McNeil, playing a hunch.

Margaret became conspiratorial.

"Well, no very many ken this, but Ah've seen her wi' him. An' Ah wouldnae be surprised. Mind you, she's probably doin' that out o' pity."

Their talk was entertaining and very little of it would ever stand up in court, but the degree to which Stone figured in the general office gossip implied that there was enough smoke to make a fire quite probable. It wasn't just the universal response to a successful, sexy, attractive woman, but a complex set of stories which cast her variously as hero and villain, mover and victim. Margaret herself, despite having been on the receiving end of her anger and sarcasm more than once, had a real regard for her and felt that she was somehow different from the rest of them.

"She'll be here when the rest are awa'," she said as McNeil at last started getting ready to leave.

"D'ye think so?"

"Aye, Ah do."

"Even though she's a woman?"

Margaret laughed and bent to pick up her bucket. She put it on the surface beside the washbasin and started rinsing the cloth in it. As she wrung it out, the laugh left her face and she turned to look directly into McNeil's eyes.

"That woman, love," she said, "has got more balls than a' the rest o' them put together." The seriousness with which she said it came as a slight surprise to McNeil. Their chat had been little more than gossip and both of them had enjoyed it at that level, but Stone's presence had been greater than could have been guessed after the initial "Bonking Barbara" tag. Margaret was willing to talk

157

about her, grateful for the color she brought to an otherwise pre-dictable set of offices but, in the end, confused about what she felt about her. None of this was articulated but McNeil sensed respect, awe, envy and a secret gratitude to Stone for putting the men of Dempster Associates in their place.

The mood at that evening's briefing seemed particularly good. Fraser and Spurle weren't there, of course, and Carston, Ross and McNeil had all had a fruitful day. Carston was still in his unaccus-tomed smart-suited mode but he'd loosened his tie, taken off his jacket and seemed almost excited.

"OK, McNeil," he said. "What've you got?"

She told him about Burnham's refusal to hand over his diary. Carston smiled and shook his head.

"Doesn't matter," he said. "We'll have it soon. How about Mrs. Stone?"

McNeil had spent her lunch hour writing up her notes about the visit to Dempster's and adding her own thoughts and guesses to them. She'd had to do some more counseling with the woman in DCI Baxter's rape inquiry during the afternoon and so she had to keep referring to her notes to refresh her memory.

"Some woman," she said. "Seems you either love her or hate her guts."

Carston nodded. The news didn't surprise him.

"What're the details?" he asked.

McNeil told them what people had said, painting a picture of a strong, ambitious, successful salesperson well able to hold her own in the macho boardrooms of the oil companies. She didn't hesitate to use labels like ruthless and aggressive and relayed the story of Pickard's broken arm as well as the sexual antics that were supposed to have preceded it. She finished her sketch by offering her personal opinion that Stone was too much woman for Burnham to handle.

Carston thanked her and turned to Ross. Before he could say anything, Ross held up a sheaf of papers.

"Everything's ready," he said. "We can pick him up any time."

Carston smiled.

"Thanks, Jim," he said. "That's exactly what I had in mind."

He was obviously pleased with himself. After leaving Nichol's office and shaking off his dislike for the man, he'd had an excellent day. The lab had been very co-operative. He'd left the jumper with them and had a long, self-indulgent lunch with Kath. He held up a piece of paper.

"Lab report on Burnham's jumper," he said. "Surprise, surprise, the fibers are identical to the ones we found in her hand and in the study. Same wool, same sort of twist, same vegetable dyes, everything. You know what they're usually like, humming and hawing. Not this time. Categorical. This is an exact match."

"And the prints on the gun?" asked Ross, knowing the answer.

"Yep. All his. Every one," said Carston. So, let's get him interviewed, taped and on the spot before he's got time to know where he is. You got a warrant amongst that lot?"

By way of answer, Ross held up a single sheet.

"OK," said Carston. "Let's do it."

Chapter Seven

The red Porsche was parked once again in Stone's drive. It looked like an ad, shining against the beech hedge and the granite wall, its bodywork reflecting the damp, amber scatterings of fallen leaves. Up in Stone's bedroom, the naked body on the bed had a red line running from a dark circle at the base of the neck down the groove of the spinal column into the valley between the two buttocks. Stone was standing beside the bed, a Kir Royale in her left hand, a tube of lipstick in her right. She looked down at the still figure.

"Christ, Steve," she said, her voice a growl, "you're almost as beautiful as I am."

Steve looked up at her and smiled.

Stone sat down on the side of the bed. She touched the cold bottom of the glass to her new lover's shoulder then put the lipstick at the base of the line she'd already drawn, sliding it down between the buttocks, easing the legs apart. She let the lipstick fall onto the sheet and traced her fingers over warm skin that was still wet from their lovemaking. Steve pushed gently against her hand, called her an insatiable bitch and turned away into the pillow again.

Stone took a mouthful of the cool wine and put the glass on the bedside table. She moved to kneel beside the bed, bent over and allowed the wine to dribble from her mouth into the small of Steve's back. Her right hand began massaging the pink liquid into the red smear of lipstick as Steve, after starting at the first touch of the liquid, relaxed into the sheets again under hands that were so good at inventing new pleasures.

The telephone made them both jump and was hugely irritating

until the answering machine clicked, the ringing stopped and Stone's recorded message said, "Barbara Stone here. I can't take your call right now. Leave a message after the beep."

They listened as the machine flashed and chirped. At last, the caller came on. It was Burnham.

"Barbara. It's me. Michael. Please pick up the phone."

He paused. His voice was pleading, pathetic.

"Please, darling. Please, please, please. I know you're there. Please."

He stopped again. Steve looked at Stone, who made a funny face and performed an extravagant "please, please, please" mime.

"I'm missing you so much. I really need to see you. Just to ... We need to straighten things out. I can't manage without you. Please, Barbara. Please. It's nearly over now. We can go away. Soon it'll be ..."

As his breaking voice went on, Stone rolled Steve gently over and leaned down across the bed, her mouth soft and open, ready with the first of many butterfly kisses. Their tongues danced lightly against each other.

"I'm so sorry, darling. Sorry I did it," said Burnham. "I should've known. Now I've killed everything. It's all ... Oh Barbara. Please speak to me."

Burnham was at his whisky again. That was what had made him ring her. He'd forced himself to stay away from the phone all day but, as usual, the loosening effect of the alcohol broke down his self-awareness and brought back to the surface his desolation. As he spoke, he began to explain things, to detail the power she'd given him, imagining he was actually speaking to her, convinced that she was listening in her house and that she would eventually soften, pick up the phone and make everything good again. He couldn't know that Stone had already turned the volume down on her answering machine so that his droning would no longer grate against the murmurings of her pleasure.

In the end, it was the doorbell that interrupted him. With one last promise to do anything she wanted, even more than he'd already done for her, if only she'd call him, he banged the phone down and went angrily to the door. When he saw Carston, he was tempted to slam it on him again. Instead, he turned on his heel and went back inside, leaving them on the step.

"What the hell is it this time?" he said. "Why can't you leave me alone? This is bloody victimization."

His words showed how close he was to losing his temper completely and he spun round and made for Carston, who'd stepped inside the door. Ross moved forward, anticipating trouble, but Carston put a hand out to stop him.

"Michael Burnham," he said, "I have a warrant for your arrest for the murder of your wife, Stephanie Burnham, on Wednesday last. You have the right to remain silent …"

As he continued to recite the familiar caution, the blood drained from Burnham's face and he fell sideways, supporting himself by putting a hand on the wall. When Carston had finished, he said nothing. He was looking at the carpet, his head shaking slowly from side to side.

"No," he said at last, adding after more shakes of the head. "Oh Barbara …"

Then the tears began.

Carston, Ross and McNeil could only stand there at first as he leaned harder against the wall and turned his face to it. He said Stone's name twice more, then with an angry shake of the whole of his upper body, he pushed himself upright, took a deep, harsh breath to gulp back the rest of his tears and stood looking Carston straight in the eye.

"This is a farce," he said, his voice higher than usual with the strain of containing his crying. "A bloody disaster. OK. What's next?"

Carston explained the protocol, noticing that as he did so, Burnham reassembled himself very quickly. He was a man of very rapid changes of mood. The apparent wreck of moments before was once again defiant. When Carston had finished and suggested that he get a coat to wear to the station, he reached into the hall cupboard and took out a tweed overcoat. He went back into the lounge and kitchen to turn off the lights he'd left on then came back out. At the front door, with the other three already on the path outside, he switched off the hall light but then immediately switched it back on again, before shutting the door.

"Better leave it on," he said. "Lots of villains about." Carston suspected that it might be a trying night.

As it happened, the interview was more straightforward than Carston expected it to be. In the car on the way to the station, Burnham had said nothing but Carston noticed how frequently he wiped his eyes to push away the tears that kept coming. By the time they'd settled him in the interview room, the residual effects of the whisky had vanished and he was subdued, tired, even compliant. It bothered Carston. The swings from mood to mood might well help him to establish a case; it would be easy to show how unstable the man's character was. On the other hand, he couldn't help feeling a little sympathy for someone whose spirit had so clearly been broken and if that was the way he, the arresting officer, felt, what sort of response would Burnham provoke in a jury which had been nudged in the right direction by the defense? They'd probably want to adopt the bugger.

There were five of them in the room: Carston, Ross, a constable at the door, Burnham and his solicitor, David Braithwaite. The tape reels were turning and Carston had been careful to do everything exactly by the book. He didn't mind not getting a conviction through the arguments in court, but he hated being thwarted by incorrect procedures and technicalities, and Scots law was careful to ensure that the administration of justice was matched by an equally powerful guarantee of fairness for the accused.

Burnham answered every question he was asked and his solicitor rarely had to intervene to protest in any way. In essence, the story he told was exactly that which he'd given to Ross in that first interview. He'd been gardening, stopped to drive to the races in Edinburgh and was late in setting out because his wife had wanted sex. In the end, he'd left just after midday, only just making the first race. He'd lost on four races, betting a hundred pounds on each, then driven home and found her in the study. Carston let him tell the whole story, then went back over it to fill in more details.

"I'd just like to clear up the business about what you were wearing."

Burnham sighed.

"My gardening gear."

"Which was?"

"Blue cords, my thick shirt—an American thing, chamois shirts, they call them, I get them mail-order, from L.L.Bean—and a sweater."

"Right. And you said you took the sweater off."

"Yes. I was mowing the lawn, I got sweaty."

"So when you came back into the house, where was it?"

"I've told you. I must have left it outside."

Carston made a note on a pad in front of him. It said nothing special but allowed a pause to build in which Burnham could worry about the sweater and Carston could change tack.

"About your wife wanting intercourse ... I believe you told my sergeant that it took you by surprise."

Burnham nodded.

"We didn't do it very often."

"So this was ... abnormal, would you say?"

Burnham nodded again and, for once, lifted his eyes from the table and held Carston's gaze.

"Yes, it was abnormal. First, that she wanted it, then that she was so violent."

"I see," said Carston, keeping his expression neutral to hide the fact that he was pleased that it was Burnham who'd introduced the theme of violence. "That was unusual, was it?"

Burnham's eyes dropped again.

"Stephanie was never a passionate woman. We ..." He stopped, unsure of what he wanted to say. The fingers of his right hand traced patterns on the table. In the end he simply added, "Sex was always ordinary."

"But not last Wednesday?" Carston prompted.

"No. She was crazy. I don't know what had got into her. It was like she was desperate for it."

"And so ... what? You struggled? Or what?"

Carston ignored the look Braithwaite gave him.

"Struggled? What do you mean?" asked Burnham. "There was no struggling. I didn't want it and she grabbed at me, but it wasn't a struggle. She pulled my clothes about, dragged my shirt out. I don't know … In the end we just had sex there on the floor. I left right away." He paused. "It wasn't nice. I didn't enjoy it."

"How about your wife?"

"I don't know," said Burnham, in the same low, even tone he'd used throughout the interview. "I didn't ask her. I just left."

Carston watched him carefully as he asked the next question. He wanted to be sure to catch the slightest reaction.

"Was there a fork in the study?"

Burnham did react. It might have been guilt but equally it might just have been surprise at the incongruity. It was enough to allow him a pause before he answered.

"I wouldn't have thought so. Why?"

"Nothing really," said Carston, wanting to keep his options open. "And how about the state of the study, the books thrown around the place? Any ideas how that happened?"

Burnham shook his head.

"No. There was nothing like that when I left. Maybe Stephanie … She was drunk. I don't know. Maybe she threw them around."

"Why would she do that?"

This time Braithwaite insisted.

"Really, Chief Inspector."

Carston looked at him, all innocence.

"It was Mr. Burnham's idea. I just wondered why he thought that."

"I don't know," said Burnham. "I don't know why I said that. OK, maybe it wasn't her. Maybe it was whoever killed her. Did that occur to you? It's the obvious thing, isn't it?"

"Yes, it is," said Carston. "Can I just go back on one thing? Something I'd like to clear up. You said—correct me if I'm wrong—you said your relations with your wife were rather cool."

"Did I?"

"I think so. You certainly implied it."

"Is that what we're after, Chief Inspector? Implications?" asked Braithwaite.

"No, Mr. Braithwaite, but we all need to know everything we can to help us, don't we?"

"As long as they're facts, yes."

"Right, Mr. Burnham. How about it then? What were relations like between you and Mrs. Burnham?"

Burnham shook his head again and went back to making patterns on the table.

"I'll tell you what they were like, Carston. We were getting in each other's way."

Braithwaite made to interrupt but Burnham ignored him.

"Living separate lives. I didn't know what she was doing. She didn't know what I was doing. And neither of us cared."

"You didn't go out together? Didn't have any interests in common?"

Again, a brief shake of the head.

"What about the baby?" asked Carston, gently. The hand on the table stopped moving. The fingers clenched into a fist but, when Burnham continued, there was no change in his voice.

"Yes. For a couple of weeks we had that, didn't we? Didn't last, though. We even disagreed on that in the end." He shook his head. "No. We were both living with a stranger."

Carston didn't like the submission that Burnham was showing. He was just answering the questions, either controlling his responses or anesthetized by the context into a dullness that he hadn't shown in any of the previous contacts they'd had with him. When the drink or his temper came into play he was unpleasant but at least he gave them some leverage, opened gaps into which they could push the irritants of their questions. This Burnham had quickly been sobered by his arrest and was reacting like an automaton. He was either in shock or a bloody good actor. Carston changed his approach, introducing a subject that he knew might light some sort of fire.

"Can we turn to your lunch date?" he asked.

Burnham looked at him with apparent incomprehension.

"Last Wednesday. With Mrs. Stone," Carston prompted.

Burnham didn't reply. Carston let the silence last, waiting for it to work. Burnham's fist was still clenched. He was tense, immobile. Ross noticed that his own breathing was shallow. Carston stared hard at Burnham's lowered head and saw a tear form in his left eye

166

and run down his cheek. It dropped onto his sleeve. When he spoke, his voice was very quiet.

"We had no lunch date. There was no lunch date. I don't know why Barbara told you that."

"She was lying then, was she?"

"I don't know," said Burnham. "Maybe she mixed it up with another day."

"Which other days had you arranged to meet for lunch then?"

In reply, Burnham just shook his head.

"Maybe she was thinking of someone else?" Carston offered.

It produced another tear. Burnham wiped it away with a quick, impatient gesture. He sat back and lifted his head. The defiance was back.

"Carston, I don't give a shit," he said. "Stephanie, Barbara, it's all gone. I was in the garden, I fucked her, I lost four hundred quid. Now, I'm a widower and I'm inside. Get on with it."

Braithwaite was alarmed at the aggression in his tone. He tried to head it off.

"Chief Inspector," he said, "you can see that my client's still suffering from the shock of all this. He's been very open with you, but ..."

He was silenced by Burnham.

"No, David. Let the bugger get to work. Checked out the insurance policies, have you, Carston? I get the lot. Seventy or eighty grand, mortgage paid off, the lot. Handy motive, eh? I can probably retire on what's coming to me."

It was Braithwaite's turn to interrupt.

"Michael, be quiet," he said, his voice sharp to cut across Burnham's ranting. He got up and went round the table to stand beside Carston.

"I want this stopped for a while. I'd like a word with my client. It's obvious that he's still under considerable stress."

Carston was tempted to refuse the request in the hope that the revitalized Burnham might reveal more than he wanted. On the other hand, to resist the seemingly reasonable demand could be construed as an infringement of the prisoner's rights. And still, under all the evidence that was gathering to submerge Burnham,

Carston felt the same uneasiness that had been with him from the start. After a small hesitation, he noted the time, recorded it on the tape, added that the interview had been suspended and switched the machine off.

"He's all yours," he said. "We'll want a blood sample when he's ready."

He flicked his head to tell Ross to follow and went out into the corridor and along to his own office.

The squad room was empty. McNeil had gone back to Dyson Close with a uniformed constable to conduct a full search. They were looking for the diary and anything else that might be useful or interesting. Carston had put McNeil in charge and trusted her to use her discretion in deciding what "useful" and "interesting" might mean.

It was twenty to eleven. He thought briefly of how much more he'd prefer to be propped up in bed beside Kath reading the thriller he'd started the previous evening. He dialed his home number, not with any particular message to convey but almost as a reflex. Kath was a long time in answering and he began to regret the call, thinking that she was maybe in the shower. At last she answered.

"Sorry, love. It's me," he said. "Have I disturbed something?"

"No, no. It's all right. I was just doing a test strip."

"A what?"

"In the darkroom. To see what exposure these shots of the river need. There are a couple that are looking quite nice. I want to get them right."

"Sorry," said Carston. "It was just to say that I've no idea what time I'll be back, if at all."

"You told me that before you left," said Kath. "I don't care. Who needs you? What time is it, anyway?"

"Nearly quarter to eleven."

"My God! Is it really? I had no idea. How's it going?"

"What, Burnham? Slow."

"Well, I'll be another hour on these prints anyway so I'll probably still be up when you get back."

"OK, love," said Carston. "Take care."

"Bye," said Kath.

Carston put back the receiver and hauled himself up to go to switch on the kettle. It was an automatic procedure, reassuring even. All the offices he saw on television had dispensing machines nowadays, or proper coffee-making equipment. He didn't want that sort of progress; he was too used to the familiarity of making the instant stuff, accepting the fact that it tasted like paint rather than coffee. He looked at his reflection in the window pane and ran his fingers through his hair. Outside, the air looked to be saturated with droplets and hung around the sodium lamps in thick orange clumps. There was little traffic and few people about. Some sanitized middle-class drinking was going on in the two private golf clubs and the three main hotels, while drinkers with fewer pretensions risked the pubs in the streets around where the canal met the river. Most Cairnburghers, however, were in front of their tellies.

The conversation between Carston and Kath had been a part of that same predictability. Nothing essential had been conveyed, no news or messages, but Carston felt better for the contact with the small reality on which he relied so heavily. The contrast between his marriage and that of the Burnhams could hardly be greater. The thought of two people living together and yet brushing past one another's lives day after day without raising any ripples of interest was hard for him to comprehend. He had no illusions about marriage; he knew the torments and tiny defeats and victories that were strung through the lives lived behind the curtains, but arguments meant passions and passions meant life. His job showed him often enough the explosions that sometimes took place. The fallout from these made him sad, but a much deeper chill spread from the strange intimacy of indifference.

The following morning, Carston was in early. They'd taken a blood sample from Burnham and, after getting him to sign an undertaking to appear when next summoned, had released him. Braithwaite had driven him home. When they were halfway through the preparation of the material they had to send to the procurator fiscal, McNeil arrived back with a cardboard box. It contained not only Burnham's current diary, but others going back over twelve years. Carston had left Ross with the paperwork and taken the box home.

He'd been reading until two in the morning, but at seven-thirty he was wide awake and eager to keep the impetus going. When Ross arrived, he stood up at once and said, "Don't take your coat off. I think we should go for a walk."

Obediently, Ross followed him out into the street.

"Let's talk through it a bit," said Carston as they turned to walk up towards the Macaulay Park whose gates were at the top of the hill. "Get a bit of air. Without any interruptions."

Carston wasn't concerned about anything to do with fitness but he didn't mind walking. It let him wander about mentally, trying out ideas, speculating, without the distractions of notes, telephones or actual points of reference. Like an owner taking his dog for a run, Carston could free his imagination. Ross, on the other hand, although he was used to the process, thought that it wasted a lot of time and that it could be done more efficiently back in the office, where they could refer to documents, statements, reports and keep the discussion focused.

They said little as they turned through the gate and began their slow amble through the avenue of rhododendrons that led to the central area of rockeries and rose beds. As always, Ross was waiting to find out where they were going to start. Carston's first question surprised him.

"Do you keep a diary, Jim?"

"No. Why, was Burnham's interesting?"

Carston nodded but, instead of answering the question, continued to follow his previous train of thought.

"Why d'you suppose people do it? Every night, religiously, they write stuff in it. What for?"

Ross shrugged. It had never occurred to him to think about it. Carston went on, almost talking to himself.

"I mean, politicians and writers and artists, people like that, it's sort of part of their job. They're all going to write their memoirs, or they're part of history or something. But people like you and me? People like Burnham?"

A toddler running towards them ahead of its mother and pushchair fell on its face and, after that strange delay between a sensation and its expression that always seems to occur with kids, started to cry in a way that suggested the entire world had disintegrated. Images of Kirsty doing the same sort of thing jumped into Ross's mind.

"Who's it for? Who's going to read them?" asked Carston.

He'd paused only briefly for the mini-tragedy. His pace increased to take them past and away from the screaming. Ross tried to hurry towards the point of Carston's line of thinking.

"It's just a habit, surely. Maybe they're lonely. Use the diary like a friend. Pour out their problems. Is that what Burnham did?"

"That's why I'm asking. I don't know what he did. He did it for twelve years, though."

"A bit obsessive," said Ross, curious himself now about the subject.

"I haven't read all of them," Carston went on. "Just flipped through them. That's the point, though. There's nothing there to read. It's all 'had a phone call from so-and-so,' 'went to Mario's for dinner,' 'meeting with some company or other.' Nothing special."

The screams from the toddler were still scouring across the park. Ross frowned.

"Strange that he thought of taking it with him last week when he went to the hotel," he said. "You'd think that that sort of trivial stuff wouldn't occur to him, not when he's under stress like that."

"No, it's a funny thing, Jim. Even though there's not much there, when you read it, you do get a sort of picture of the bloke. It … creeps up on you. Builds up gradually."

Ross wished they were back in the office so that he could look at the diary to see what Carston meant.

"There's a sort of honesty about it. He writes about how fat he's getting, little worries about his health …" Carston stopped walking for a moment.

"You know," he went on, "it's only just occurred to me but I felt a bit like an intruder when I was reading some of it. He does get very personal sometimes."

"It's a bloody diary," said Ross. "It's supposed to be personal."

Carston started walking again.

"I know," he said, "but it's personal in a different way when somebody else is reading it. D'you see what I mean?"

Ross couldn't be bothered to see what Carston meant. He wanted this detour to come back to some sort of relevance. He ignored the question.

"What did he write the day his wife died?" he asked.

"He didn't," said Carston.

The dead leaves which had piled up along one side of the central rose bed began to lift as a breeze started plucking at them. Carston picked up a sheet of newspaper which had blown onto the path in front of them and shoved it into a litter bin.

"What d'you make of that?" he went on. "The one day when something's really happened, a major event with a vengeance. He makes sure he takes the diary to the hotel with him but he writes nothing in it."

"Doesn't mean anything," said Ross, thinking over the possibilities. "Too upset to write. It's too big a thing altogether, bigger than the other sort of stuff you said he wrote. Or maybe he doesn't want to confess. It's not proof of anything but it doesn't help him, does it?"

Carston shook his head.

"I don't know, Jim," he said. "For me, it confuses the whole bloody thing even more. I mean, it was like reading a book. Well, that's daft, I was reading a book, but I mean, it's like characters in novels, they're different from real people. They're more real."

This was making Ross impatient. He couldn't see how airy-fairy talk about stories was contributing to their case against Burnham.

"With respect, sir," he said, "we're losing the thread a bit here. The procurator fiscal isn't going to want to know about novels, is he?"

Carston smiled. He knew how this sort of thing went against Ross's methods and instincts.

"I'm not talking about him. I'm not even sure it's evidence. What I'm saying is that reading his diary has made Burnham a different person for me. We look at him and he's a businessman, plenty of cash, swigging whisky out of crystal glasses, nice house, bit on the side. Then, in the diary, there's this different bloke, worried about going bald, feeling middle-aged, using stupid codes to mention the

172

Stone woman and what they've been up to, frustrated by colleagues at work, looking at himself night after night, writing down his life. It makes it all much more complicated."

"No, you're making it complicated. We wanted that book to see whether there's anything in it that can help us with his wife's murder, that's all."

"Yes. That's what I'm saying. There is. Not what we were expecting though. What did you want, Jim? 'Today I shot her indoors'?"

Ross looked away, wanting to hide his impatience.

"I don't think there's much I can say about it until I've looked at it, is there?"

"No, you're right. You can have a glance at it when we get back. See what your reaction is. I don't think it makes the case easier, though."

It was a big understatement. Carston's reading of the diary had increased his uneasiness about the whole affair. There was plenty there which showed the distances that had grown between Burnham and his wife and which the prosecution would no doubt use to evoke the bitterness and potential for conflict between them, but, more importantly, there were sketches of and insights into the writer which made him real, gave his life a peculiar substance, revealed a man who was certainly self-obsessed but also vulnerable. In the flesh, there'd been blustering aggression; in these pages there were fragile, childish joys, scatterings of tiny pains and some underlying regret which he never properly expressed and which fascinated Carston.

They'd reached a fountain which had been unveiled by a local dignitary in 1862 to mark a visit by Queen Victoria. It was presumably a water nymph of some sort but it was weighed down by so many decorative whorls and flourishes that anything that might have given it identity—size, gender, age—was obscured by the sculptor's exuberance. In the pool at its base were the usual, inexplicable coins thrown to finance wishes and regularly stolen by the less fanciful children of Cairnburgh's enterprise culture. Carston had lapsed into silence, still thinking about diaries and what they signified. Ross wanted to hurry things on.

"Any other problems?" he asked.

173

Carston shook his head.

"Not specifically, no."

Another alarm bell rang in Ross's head.

"What d'you mean?"

"Don't know," said Carston. "The case is there. We've charged him. It's all too pat."

"Why?"

"That sweater. Why didn't he get rid of it? Why just hand it over when we asked. He didn't need to."

"He didn't know about the bits in her hand. Why should he worry about the sweater? The bits of it we found around the study, he could just say he'd worn it there lots of times."

"He couldn't even remember if he was wearing it, though. Surely he's bright enough to have come up with something more definite than that. And just leaving the gun there. It's so bloody obvious. There are so many things ..."

Ross tried to stay reasonable.

"You're getting ahead of yourself again," he said. "There's nothing that says anybody else did it. Nobody came in or out except him ..."

"If we believe the gardener," said Carston.

"Is he a suspect too?" Ross asked.

Carston stopped again.

"Look, Jim," he said, "you're so set on these bloody facts of yours that sometimes you let them dictate to you. For instance, OK, nobody came in or out, but what about round the back?"

"There's a bloody canal."

"So? None of the neighbors were home. Nobody can see round the back of the houses. Easiest thing in the world to get in and out and across to the other side."

"So he swam across, did he? Find any water stains?"

Carston shook his head.

"OK, mooring ropes? Or any other traces from this phantom navigator? Did forensics find anything?"

Carston shook his head again. "Muck from outside that anybody could've brought in," he said. "Fibers from him and her, general stuff ..."

174

"See?" said Ross.

Carston had been saving the last point.

"And five sets of prints," he said, turning away and walking on down the path.

Ross followed, smiling despite himself at Carston's deliberately timed surprise. He'd seen the initial report from the scenes of crime squad but, at that stage, there had been no definitive classification of prints.

"Five?" he said. "Whose?"

"That's the question, isn't it? His and hers, and there's a cleaning lady who comes in every Monday. We'll check her out. But that leaves two more."

"OK, so who else is in the frame?"

"Who knows?" said Carston. "As far as I can make out, they didn't have any friends. Nobody much came visiting. I'm waiting for the DNA check on the fetus she was carrying to come through. We can try to sort out who the father was. We've got Burnham's sample and I want to get that bloke Sleeman tested if he'll co-operate. We have to check Burnham against the semen we found. Mind you, he's already admitted that they had sex."

"Yes. Good thinking, that. He knew we'd find that out easily enough."

"Jim," said Carston, "Don't rule out the other possibilities. I know you're right. I know that there's a lot going against him. I arrested him, for Christ's sake, so I'm not exactly defending him. I'm just concerned that we cover everything, think of all the angles."

"Aye, I know that," said Ross.

They stopped at a turn of the path that gave them a view over the town and on to the Cairngorms in the distance. The buildings sat well against the hills, the grays of Welsh slate and the pinks of Peterhead granite blending into a soft, variegated wash. Yesterday's mists had gone, leaving the air rinsed and clean, and the gentleness of late September light had taken over.

"Not bad, is it?" said Carston.

Ross nodded. His mind was still with Burnham.

"D'you think the fiscal will go for it?" he asked.

"Don't know," said Carston.

He'd had to learn the very different procedures for bringing prosecutions that operate under Scots law. In England, he'd initiated criminal proceedings himself as a police officer. Up here, he had to report the results of his investigations to the procurator fiscal. It was he who then decided whether or not to prosecute. They had to convince him that they had a case.

Extending his fingers one by one, Ross listed the evidence they'd got.

"No alibi. A witness puts him at the scene at the right time and swears nobody else was there. Shotgun with his prints all over it. Plenty of motives to choose from …"

"Like what?" Carston interrupted.

Ross used more fingers.

"Get rid of her to go off with his bit on the side. Insurance money—he gave us that one himself. Domestic. Found out she was having it off with Sleeman. Found out it was Sleeman's baby …"

"We don't know any of this."

"No, but you asked me. I'm just giving you possibles. There are plenty of them. And he's capable of violence; he beat up the other woman, Stone. Then there are the bits of his jumper in his wife's hand. That's the clincher, isn't it?"

Carston nodded, then started extending his own fingers in the same way.

"He doesn't get rid of the jumper. Why not? Somebody else wore it to set him up? An intruder could've got in the back way—"

"Got dressed up in Burnham's jumper, shot his wife. then floated off down the canal again," said Ross with very heavy sarcasm.

Carston dropped his hand back to his side. He knew Ross's version was more persuasive. He *agreed* with it, for God's sake! Why else had he arrested Burnham? But, for all sorts of reasons, he still wasn't satisfied.

"You haven't seen his bit on the side yet, have you?" he said.

"No."

"You should. She's something else. Sex on a stick. So, if he's having it off with her regularly, what the bloody hell does he want to rape his wife for?"

"Rape's not sex, it's power," said Ross.

"I know, but you've still got to get it up. You've heard him say what their sex life was like."

"Yes. But he wants us to think that, doesn't he? How much can we believe him?"

Carston shook his head again and turned to start back for the station.

"I don't know, Jim," he said. "Let's see what the fiscal does with it."

Once the process had been started, everything began to move far too quickly for Carston to indulge in doubts and reservations about the arrest. The procurator fiscal arranged for Burnham to appear in private before a sheriff for a judicial examination. Apart from Burnham and the policemen escorting him, only the procurator fiscal, Burnham's solicitor and the sheriff were present. The idea of such examinations is to pre-empt any surprise Perry Mason-style revelations if and when the case comes to trial and also to give the accused a chance to offer explanations which he might not be able to state in open court. In Burnham's case, the truculent attitude he adopted to the anodyne questions that were put to him helped the procurator fiscal to decide that there was indeed a case to answer. Braithwaite's efforts to reason with his client were met with impatience and arrogance. Burnham seemed to be unaware of the damage he was doing to his cause by treating the whole thing as if it were some sort of arcane ritual that was relevant to everyone present except himself. In fact, as Braithwaite told him when it was over, the attitude he'd adopted was the judicial equivalent of a death-wish.

He was released on bail and instructed to make himself available for trial in the High Court at a date that would be intimated to him at the earliest opportunity. He'd listened to all the strictures and conditions of his bail with the same irritated air that had been with him throughout. His most outraged reaction was provoked by the information that he must not seek to interfere with any of the witnesses. Since one of these was Barbara Stone and he would therefore not even be allowed to speak to her on the telephone, he felt that they were already punishing him for a crime they had yet to prove he'd committed. By telling the sheriff as much, he simply elicited from him not the understanding he expected but a short, tetchy lecture on justice and morality in Scottish jurisprudence.

He went back to work and endured the notoriety of his condition. The usual restrictions on reporting made sure that no one knew the facts of the indictment. The idea of that was to avoid the possible contamination of potential jurors by press speculations but, when the imaginations of people who already had warped views of him and his carryings-on were let loose, his status as a mad axman, sadist and pervert was quickly established. In turn, his own scorn for the whisperers made his comments to them sharper and his whole disposition much more bitter. Whatever the rights and wrongs of the case, he would not get through it unscathed.

Carston and his team now had some time to firm up their case. McNeil was, for the moment, on permanent loan to DCI Baxter. Fraser had been warned that if he spoke any more of his bad French in the squad room he'd be transferred to traffic control and, while continuing to pursue the perpetrators of other Cairnburgh and district crimes, he and Spurle had been advised to check over all their notes and read up the files so that, if they had to give evidence, they didn't look like pillocks. And, between other investigations and writing reports on the proposed restructuring of divisional areas of responsibility, Carston and Ross concentrated on tying up the loose ends of the Burnham evidence, of which there were still far too many for Carston's liking.

Two weeks had passed after Burnham had been charged before Carston was able to pin down Sleeman. The marine biologist had taken his boat up to the Marina at the northern end of Loch Ness and left her there while he spent time on board the aquarium ship which had been sent up to Loch Linnhe by the marine laboratories in Plymouth. There had been a series of real-time experiments which had required his exclusive attention and he'd been unable to free any time to meet Carston. He'd given a statement to the procurator fiscal about his acquaintance with Mrs. Burnham but it was a thin document and no one had yet touched on the subject of a possible DNA test.

178

He was due to be in the Aberdeen laboratories towards the end of November and Carston made an appointment to meet him at Grampian Police headquarters on the twenty-second. This time, he took Ross with him, partly to make sure that the dislike he'd developed for the man on their first meeting didn't cloud their contact and partly to get a fresh perspective on him. They waited in the reception area, chatting to a constable on duty at the desk and watching the continuous trickle of people coming in to report problems, look for lost property, show driving licenses and altogether keep the staff busy with activities far removed from the glamour and gore of crime fighting. Carston noticed, not for the first time, that the majority of the visitors somehow looked cowed, uncertain. None of them seemed to belong to the privileged classes and the moment they entered police headquarters, an unspecified guilt bent and confused them even further. Their gratitude for help was excessive, their respect for the uniforms would have graced a Sandhurst reunion and their uneasiness translated into the shufflings and shiftiness of irredeemable culpability.

Of course, when Sleeman arrived, the mold was broken. There was no stooping with him, no apology in his demeanor. He came in and walked easily up to them, looking as relaxed in his charcoal gray suit as he had in the jeans and sweater he'd worn on his boat. The wind-tanned features gave him a robustness that looked artificial amongst the winter-pale Aberdonians standing at various points around the foyer. But there was no smile, no pretence that their meeting gave him any pleasure. He stopped in front of Carston and immediately let them know where they stood.

"I hope this won't take long. I've set up three experiments to run this morning. I need to get back and check the data before lunch time."

"Good morning, sir," said Carston, with glutinous politeness. "You haven't met Sergeant Ross, have you?"

Sleeman looked at Ross, gave the slightest of nods to acknowledge him and turned back to Carston, waiting. All the irritations that Carston had felt in Findhorn came back to him. He smiled.

"Wonderful day, isn't it?" he said. "Pity you can't be out on your boat, eh?"

Sleeman said nothing.

"Yep. Nice little breeze out in the firth I should think. Just right for your … what's she called? I've forgotten."

Sleeman was still silent, staring at Carston, waiting for him to finish his game. Ross sensed the antagonism between the two of them right away, but there was not much he could do to get things going. Carston was an annoying bugger at times like this. It didn't get him anywhere and it could alienate people so that you got nothing out of them. On the other hand, he'd known it to provoke them so much that they lost their rag and gave away things that might otherwise have remained unsaid. Somehow, though, he didn't think that this time there was any strategy involved. Carston just didn't like the man. Simple as that.

"Shall we go through, sir?" Ross asked, as the pause was prolonged. The "sir" could have applied equally to Carston or Sleeman. Carston's response was an even wider smile and a gesture of invitation to Sleeman that wouldn't have been out of place if he'd been a wine merchant offering him access to his most prized vintage.

They went through to a small room just off the corridor that led away to the right of the reception area. Sleeman refused the offer of coffee.

"Can we stop the nonsense, Chief Inspector?" he asked as soon as the door closed behind them. "I really am very busy."

"Of course, of course," said Carston, satisfied that he'd managed to irritate Sleeman but also annoyed with himself for giving in to his own childishness. He sensed Ross's disapproval and knew that he was right.

"This really shouldn't detain you too long," he went on briskly. "Really, it all boils down to just a few questions."

Sleeman waited. Carston's attitude had killed any likelihood that he would open up willingly for them.

"I didn't ask you when I met you in Findhorn, but did you ever go to visit Mrs. Burnham at her home?" Carston asked.

Sleeman thought about the question.

"Why?" he asked.

Neither of the policemen answered. It was their turn to wait.

Carston held Sleeman's stare until it flicked away from him as frustration took over.

"Only once," he said.

"And when was that?"

"No idea. A week or so before we split up, I'd guess."

"May I ask why you went there?"

"A fuck," said Sleeman. "I was driving up to Inverness. It was on my way."

Carston knew that the coarseness was a deliberate response to his own provocations.

"Yes. Handy," he said. "I can see that."

Ross wasn't interested in their sparring.

"Sorry to be indiscreet, sir, but it is important. During your visit, were you just in the one room? Or what?"

Sleeman turned to look at him. Ross noticed the puckering of his brows as he thought about the question and the suggestion of amusement as his lips drew back slightly.

"No sex with Steph was ever very confined," he said. "She was a mover. A heaver."

Again, the desire was to create an effect. Ross was patient.

"So, which rooms then?" he asked. Sleeman wrinkled his handsome face and thought some more.

"We certainly didn't go near the bedroom," he said at last. "But, as for details … We started in the kitchen as far as I remember. Finished off upstairs. A room at the back. Some sort of study by the look of it. Books and things."

"Yes. Thank you," said Ross.

There was a small pause.

"Since we're being indiscreet," said Carston, in a quieter voice than before, "you mentioned Mrs. Burnham's … energy during your meetings. I wonder if you remember … Did she have any … what you might call peculiar tastes? Sexually, I mean."

It took both Sleeman and Ross by surprise.

"Like what?" asked Sleeman, seeming to be more amused by the question than anything else.

Carston shrugged.

"Anything at all. I mean, was it always just straight … sex?"

"Depends, doesn't it? What do you call straight?"

He waited for an answer. The question was insolent. Carston shrugged and spread his hands. Sleeman nodded slightly and smiled his superiority again.

"She liked it. We had a good time. What can I tell you?"

"No … S and M tendencies?" Carston persisted.

Sleeman's amusement died.

"Absolutely not," he said, his voice guarded.

"I see," said Carston.

Sleeman didn't trust the motives behind such a loaded question.

"Look, what's going on?" he asked, looking from one to the other of them. "I've given up time to come here. You've charged her old man with murder, why the hell are you asking me questions like this now?"

Ross tried to reassure him.

"Background, sir. Important, but just background. The more details we can fill in, the better our case. Can't say much more, as you'll appreciate."

"And we have been trying to get in touch for a while, Dr. Sleeman. You've been rather … elusive."

Sleeman's head was shaking back and forth.

"Look, either you've charged the guy or you haven't. Bit late to be getting a case together now, isn't it?"

"We've got a case," said Carston. "As Sergeant Ross says, the rest is background. That's what we were hoping you'd help us with."

"There's nothing else I know. I don't see how …"

Carston raised a hand to interrupt him.

"There are two other areas, both a bit sensitive," he said.

He paused, for once not certain how to approach the next question. Sleeman was right. They had their case, so what the hell was this extra questioning about? It was all stuff that should have been cleared up in the first round of interviews. Both technically and actually, none of it was material to the case they had against Burnham. But he really did want to understand the whole thing a bit better. It was information he needed to firm up his convictions, to give real, believable substance to the accusations that would be made in court, to turn the scraps of evidence they had into visible

182

fragments of events he could confidently reconstruct. So far he was hearing echoes. He wanted voices.

"There's no point in talking round it," he said at last. "We were wondering if you'd mind giving us two things, your fingerprints and a blood sample."

"What?" It was an explosion rather than a question. Sleeman was on his feet. "What the bloody hell for?"

Carston nodded his head and held up both hands, both gestures admitting that he realized that the request seemed strange.

"Elimination, that's all. As the sergeant said, the more things we can tidy away, the better."

"And exactly what is a blood sample from me going to tell you?"

"The pregnancy," said Carston. "We need to know whose child it was."

"What for?"

"Really, sir," said Ross, trying to help out, "we can't go into details but it would be very helpful if you'd co-operate."

Sleeman walked away from the table, stood looking down at the floor for a moment, then turned back to them.

"Just try to shift your perspective for a moment, Sergeant. I'm a member of the public. I'm in a police station. I was having an affair with a woman who's been murdered. Now you're asking for finger-prints and blood samples. How do you think that strikes me? Don't you think I should be asking for a solicitor?"

Ross's tone was even.

"No, sir," he said. "As you said yourself, someone's already been charged with the crime. We've got our case. We're not looking for any other suspects."

Carston was watching carefully. Sleeman's initial shock at the request had quickly been replaced with a measured calculation. It was as if he was already in the courtroom, treading carefully through the questioning and cross-examinations.

"Nevertheless," said Sleeman, still addressing himself to Ross, "I feel threatened. And who've I got as a witness to the fact that you don't think I'm under suspicion?"

"Are there any reassurances we can give you, Dr. Sleeman?" asked Carston.

"Like what?" said Sleeman, turning to him. "That if you suddenly find that I did it after all you won't tell anyone?"

"You didn't do it," said Ross. "Someone else did. He's been charged."

Sleeman looked at him and tutted.

"Wrong, Sergeant," he said. "He's as innocent as I am until the jury says otherwise, isn't he? Your prejudging the issue isn't very reassuring."

Carston suspected that he was starting to enjoy this.

"So you won't help us then, Dr. Sleeman?" he said.

Sleeman looked at him then turned away from them again, looking down once more at the floor and seeming to contemplate a response. They waited, knowing that there was nothing else for them to say. After what seemed a very long time, Sleeman lifted his head and, without turning round, said, "Of course I'll help you. I'm a good citizen."

Carston and Ross looked at one another. They were both too relieved to show any reactions.

"That's very good of you, sir," said Ross.

His words were cut short by Sleeman as he turned round and came back to the table.

"So can we get it done and let me get back to my experiments?" he asked, his earlier impatience back in his voice. "This whole damned thing has taken up too much of my time already."

Carston was too relieved to risk losing Sleeman's co-operation again by asking him more questions and he left Ross with him while he himself went to the front desk to telephone and make all the arrangements. It also gave him time to think about Sleeman's sudden co-operation and seeming change of attitude. Almost everything about his reactions had puzzled Carston. They lacked consistency. Anger at being required to give samples, anxiety at some implied accusation, suspicion of their motives, willing acquiescence, any of these things would have been understandable, but the way in which he'd spun from one to the other left him wondering where Sleeman really stood in relation to the affair.

When he got back to the interview room, Sleeman was talking to Ross about the experiments he was working on. Ross had obviously asked the right questions because the superior, irritating Sleeman had been replaced by one who still treated Ross like a lesser intelligence but did at least speak with some enthusiasm about the planktonic variations they were finding in Loch Linnhe as a result of the nitrogen in the local farmers' fertilizer being washed down into the rivers and joining all the other nutrients falling like some underwater mist from the cages of the salmon farms. Ross's genuine interest enabled him to continue with appropriate questions until the nurse came.

By the time she'd taken the samples they needed and a constable from the duty room had brought the pad along for the fingerprinting, Sleeman had reverted to his former brusqueness. As he finished drying his hands on the paper towel, he looked at his watch.

"Chief Inspector," he said. "I hope this'll be the last of these little surprises. I really don't have this sort of time to spare."

Carston reluctantly acknowledged his assistance.

"You've been very helpful, Dr. Sleeman. We really do appreciate your time and trouble."

Sleeman looked to see whether there was any irony in his words, decided that, this time, there wasn't, and made for the door. Ross opened it for him.

"See you in court," said Carston, unable to resist it.

Sleeman turned at the door and, to Carston's surprise, smiled at him.

"You're a bloody chancer, Carston," he said.

"He's right, sir," said Ross as he rejoined Carston at the desk.

"About what?"

"You are a chancer."

Carston grinned.

Their business in Aberdeen was only half done. They still wanted to see Stone but Carston hadn't been able to contact her before they'd left Cairnburgh. He asked the duty constable if he could use the phone. The young man pushed it towards him as Carston reached for the directory that was in a brown holder at the end of the desk. He looked up Dempster Associates and dialed the number. The luck they'd had with Sleeman's co-operation held.

Stone was in the office and, when he was put through to her, sounded as if she'd been waiting for his call since their previous meeting. He arranged to come straight to her office, declining her (he presumed) playful suggestion that a motel might be more comfortable and, to Ross's incomprehension, giving as his own playful excuse the fact that the sergeant was with him. As he should have known, this simply produced the suggestion that a session in the motel might therefore be even more piquant. As he rang off, he wondered briefly at the woman's gift for brightening the slightest, most mundane contacts. She was only flirting, playing a game they both knew was just that, but to be a player, you had to have the equipment. He had had no desire to deceive Kath for years and the universal fear of AIDS was a powerful argument for fidelity, but he knew bloody well that, if anybody could try his resolve, Stone could.

Her office was in a large modern block that overlooked the harbor. This also meant that it was near the railway station and, perhaps because of this, parking facilities were limited. When they arrived, a security man at the gate directed them to a public multi-story car park just around the corner. They left the car there and walked back, Ross remarking on the fact that the amount of commercial traffic, mostly oil-related to judge from the names on the sides of vans and lorries, indicated that in Aberdeen at least, there was still plenty of money about.

It was an impression that was fortified by Stone's office when they got there. She was high enough in the hierarchy to have a room to herself. Its fittings were predominantly black against walls lined with pale beige, lightly textured linen. Three dramatic color high-lights were provided by prints on the wall opposite the window. Two of them showed oil platforms in impossible seas, the third a tangle of pipework that was either the artist's idea of a refinery at night or a set design for a Ridley Scott movie. Stone fitted perfectly into the setting. She was wearing a beautifully tailored maroon jacket over a loose silk blouse. Her black skirt was snug over her hips and thighs and emphasized the taper of her long legs. As she moved to greet them, her hand outstretched, Carston couldn't help returning her smile.

"You haven't met my sergeant," he said.

Briefly, Ross noted the "my sergeant," a formulation Carston rarely used, but there was no time to wonder about it because Stone turned her smile on him and he was immediately on his guard.

"A pleasure to meet you, Sergeant," said Stone.

Ross simply nodded. She led them to a low coffee table in the corner by the window, sat down and invited them to join her. Outside, the harbor was full of supply vessels except for one quay, along which the Orkney ferry was taking on cars and passengers. It was an impressive view but both Carston and Ross turned their attention quickly back from it to Stone. She'd let a phantom of the smile stay with her and sat looking expectantly at Carston. Neither of the men knew where it came from, but she radiated a sexuality it was hard to ignore. Ross now understood all the innuendoes that had suffused any talk they'd had of her in the course of their discussions about Burnham. Carston had to acknowledge that the skittishness that had characterized his own brief contacts with her was still childish but utterly excusable.

"Well then?" said Stone, making Carston uncomfortably aware that they'd been sitting looking at her slightly longer than they should have.

"Sorry to bother you," he said, hurrying on now, "but we'd appreciate your help."

"I'm entirely at your disposal," she said.

"Yes," said Carston. "Good. Er … as you know, we've charged Mr. Burnham and …"

"I am being called as a witness, Chief Inspector," she said sweetly. "So I think you can assume that I'm aware of the basics."

To his disgust, Carston felt a blush across his cheeks.

"Yes," he said. "Well, there are one or two things we need to clear up."

He stopped. She waited.

"Odds and ends," he added.

"Like what?" she asked, helpfully.

"Fingerprints," said Ross.

He had left no pause between question and answer. His voice was harder than usual, tightly controlled. In the few seconds of conversation he'd heard, he was already aware of the power the woman was exercising and resented the fact that she was making a game out of it. He was as susceptible as Carston to the sex appeal she generated and knew how easy and pleasurable it would be to step aside from duty for a moment and indulge in some old-fashioned flirting. It was precisely that recognition that put him on his guard. Consciously, deliberately, he looked directly at her and made himself see a witness whose co-operation they needed. Stone sensed some of this, looked straight into his eyes and turned up the power.

"How exciting," she said. "I've been asked for lots of things in the past, but never fingerprints. What do you want me to do?"

Ross was unimpressed. He opened the briefcase he'd brought with him and started to take out the kit they'd borrowed from the station.

"It won't take long," said Carston.

"It rarely does, more's the pity," she said, flicking a sideways look at him.

She smiled and watched as Ross spread a strip of paper on the table.

"It may be old-fashioned of me," she went on, "but I thought the only people who had their fingerprints taken were criminals. And corpses of course."

"No, no," said Carston. "It proves innocence as well as guilt."

"Is that what you're doing then? Proving my innocence?"

Although she gave him her devastating smile as she said it, Carston found the conversational turn a little strange. The thought also occurred to him that innocence was the last quality he'd associate with such a woman. He resisted saying so and tried to catch her off guard.

"Have you ever been to Mr. Burnham's house?" he asked.

Stone paused only briefly.

"In Cairnburgh? No, I don't think so. Not exactly politic, is it? The other woman wandering into the happy home."

Ross was leaning forward to put an ink pad beside the piece of paper. Stone watched with interest.

"Why do you ask?" she asked, still studying the items Ross was arranging.

"Oh, we just wondered," said Carston. "We need to find out who's been there, eliminate all the people we know of. Just in case there are any … well, unforeseen factors waiting to surprise us."

"Like what?" asked Stone.

This time it was Ross who noticed a change in her. She was forgetting to emit charm. She seemed genuinely interested in Carston's answers.

"If they're surprises, we don't know," he said.

She looked up at him. Momentarily, her eyes were guarded but the smile came back almost at once.

"What an invaluable assistant you have, Chief Inspector," she said. "A bit literal-minded, but something of a treasure I should think."

Carston knew what lay beneath the exchange and was interested by it. It also allowed him to shake off some of the spell she'd woven.

"So you've never visited Mr. Burnham at home?" he asked again.

She looked at her sleeve and brushed some invisible specks from the cuff.

"Once," she said, with no acknowledgment of the fact that she was changing her answer. "Poor Michael was so insistent. He was like a baby so much of the time. He wanted me to go there just to … you mustn't laugh at this, Chief Inspector … to leave something of me there."

Carston didn't feel in the least like laughing.

"I'm not sure I understand," he said.

Stone pushed her chair back, got up and turned to the window.

"He said the place was sterile, bleak. Those were his words. He said he wanted to be able to come home to something of me, my perfume, my presence. It sounds like Mills and Boon, I know, but those were the things he was saying. I told you, he was like a baby."

She went to her desk, took a tissue from a box and came back to sit down again.

"So you did go, then?" asked Ross.

"Yes. To humor him." Her voice was gentle. It carried none of the scorn that her words might have implied. "It was sad really. That marriage … desolate. No wonder he …"

She shook her head. Carston knew that there was no point in asking her to finish the sentence.

"You told me you'd never met Mrs. Burnham, didn't you?" he asked.

"Yes. I was wrong though." The gentleness had gone and, once again, there was no acknowledgment that her story was changing.

"I did see her once or twice. At seminar things in town. Michael told me all about her, though. She was weird."

"Weird?"

"You want me to speak ill of the dead, Chief Inspector? OK. Yes, weird. Round the bend. Frustrated at work. Classic menopause. Didn't know what she wanted but making sure that no one else got it either. They were poison for each other, you know. I was a therapist as much as a lover. Reminding him of how to live. Showing him it didn't have to be all mud and despondency. Did too good a job, didn't I?"

She stopped. Again, Carston knew instinctively that pursuing the question would produce nothing. In any case, Stone forestalled him. With an instantaneous change back to a tone thick with bedroom resonance that struck both the men, she said, "And now, Sergeant, you look ready to take me."

Ross had decided he definitely didn't like her. There was no danger of his being caught up in her games. He explained what she had to do and, when he took her hand to press each finger on the pad, he was quick, businesslike and, for all the effect the contact had, might have been a fishmonger weighing haddock. Stone sensed the antagonism and reacted to it. When the last print was taken, she got to her feet immediately, wiping her fingers on the tissue she was holding.

"Well then," she said, the voice now that of a busy executive. "If that's everything, there are wheels of commerce that need to be turned."

Carston and Ross were being summarily dismissed. So comprehensive was the change of mood that Ross found himself hurrying to pack away his gear as Carston stood helpless, feeling that he was an intruder. The woman really was something else. She stood by her desk, waiting for Ross. When his briefcase clicked shut at last, she switched on a wide smile which carried no trace of sexuality and led them to the door. There, she gave Ross the barest of nods and held out her hand to Carston.

"Thank you for your time," he said, as he took it and felt (or imagined) the extra pressure of her thumb in his palm.

"Anything to help the police," said Stone. "Anything at all."

Outside, walking back to the car, neither of them said anything at first. Stone had a way of troubling people, making them wonder about their own attitudes, distorting their perceptions so that it took a while to reorient themselves. For both of them, reintegration into normality was helped by a couple who came up the steps from the railway station as they passed. They looked to be in their fifties but were probably younger. The man, short, aggressive, his shirt collar out over the lapels of his jacket, walked ahead. The woman, gray and thin, stumbled after him.

"D'ye want yer Export?" she asked as they got to the pavement.

"Course I want ma fuckin' Export," he replied, not breaking his step.

From her handbag, the woman took a can of McEwans Export, already opened, and quickened her pace to hand it to him. He took it gracelessly and swigged from it on the move as she fell into step just behind him again. As they moved away up towards the railway bridge, Carston and Ross looked at each other, shook their heads and smiled.

"Just like home," said Carston.

Chapter Eight

For all the speed with which they'd got their evidence together and charged Burnham, it was spring before the indictment was served on him. Carston was standing in front of a picture of a plow when Ross gave him the news. They were in the lower gallery rooms of the Cairnburgh Arts Center on Rose Street where Kath was exhibiting two of her pictures in the Cairnburgh Photographic Society's annual show. Her sepia study of the town's famous Bridge of Beedon had won a commendation and a local printer wanted to reproduce it on some greetings cards. The plow was the sole exhibit of an eleven-year-old girl and Kath was trying to educate Carston into appreciating the freshness of its vision.

"The handle, look, that single sort of arrow shape pointing up to the right, it lifts your eye up, back into the picture."

Carston looked, considered, and agreed.

"And the two shoulders of the plow, or whatever they're called, they're swept back as if it's traveling fast."

From Carston, more agreement but muted enthusiasm.

"Oh Jack, look at it."

"I am. And it's very nice, but I still don't see the …"

Kath held up a finger.

"Which way do plows go?" she asked.

Carston frowned.

"Whichever way they're pulled," he said.

Kath gave one triumphant nod of the head.

"Precisely," she said, her finger swiveling to take his eyes back to the photograph. "And this one would be pulled the other way from the way it seems to be moving. The handle's at the back, remember."

192

Carston saw what she meant and, as she moved into the next room, he remained in front of the picture and let his mind work on rearranging his reactions to this new angle on it. The more he thought about it, the more abstract the pattern became and he was trying to bring the object and the image back together when Ross arrived.

"Sandy said you were here," he said. "Into art now, are you?"

"What d'you think of this?" asked Carston, pointing at the picture.

"It's all right. What am I supposed to think? It's just a plow."

"Wrong, Jim. Apparently, it's an exercise in contrapuntal dynamics."

Ross looked at the picture again.

"Of course. Why did I no see that right away?" he said.

The two of them turned away.

"What's the news then?" asked Carston.

"April the fourteenth," said Ross.

"In a hurry all of a sudden, aren't they?"

"I think there's a backlog building up."

"Does the team know about the date?"

"Fraser and Spurle do. McNeil's been in court today. The rape case."

"Oh, right. Any news?"

"No."

"Well, I'm glad to be getting on with it. I've almost forgotten the bloody thing."

They walked into the next room.

"Did you come here specially to tell me about Burnham?" Carston asked.

"No. I'm just on my way home. It's Jean's night-school class."

Kath smiled at Ross as the two of them came up to her.

"Congratulations on the news, Jim," she said.

Carston looked at them both.

"What news?" he said.

"The baby," said Kath.

Ross smiled broadly and Carston felt briefly excluded from the secret the two of them seemed to have.

"You mean Jean's ...?"

He stopped, letting a facial expression and a gesture which sketched a balloon in front of his abdomen complete his question. Ross nodded. Kath laughed.

"Didn't you know?" she asked.

"No," said Carston. "I'm a detective. I'm supposed to find out these things for myself."

"Jean told me yesterday," said Kath. "I rang her up to fix a day to come round. I'm taking some shots of Kirsty."

"Aye. She said."

Carston held out his hand.

"Well, congratulations, you dirty sod," he said.

The handshake was brief. The physical contact embarrassed Ross.

"August, isn't it?" said Kath.

"Aye," said Ross, a grin showing the pleasure the thought gave him.

"Come on then," Carston said, taking each of them by the arm and rekindling his sergeant's embarrassment. "Enough of this art business. A quick drink to celebrate."

As he helped Kath on with her coat in the foyer, Carston reflected on how Ross's tendency to organize things seemed to extend even into his private life. Kirsty's birthday was in August. So was Jean's. It was as if he'd used his computer to generate some sort of optimal family. Two years between each child, all the family birthdays concentrated in high summer. Precise planning for maximum efficiency. It was a frivolous, unworthy thought but one which might well carry some truth. Nonetheless, he kept it to himself. Ross's fierce protectiveness about Jean and Kirsty was an area into which only Spurle was stupid enough to stray and even he didn't risk it often. Ross's voice came right on cue.

"One drink, and I'm buying," he said. "Then I'm off. Jean won't want to be late for her class."

As they walked through the March evening towards the pub, Kath and Ross talked about the classes Jean was following. Carston barely listened. His earlier claim that he'd almost forgotten about Burnham was pure invention. The whole affair still fascinated him and he was eager to have all the pieces brought together, not only for the sake of justice but also to offer him the coherence he'd not yet managed to achieve in his frequent speculations about the people who'd circled around Stephanie Burnham's chaos.

The coverage of the case in the *Aberdeen Press and Journal* made sure that there were plenty of interested spectators in the public seats of the High Court. In the dock, Burnham looked impeccable. His three-piece suit was a mid-gray woolen mixture, his tie a dark blue with a faint Cambridge blue stripe, his cotton shirt a rich cream color, his shoes brushed black pigskin. It had all been selected on the advice of the advocate who was defending him, John Maunder, who insisted that the impression they needed to create was that of a correct, sober businessman against whom circumstances had conspired. Nothing must look too expensive for fear of releasing in a jury the natural desire to see someone better off than themselves brought down to size. Burnham had accepted the advice quietly, calmly, recognizing that, from the moment the indictment was served, he was simply an object that would be part of the manipulations of people whose skills were of a different world from his own. In the months since Stephanie's death, he'd been forced further and further into himself and had effectively become a recluse. Deprived of the company and excitements of Stone, he'd been twice to prostitutes in Aberdeen and once to a hotel in Glasgow a colleague had recommended to him at the firm's Christmas party. On each occasion, the hunger that had driven him there abated the minute he was alone with the woman and he found himself lying back and feeling dirty and miserable as she went about her business. All his social contacts had been work-related and now most of his spare time was spent in his Dyson Close home with radios or TV sets on in every room and a bottle of Chivas Regal always close to hand.

The prosecuting Crown Counsel, Andrew Milne, was a mature, imposing figure with a rich Edinburgh accent. He drew verbal pictures of the murder scene for the jury, his refinement and restraint giving greater piquancy to the brutality of what had happened than more colorful language might have done. He conveyed the disarray of the study, the damage inflicted on the victim, and underlined the fact that forensic evidence suggested

195

very strongly that the only recent visitors to the room had been Mr. and Mrs. Burnham and that fingerprint experts would testify that the last person to handle the fork, plunger and gun had been the accused.

Right from the start, his attack was uncompromising. With the help of Carston, he used extracts from Burnham's diary to create a powerful image, that of a callous, adulterous individual whose attitude to his wife was hateful and venomous. Carston was uncomfortable as Milne asked him to read selected passages.

"Eight-thirty pm. In the study. Trying to finish the Bailey account. S is in the kitchen. The bitch knows I've got to get this done so she arranges a fucking meal with Ben and Joanna. Christ, I get so angry with her pissing me about like that."

The judge looked at Milne, unhappy about the obscenities. Milne refused to meet his eye and invited Carston to read fresh extracts.

"Jesus, S makes me sick. Another bloody row about France. What the fuck do I care about it? Why doesn't she just piss off? It'd be so much simpler. She does it on purpose, I'm sure. A pity because it was a good day. Productive. Jerry brought the new figures to the meeting and they were better than I thought they'd be. Twelve percent up. The market must have steadied. That fucking awful bitch ..."

This time, Milne anticipated the judge's displeasure and hurried him on to the last passage, written just three days before his wife's death.

"What a day! What a day! Finished the Tranter account early and meeting with B in Aberdeen for extended(!) lunch. Everything! Everything! Why didn't I get this earlier? S has always been there, that's why. In the fucking way. She's got to go. I need space for B. We do so much. Unbelievably good! Talk about alpha and omega!"

In a very short space of time, Milne had established Burnham as a foul-mouthed, egocentric monster who'd actually articulated his desire to get rid of his wife. With hardly a pause, he continued his attack, now sketching a picture of the person he called "the savagely wronged woman." He called Borney and Mrs. Napier, both of whom evoked Mrs. Burnham's intellect, charm and professional

196

expertise and stressed how efficiently she'd serviced her clients and how pleasant she'd made life for everyone who worked with her. He showed how inappropriate the term "bitch" was when applied to such a paragon and did such a good job that Maunder's attempts, during cross-examination, to highlight her ambition, the ruthlessness she'd used to get promoted ahead of Roach and the drink-related interludes, were seen as irrelevancies by a jury already heavily predisposed against the silent man in the dock.

The tone had been set and the prosecution went confidently forward. The only hitch occurred towards the end of the first session. Willie Hardie, the gardener who'd seen Burnham leave his house on the day of the crime, was on the stand. He was wearing his only suit, an ill-fitting brown affair, and Milne had been careful to establish his down-to-earth reliability. Hardie told how he'd seen Burnham come out of his house just after twelve in "a muckle hurry" and drive quickly away. His certainty regarding times and what had happened was legitimized by the fact that his days and actions were regular, standardized, reliable. He knew he'd seen Burnham just after twelve not by referring to any clock but by the fact that he was just taking out his sandwiches.

The problem arose when they moved to questions about shots being fired. Milne had established that the presence of the gun club made gunfire a frequent occurrence in the area and therefore part of simply being there. Hardie agreed that, just because he didn't remember having heard anything, that didn't mean that no one had been shooting. You just got so used to it that in the end, you took no notice. But, during his cross examination, Maunder wasn't satisfied with that sort of fudging.

"Look," said Hardie, "Ah may have heard something and Ah may not. Ah canna be sure. Ah'm under oath here. Ah'm nae wantin' to tell nae lies."

"I appreciate that, Mr. Hardie, but it's something the rest of us find difficult to understand. I mean, cars seem to backfire less nowadays, and gunshots can hardly be confused with anything else, can they?"

By way of answer, Hardie suddenly snapped his fingers.

"My God," he said.

"Yes, Mr. Hardie?" said Maunder, having no idea of what he was inviting.

"Backfire. Ye're right. I did hear a shot that day."

Along with everybody else in the court, Carston focused his attention more sharply on the man. He noticed that Burnham had looked up too and was staring intently at Hardie. Maunder trod carefully.

"Now let's be clear about this. You've said you couldn't be sure."

"Aye, but it was when I got in the van. It'd just gone clean out o' mah mind before you said about backfires."

"All right, Mr. Hardie, so you did hear a shot. One shot?"

"Aye."

"And what time would that be?"

"Just after two."

"Two o'clock in the afternoon?" said Maunder, unable to suppress completely the pleasure the news gave him.

"Aye. Ah got in the van and turned the key an' there was an almighty bang. At first, Ah thought it was the van backfirin' but then Ah realized it was yon club again."

"The club. You're sure it was from the club?"

"Well, what else would it be?"

"It couldn't perhaps have been a shot fired in the Burnhams' house?"

"Aye, maybe. I was just glad it wasnae the van."

The man's priorities helped to defuse some of the tension that his revelation had introduced. A prosecution witness had just offered the accused an alibi and yet he was more concerned that his van didn't need servicing. When the court rose for lunch, it was the image of the red-faced figure in the brown suit that stayed with everyone.

The afternoon session began with the pathologist, Brian McIntosh. Milne wanted to re-establish the horror of Stephanie Burnham's death. In clear, simple terms and with the use of diagrams, McIntosh showed how the muzzle of the shotgun had been placed against her back just below her right shoulder blade. The charge had torn through the tissue of her lungs and hit her heart, which indicated that the gun had been pointing at a slight angle up and across her chest cavity. His description of the wound and the massive tissue damage brought a chill to the court which deepened when Milne led him into some of the other events and actions of that Wednesday. He described the bruising he'd found around her vagina and anus which was consistent not just with sexual intercourse and sodomy but also with the use of both the barrel of a gun and a blunt instrument made of wood. There were also the stab-marks on her legs from the kitchen fork, all pre-mortem. The condition of her skirt and panties clearly showed that they had been torn from her. By the time he'd finished his methodical, scientific reconstruction of the last, fear-crammed moments of Stephanie Burnham, there was no longer any doubt where the court's sympathies lay. Equally, the hostility of those on the public benches was stoked higher against the presumed perpetrator of it all.

Throughout McIntosh's evidence, Carston was watching Burnham very closely. He showed an astonishing degree of control. Once or twice, his head shook, almost involuntarily, and when the fork wounds and sodomy were being described, he brought both hands up to his face and massaged his forehead. Throughout all the other details of pain and destruction, he looked across at McIntosh, his eyes showing nothing.

There were two other pieces of McIntosh's evidence that aroused interest. First, he helped to establish that death had occurred between twelve and two o'clock and then he turned to the phenomenon of cadaveric spasm. Milne asked him to explain it and then to confirm that the fibers which had been found in the victim's hand had indeed been clutched at the moment of death. This so clearly implicated Burnham that everyone was surprised to hear his advocate ask McIntosh to repeat it. When he did, Maunder persisted.

"These fibers couldn't have been put into her hand by a third party and the fingers made to close around them?" he said.

"Impossible," said McIntosh.

Maunder smiled at him then at the judge.

"Thank you," he said.

In his seat, Milne frowned, wondering what sort of point Maunder might be planning to make by strengthening one of the prosecution's hardest pieces of evidence. But Maunder didn't pursue the matter. He had nothing more to ask.

The prosecution ground steadily on, building a solid structure of facts. William Cowie, a ballistics expert from the engineering department of Robert Gordon's University, confirmed that the amount of lead found suggested that the type of shot fired into Mrs. Burnham's chest had been a Winchester Superspeed, in which thirty-six grams of powder were used instead of the usual twenty-eight. When questioned by Maunder, he offered the opinion that this would cause much greater damage to the "target" and also that it would mean a more powerful recoil. To demonstrate the effects of such a recoil, Maunder got him to take the gun, adopt the usual shooting stance and describe its main aspects for the jury. Cowie, small, bald, embarrassed, recited a quick litany.

"Stock tight into the shoulder, hands firm but relaxed, body slightly forward, leaning into the shot, left leg forward, both legs braced."

"Thank you, Mr. Cowie," said the smiling Maunder. "Very illuminating. There's just one other point I'd like you to clear up for me. Shotguns are quite large, aren't they? How big is that one?"

Cowie held the gun in front of him.

"They vary a lot. This one's got a 32-inch barrel ..."

Maunder was satisfied.

"Fascinating. Thank you very much, Mr. Cowie," he said.

The day ended with another expert; Dr. Marchant, a forensic scientist. The main thrust of his contribution concerned two areas, fingerprints and fibers. He confirmed that five different sets of prints had been found in the study, those of Mr. and Mrs. Burnham predominating, as one would expect, those of Mrs. Wedderburn, their cleaning lady, being almost as numerous, and two others which had since been identified as those of Mrs. Stone and Dr. Sleeman. Milne interrupted him at this point to tell the court that both those individuals were friends of the Burnhams and that they would be hearing from them in due course. In Sleeman's case there was a single palm print on the underside of a shelf but Stone had left several impressions, most of them on the legs of the desk and the skirting board behind it. Prompted by Milne, Marchant pointed out that, of all these findings, those of the Burnhams were the most recent.

His evidence on the fibers found in the victim's hand and elsewhere in the study was equally concise. He first quoted the formulae of the vegetable dyes used to color them, then the constituent parts of the material itself. Under gentle prompting from Milne, he stated categorically that the fibers were identical with those of Burnham's gardening sweater and that he was absolutely certain that the ones in the victim's hand had been pulled from the garment with considerable force.

It was the end of a fascinating day. Ross and Carston drove back to Cairnburgh together with Ross, as usual, at the wheel. They said little until they were clear of Hazlehead and heading into the country. The contrast between the open April sky and the restricted, crowded room they'd been in made Carston's mind feel dusty, as if the two lawyers had thrown webs over it and drawn it into a tight pattern of their making.

"What d'you think, then?" asked Ross at last.

Carston kept his gaze on the hillside on their left.

"Clever buggers, both of them. Wish I knew where Maunder's heading, though. He's acting as if Milne's making a case for the defense."

Ross snorted.

"He was for a minute, with yon bloody gardener."

Carston smiled.

"Marvelous, isn't it? The number of times we asked him about that, and he only remembers in court."

They were silent again, both reflecting on the gardener's evidence. When Carston spoke again, his voice was quiet.

"It's thin, Jim, isn't it?"

Ross gave a small shrug but didn't contradict him.

"The only thing we've got is that bloody jumper. It was there when she was killed." He paused, then continued. "Trouble is, who was wearing it?"

"Why should it be anybody else?" asked Ross, aware in spite of his question that it could be a problem for the prosecution.

"That's not the point. They've got to prove it was him. That was a big time-window that Brian McIntosh opened. Burnham was there for part of it, but there's proof he wasn't for the last bit. Up till two o'clock, for Christ's sake. That's plenty of time for somebody else to get in and ..."

His hands sketched the rest of his thought.

"Why, though?" said Ross. "And why put on Burnham's jumper? No, that's thriller material, that."

Carston nodded, but the gremlins in his mind kept on turning.

The following day, Ross stayed in Cairnburgh and Carston was driven in by McNeil. Their conversation centered at first around the wonderful properties of garlic. His dinner the night before had been liberally flavored with it and McNeil had let him know, discreetly but unmistakably, that its familiar pungency lingered with him. The result was that he kept his head turned towards his window most of the way into Aberdeen.

On the outskirts, he remembered the rape trial she'd been attending and asked her about it. Her change of mood told him as much as her answer.

"Acquitted, sir," she said.

"Why?"

"The usual. Unsubstantiated evidence, and the wife refusing to testify."

Carston shook his head.

"I thought you said she'd started coming round. She was co-operating with you all right, wasn't she?"

"Aye, she was. But as soon as she had to start giving the details to her brief again, she started to back off from them. Didn't remember properly, she said. Didn't want to, more like. And she was feart of him, of course."

Carston didn't understand.

"Her brief?" he said.

"Her man," replied McNeil, not trying very hard to keep all the scorn out of her tone.

She tapped her fingers on the steering wheel and he saw that her eyes were flicking about as she stared at the road.

202

"Same every time. It never changes," she said. "I don't know what we've got to do to get to grips with it."

"Education," said Carston. "And lobotomies for half the male population."

"Only half?" she said, appreciating his understanding.

"Many as you like, except me, Sergeant Ross and maybe the guy who's trying to teach me to play golf," he added.

In the courtroom, Carston watched Burnham's arrival with interest. He was wearing the same mid-gray suit but the shirt was now a dusty pink and the tie a dark blue, unpatterned silk. He still had the same air of quiet defeat and paid no attention to any of the people in the room. Carston guessed that his stillness might be a result of some coaching from Maunder because it did give him the sort of gravity that had rarely been apparent in his volatile behavior towards Carston and Ross in their various interviews.

Milne had chosen a star witness to open the proceedings. Having sanctified Stephanie Burnham and spelled out the horrors of her agony, he now wanted the court to know the extent of the depravity and deceit of which Burnham was capable. To convey that information, he called Barbara Stone.

As she came in, Carston saw at once that this was yet another of her incarnations. She wore a black Venetian wool double-breasted suit over a cream linen shirt. From her ears hung two small, jet-black drops on tiny gold chains. The only colors to provide tonal variations were those of her eyes and her lips but her make-up had been applied very discreetly and the strong impression she conveyed was of a striking woman who was careful about her appearance but without vanity. There was no smile on her face and her expression showed that she knew the gravity of the situation into which she was walking. She gave Burnham a little look as she passed him and immediately dropped her eyes away again, even managing a little blush across her neck as she did so. Carston watched it all, absorbed by the performance (which he knew it was), and drawn by the same chemistry that he'd felt on their other meetings.

As she answered Milne's gentle questions about who she was, where she worked and the nature of her relations with the accused, her voice was steady, mature, but held at a lower pitch which kept it audible but reserved. When she admitted that she'd been having an affair with Burnham, she did so without implying that she was ashamed of it or that there was indeed any guilt involved on either side. She offered the picture of herself as a no-longer-married woman in the world of business where the need to survive and the avoidance of stress sometimes led people beyond the correctives of morality. She was careful to point out that she had entered the affair with her eyes open, but the quiet voice and the taut, defensive fragility she was projecting left few in any doubt that the man in the dock had driven the bargains.

As Milne questioned her, his courteous phrasing and gentleman's manner gave darker definition to their indiscretions.

"I think you've been made aware by the police of the fact that you're frequently referred to in the accused's diary. Is that right?" he asked.

"Yes," said Stone.

"Would you mind if I read some of those entries to you?"

Stone shook her head. The chains of her ear-drops sparkled.

"For example, part of the entry for August the eighteenth reads, 'B came home. Deskbound with a vengeance.' Does that mean anything to you?"

"Yes. I went to Michael's home. We were in the study, he wanted me to … play a game."

"What sort of game?"

"Sort of bondage. Tying me to the desk. It was harmless. Stupid. Nothing sinister. Just … silly games."

She seemed mildly embarrassed by the admission. Milne turned to another page.

"The previous month, you'd apparently been to a hotel in the Lake District."

"Yes," said Stone. "The Lovelady, in the hills near Ullswater."

"Yes," said Milne, studying the entry. "I note that the accused writes here, 'B's inventions.' Then there's an exclamation mark. Do you remember what this might be referring to?"

In the dock, Burnham brought his hands up to his face and kept his head bowed. Stone didn't flinch.

"Yes, I do," she said.

Milne waited and Stone, in quiet, controlled tones described a series of sexual games in which she'd had to play various roles. The games were standard, unimaginative affairs, their only real interest lying in the fact that each had contained an element of danger, sometimes ropes, sometimes electricity, and once, six knives arranged around the edges of the rug on which they were making love. In the courtroom, the silence almost crackled.

"I don't understand," said Milne. "The entry seems to credit you with the inventions."

Stone let her eyes drop. She wasn't crying but the hunch of her shoulders suggested that tears weren't far away. She shook her head and straightened up once more.

"I … I had to. Michael … made me … He wouldn't …"

Burnham raised his head from his hands, kept his fingers over his lips and looked hard at her.

"He kept shouting at me. Making me think of more things."

"But surely you could have just stopped," said Milne.

Stone shook her head.

"He hit me," she said, making an obvious effort to control her voice. "Not hard, but not playful either."

Burnham's hands dropped away from his face. His mouth was half-open and his eyebrows were drawn down into a frown.

"Didn't you try to leave the room?"

"Yes. But then he had the knife."

Burnham's eyes closed and he sat back in the dock with a sigh, opening them again and looking up at the ceiling.

"He had it in his case beside the bed," Stone went on. "He took it out and said that if I stopped … he'd cut me."

"And what happened?" Milne prompted.

"There was a balcony. A view out over the valley. He'd asked for it specially. He made me take off all my clothes and go out onto it."

Her delivery was in cropped, breathy tones. Carston was watching it with a different type of interest now. It wasn't the pull of her sexuality that held him but the power of her presentation. He had only met her a few times, but he was convinced that any attempt by Burnham to impose his will on her, with or without armaments, would be deflected without even a thought on her part of how to effect it. He was sure that there was only one controller in this relationship. She was lying. But the show was amazing.

Once more, she'd stopped, apparently stilled by her memories. When she spoke again, her voice was steady, flat, the expression on her face was neutral, and yet tears were slipping down her cheeks. They were the only sign that she was crying. It was a wonderful skill to have acquired and its impact on the jury was immediate.

"I had to pretend to be a high diver. He made me stand on the top rail with my legs apart while he ..."

The thought was too much for her. The words stopped, the expression remained mute, but the eyelids drooped slowly shut as the tear ducts increased their productivity.

Carston almost applauded.

The judge seemed to have none of the cynicism that usually goes with the job and asked Stone if she wanted a break. She shook her head and smiled at him in a way that left him with a feeling which he didn't get rid of until he was in bed that night and which came as a great surprise to his wife.

Stone had obviously retaken possession of herself. The crying stopped and she was ready for more of Milne's questions. He was quick to ask her why she hadn't immediately called off the affair with Burnham after such an evening and the reasons she gave in reply showed her once more to be a caring, understanding woman who was prepared to excuse the drunken excesses of her lover because of her fundamental belief in his goodness and also because she knew that the world was a mucky place. She seemed eager to defend Burnham by insisting, with no prompting, that he'd only threatened her with the knife on that one occasion, but Milne managed to guide her to many others when Burnham's fists had been raised and his questionable sexual appetites had demanded satisfaction from her. Throughout the whole session she'd managed to be the threatened victim of his excesses and yet still retained her strong individual presence as a self-sufficient woman making her own choices in a dangerous game.

"Can we come to September the twelfth, the day of the murder? I believe you had a lunch date that day?" asked Milne, suddenly changing tack.

"Yes," said Stone. "Michael had an appointment here in Aberdeen. He was supposed to come to my house after twelve."

The whole court was suddenly surprised by Burnham's voice from the dock. It was not shrill, not even protesting. It simply said, very quietly, "Oh please, Barbara ..."

The judge looked at him.

"The accused will refrain from commenting on the proceedings until he is called to the stand," he said.

Burnham looked at him, nodded, then looked back at Stone, who, apart from one quick glance across at him, had kept her eyes on Milne. The judge flicked a finger to indicate that they should proceed.

"And what time did he arrive for lunch?" asked Milne.

"He didn't."

"Not at all?"

"No."

"Did he phone to say why?"

"I heard nothing from him until ..."

"Yes?"

"Until the evening."

"Ah, to explain?"

"No. To ... to ask if he could come round and ... spend the night at my house."

"I'm sorry?" said Milne, seeming surprised by the news. "This was the day of his wife's death? And he asked to spend the night with you?"

"Yes," said Stone, apologetically.

Burnham sighed, put his right arm across his chest and his left hand up to his bowed forehead. Milne shuffled through some papers.

"Mrs. Stone," he went on at last. "May I ask what the nature of your relationship with the accused has been since that day?"

"It's over."

"I'm sorry?"

"I've only seen him once. He came to my house."

"And?" prompted Milne as she paused.

"Nothing. That's all," she said. "He's tried to ring me a few times since, but it's over. How could we ...? I mean, how could I ...?"

"Of course. And did the accused accept your decision?"

"Not at first. That's what the calls were about. He kept asking me to meet him again."

"And how did he react when you refused?"

Stone shrugged again.

"He was angry, of course. Said there was no point now in staying apart. Said we could get married if we wanted to … I didn't want to."

"Thank you, Mrs. Stone. You've been most helpful."

It was an understatement and Carston was anxious to see how Maunder set about repairing the damage she'd inflicted on his client. His opening was all charm, smiles and invitations. He talked of her work, the successes she'd had, her position and growing influence in Dempster Associates. In her answers, she matched his charm but just beneath her words, Carston could sense a watchfulness. At last, Maunder asked if she ever felt vulnerable as a woman in the hard world of commerce.

"I don't have time to think about things like that," she said. "I do the job."

It was simple statement, with no undue pride but with a whisper of steel in it. Maunder brought his hands up in front of his face, steepled them, then tapped the fingers together as he appeared to reflect on something.

"You see," he said finally, "I'm finding it very difficult to see how someone with your experience of dealing with people, your obvious gifts in negotiating deals, your ability to be strong in potentially stressful situations, can succumb so comprehensively to the whims of a middle-aged, middle-management man like my client."

Along with most of the jury, Carston looked at Burnham to see how he would take to the insult. There was nothing. His eyes were fixed on the ledge in front of him, his hands folded in his lap. His posture, in fact, confirmed what his counsel had just said and gave even more relevance to the question. If Stone was the hot-shot she was being billed as, what the hell was she doing messing around with such a loser? Maunder had directed the insult at Burnham, but its real target was Stone. She showed no signs of a hit.

"You're painting too crude a picture, Mr. Maunder," she said. "Yes, it's hard, yes, we often have to fight, but we're still people.

Maybe the antidote to power games is just some simple humanity. I don't know why I let Michael make me do all those things. Maybe … maybe weakness is a relief sometimes."

"Yes, of course," said Maunder, smiling his understanding. "Let's turn to something else. In fact, can we go back to February of last year. I believe you took some time off work then."

Stone straightened a little.

"Yes," she said.

"Why was that?" asked Maunder, all innocence.

"I was ill."

"What sort of illness?"

"Depression," said Stone, very firmly.

"I'm sorry to hear that. Were you treated for it?"

"Yes."

"Where?"

"Kingseat," said Stone.

To most Aberdonians, the name of the local psychiatric hospital was synonymous with out-and-out madness. They were, of course, mistaken but the myths of mental disturbance are hard to undermine. The very fact that Stone had been to Kingseat immediately halved her credibility. Carston had learned of Stone's brief bout of depression in the course of his investigations and wasn't surprised that Maunder had chosen to use it against her. In a courtroom, with its rituals and gentility, its impact was shocking. But she'd chosen to be a player. She was in court flinging handfuls of mud in Burnham's direction; Maunder had simply turned on the fan.

She looked at him now, her eyes shining, ready to be challenged and taken further into the unwelcome subject. But he had gauged her shrewdness well and knew that, given the opportunity, she would use even this new revelation to her own advantage. Having associated her with Kingseat, he was content to let the jury's own prejudices do the rest.

"Thank you, Mrs. Stone," he said. And he sat down.

Milne retrieved the situation.

"I don't wish to prolong painful recollections, Mrs. Stone," he said, rising immediately, "but would you mind telling us the cause of your depression at that time?"

This time, Stone only let the tears get as far as her eyes.

"I lost my mother," she said. "We were very close."

Milne nodded understandingly.

"Thank you," he said.

Stone was a difficult act to follow and the remainder of the prosecution's witnesses trooped through their testimony very quickly and without undue molestation from Maunder. When the last of them had been excused, it was well into the afternoon and the prosecution's case was complete.

Maunder, predictably, submitted that all that had been offered was circumstantial evidence, none of which tied his client irrevocably to any of the events in question and that there was therefore no case to answer. The judge listened patiently and attentively but, equally predictably, didn't agree with him. Maunder was invited to be ready to proceed with the defense case the following morning.

In the car on the way home, both McNeil and Carston were sorting out their reactions to what they'd heard. They were nearly eight miles out of Aberdeen before Carston asked McNeil what she thought of it all.

"Guilty," said McNeil.

Her certainty took him by surprise.

"Just like that?" he said.

"No, but on balance. He's too fond of beating up his girlfriend."

"Yes, what d'you make of her?" asked Carston.

McNeil said nothing as she pulled out and overtook a tractor with a load of foul-smelling stuff in the trailer behind it. Once she was cruising at fifty-five again, she said, "I wouldn't trust her further than I could throw her, but writing stuff about her in yon diary, he's got to be no all there."

"Bit much to condemn him because he writes a diary."

"You arrested him, sir. What do you think?"

"Good question, McNeil. I've been through all this, and now I've listened to it all again. He's probably guilty, but I still don't know."

The next day, Maunder's defense tactics began with a systematic attempt to dismantle the apparently admirable character of Stephanie Burnham. Paul Roach and Mrs. Napier testified respectively to

210

her deviousness and her drinking. Even Borney, recalled to the stand, was forced into admitting that she could be hasty and that her treatment of some clients had been less than professional. But it was the testimony of Sleeman that really confirmed her Jekyll and Hyde nature.

He looked like the sort of witness that appeared in television courtroom dramas. His thick dark hair was just long enough to start curling over his shirt collar. He wore an almost black cashmere jacket over a blue Oxford shirt and a pair of stone-washed jeans. Through him, Maunder planned to broadcast the wife's adulteries to counterbalance those of her long-suffering husband. This was going to be a strong hand to play. He started with an attention grabber.

"Dr. Sleeman. You were Mrs. Burnham's lover."

Burnham's eyes were looking down at his hands. Sleeman looked directly back at Maunder.

"Yes," he said.

"For how long?"

"About four and a half months."

"Did you know she was married?"

"Yes."

"Did you also know that at the time of her death she was pregnant?"

"No. At least I didn't then. I've been told of it since."

"I believe you've also been told the identity of the father."

"Yes. The baby would have been mine."

The *Press and Journal*'s reporter started some furious scribbling. Maunder had established a tempo he didn't want to relinquish.

"Where did your meetings with Mrs. Burnham take place?"

"Mostly on my boat. I live on board. In Findhorn Bay."

"You didn't visit her home?"

"Once. Last July, I think."

"Ah, that would explain why your fingerprints were found in the study."

"I imagine so."

Maunder paused, considering then rejecting some notes. He turned to a fresh page before him.

"We've been offered a picture of the unfortunate victim of this crime as a model employee, a wronged wife, in fact an innocent who was subjected to vile abuse. Does that coincide with your image of her?"

Sleeman shook his head.

"No. Stephanie was no saint. She knew what she wanted. She went for it."

"In what way?"

"Every way. Work, sex. Life."

"Did she ever talk about her marriage?"

"Too often. She had no time for her husband. She wanted to leave him, get rid of him. She was a very bright lady. Much too bright to be a victim."

Sleeman's hard brashness was making him very few friends. Maunder pushed on.

"Could you perhaps tell the jury the reasons why you formed such an opinion of Mrs. Burnham?"

Sleeman tapped his forefinger on the rail in front of him several times before speaking.

"I knew her. Knew her well. She was … sharp, intelligent. Not the sort of woman you push around."

"So when you heard of her death, what was your reaction?"

"I was surprised … I mean, that she let anybody do that to her. She wasn't weak. She could handle herself as well as a man if it came to it."

"What makes you say that?"

"Experience, for a start. With her. She could be … well, powerful. My yacht's not small. It's a 34-footer. She sailed it from Cromarty across the Moray Firth to Findhorn single-handed in a force seven once. A south-easterly. I was on board, but she asked me to let her do the sailing, so I did. I was a passenger. There was a long swell coming up the Firth and a chop across the top of it. But she beat all the way across with no help from me."

"Remarkable."

"I told you. She was no pushover."

With a slight inclination of the head, Maunder sat down.

Milne took over immediately and it took him no time at all to channel all the jury's negative feelings into antagonism towards the witness. His questions provoked Sleeman into expressing attitudes about marriage, the unborn child, Mrs. Burnham and women in general which alienated all the female jurors. His self-assurance had already ignited the envy and therefore resentment of some of the males, too. Sleeman himself was unaware of the impact he was having and seemed not to care about it in any case. When the judge released him, he pulled at his lapels, shrugged his shoulders inside his jacket to make them more comfortable and left the court without a glance at anyone.

Carston, well used to Sleeman's arrogance, had been less affected than the other people in the room by his evidence. Some of what he'd heard had started him thinking along the sort of speculative, creative lines that he had been trying hard to rub out of his repertoire. The problem was that these musings tended to produce scenarios that he couldn't nail down. He frequently came up with suggestions that fitted all the pieces of evidence together into a very plausible pattern but which were impossible to verify because their sole basis was his intuition. They drove Ross wild but to Carston they were irresistible. A niggling suspicion about Stephanie Burnham's death was forming but it was too unlikely to be satisfactory even as a mind game. He needed to hear more about the whole thing.

The snippets he was looking for began to come as Maunder brought Brian McIntosh back to talk about the fibers and the cadaveric spasm. Having reminded everyone of the condition, he surprised the court by asking, "Dr. McIntosh. How long is the average arm?"

McIntosh frowned, looked at his own arm and said, "Twenty-six, twenty-eight inches."

"And would you say that Mrs. Burnham was of about average size?"

"Slightly smaller, I'd say."

"I see. So, what's the furthest she'd be able to reach, with her fingers fully extended?"

McIntosh took refuge in stroking his beard.

"Fully extended? I'd say up to about thirty inches."

"Interesting," said Maunder. "You see, this causes me a bit of a problem. You've insisted that cadaveric spasm occurs at the moment of death. You've also told us that the furthest Mrs. Burnham could reach would be some thirty inches. And that with her fingers out-stretched."

He waited. McIntosh nodded.

"Now the prosecution asks us to believe that Mrs. Burnham grabbed at the killer, who was standing behind her, presumably wearing my client's sweater and holding a shotgun whose barrel was thirty-two inches long. How on earth could she reach him?"

McIntosh thought.

"If that's what happened," he said, "she couldn't."

Carston felt a gush of adrenaline. Another strand was added to his speculations. This was better than he could have expected. Maunder continued by taking McIntosh back over the details of the entry and exit wounds and reminded everyone that the shot had traveled slightly upwards through the chest.

"So we've got a shot fired which starts some—what?—let's say four feet from the ground, and then travels upwards?"

"That's right," said McIntosh.

"And we know that, because of the recoil from the Winchester Superspeed shot, the gun has to be cushioned against the killer's shoulder as he stands behind Mrs. Burnham."

"Probably."

"So, unless the person's kneeling down, that makes him less than five feet tall," said Maunder, innocently.

Milne was immediately on his feet to protest and the judge agreed that such speculation was gratuitous and should be dis-regarded. But the scene had been played into the minds of the jury. Up to that point it had been a question about which people they chose to believe; now they had to re-examine the event itself. It was no longer straightforward. It seemed that, for Maunder and Burnham, some sort of turning point had been reached.

It certainly had for Carston. The last ten minutes had nudged his imaginings about Stephanie Burnham's death from their secret place in his day-dreaming mind to downstage center. All his uneasi-ness in the early stages of their investigation was well founded. It was precisely because so many things were missing that he had been less than eager to make the arrest and he had always had the feeling that they hadn't got near the truth. He still wasn't sure that Burnham was entirely innocent, but equally, he doubted very much that he was guilty.

It was a feeling that was strengthened by something he saw outside the courtroom that evening as he was preparing to leave. In a private parking area, Sleeman and Stone were standing beside the white Honda CRX. Stone was smiling and Sleeman's finger was trailing down the side of her neck and over her shoulder. Carston didn't wait to see any more. When the Burnhams had got involved with people like these, they'd moved into a league where sudden death was no surprise.

Back in Cairnburgh, Carston found Kath waiting for him in the kitchen. She was picking bay leaves off the plant on the windowsill and dropping them into a mixture of cubed Jerusalem artichokes, onions and garlic. The smell was wonderful. He kissed her on the back of the neck.

"There's wine open in the fridge," she said, shaking him off.

"D'you want some?" he asked.

Kath answered by pointing to a glass already filled beside the draining board. Carston took the bottle of Marks and Spencer's Jeunes Vignes from the door of the fridge and poured himself a too-full glass. It was a cold, green taste and it eased him back into the safety of his world with Kath. He deliberately put Burnham and the rest from his mind.

"Ask me what I've been doing then?" said Kath.

"What have you been doing then, Kath?" he asked obediently.

"Getting a commission," she answered.

He looked at her, genuinely interested.

"What sort of commission?"

"The library. They've got a photographic archive. Stuff taken by Washington Wilson and a few others round the turn of the century. Even earlier. They're going to mount an exhibition."

"And ...?"

"They want the photographic society to look at some of the prints and take some shots from the same spots, same angles. I'm

215

doing all the water shots, the canal, river, bridge. There's dozens of them."

"That's terrific, love. Well done," said Carston, his delight and pride obvious in his voice.

Like everything else she took to, Kath's photography had flourished. She spent hours in her darkroom and the spare bedroom was beginning to look like a gallery with all the ten by eights she had stacked and propped around it. She wasn't content to keep on polishing a single technique or studying the same theme; she wanted to try everything: portraits, still lifes, landscapes, image manipulation. She'd even coated some wood and pebbles with silver emulsion and was keeping them until she found the right images to use on them. Kath lived every bit of her life. Her delight and enthusiasm were infectious and Carston knew that it was she who was keeping his awareness of middle age at bay.

He surprised her by coming up behind her again, this time to kiss the back of her head. She pushed her backside out to shove him off again.

"What's that for?" she asked.

"I want to make sure you stay with me when you're famous."

"Well, you'll have to do better than lick my hair," she said, adding immediately, "and before you say it, you're not licking anything else."

"I'll go and lick myself then."

"Bet you wish you could," said Kath.

Carston smiled, told her she was disgusting and began asking for more details about the library's exhibition. As she spoke about it, the affection she'd developed for Cairnburgh was obvious. The culture shock of the move north had been stimulating rather than disturbing and she was greedy for the new angles and insights that the Cairnburghers gave her. By the time they'd eaten and cleared everything away, Carston had once more had the negation that attended so much of his work soothed away and was feeling warm, contented and optimistic. Even about people.

Chapter Nine

The climax of the trial came with Burnham's turn to be called to the stand. He and Maunder had had a long discussion about whether it was necessary. Maunder had done such a good job of undermining the prosecution's case that he was confident that the jury would be in enough doubt to find in their favor. He didn't particularly want to bring attention back onto Burnham for fear that he might restore the unfavorable impression that Milne had worked so hard to create in the beginning. On the other hand, he knew that, in many minds, not calling the defendant was a sure indication of his guilt. The assumption was that innocent people had nothing to hide and would therefore take every chance to say so.

He had schooled Burnham very carefully and given him dire warnings about the possible consequences of losing his temper or even raising his voice. His job was to be the bewildered unfortunate who had been caught up in a nightmare which was no doubt spawned by his wife's devious dealings with the likes of Sleeman, Roach and others unknown.

Maunder's questioning was low key, anti-climactic. He drew from Burnham the story of a marriage which had simply become a drag. Burnham and his wife rarely spoke, their interests had diverged to the extent that he couldn't even answer a question about how she spent her time. When they spoke about his affair with Stone, there was no need for Burnham to act the part of a broken person. His memories of her, the ache she'd left, the incomprehensible testimony she'd given had drained all venom from him. He was a shadow and more than one of the people in court wondered how on earth she and he had ever become lovers.

He talked about why he kept the diary which seemed to be so

harmful to his case, saying that it was just a habit, with no significance. When Maunder asked why he'd made no entry since his wife's death, he seemed reluctant to reply.

"Mr. Burnham?" prompted Maunder.

Burnham sighed.

"I was going to," he said. "I always write ... used to write things in it. I was going to write that night, but ... I couldn't."

"Why was that?"

"Various things. What do you write when your wife's been killed? What do you say when you come home and find her with a hole in her back?"

It was a powerful question but the tone in which he asked it was too cold to impress. There were no tears in his eyes, there was no strain on his face. He seemed to be stating simple facts.

"So why did you take it to the hotel with you?"

"Habit, you see. I was going to write it but ... well, I didn't, that's all."

Maunder put down his notes and leaned forward, waiting. When Burnham started speaking again, the changed tone of his voice showed that he was closely tangled in thoughts of that night.

"It's automatic. I used to get into bed and just reach for the diary. I did the same thing that night. But I didn't know what to say. I couldn't just write 'Stephanie was killed today,' could I? I don't know how long I sat there with it open. Then I started looking back through it. And I read lots of the ... complaints I'd made about her, about her nagging, her moaning. And it seemed awful."

He stopped, his mind replaying the experience.

"But wasn't there one particular entry that you found especially disturbing?" asked Maunder, very gently.

Burnham nodded.

"Yes. One about choosing the baby's name. I thought it was my baby then. One night we spent a long time deciding on names and the baby sort of became real. It wasn't a stain on a testing kit or a tick on a medical chart. It was a person."

He stopped again, the whole attention of the court on him once more. Maunder let the silence stretch. It was Burnham who broke it.

"I was reading that, and thinking how awful it was, how … criminal … to have an abortion."

Maunder again rode the silence. At last, very gently, he closed the file in front of him, picked it up and stood, still and handsome, looking directly at his client.

"Mr. Burnham. Did you love your wife?"

"Yes, in the early days. But not recently, no. We'd drifted apart."

"Did you kill her?"

"No, I didn't."

Maunder nodded as if to confirm that that was what he believed too.

"Thank you," he said and sat down.

Milne was aware of the sympathy that had begun to grow for Burnham and he eased into his cross-examination with great care. Only after he'd established a sort of rapport with him did he begin the real probing.

"Did you ever see Mrs. Stone after your wife died?" he asked.

Burnham paused and then said, "Once."

"Ah. Would you tell us about that meeting?"

"It wasn't a meeting. I went to her house. I saw her there, that's all."

"I see. You saw her there."

"Yes."

"Nothing else?"

Burnham was silent, knowing what was coming.

"You didn't beat her up, Mr. Burnham? You didn't give her a black eye?"

Milne waited.

"I hit her," Burnham admitted, his hands clenched in his lap.

"I'm sorry. What did you say?"

"I said I hit her," said Burnham, his voice louder, defiant. "I hit her because she asked for it. She lies, she cheats, she …"

His voice tailed off. Maunder tried to catch his eye to flash a warning at him, but Milne was in pursuit.

"And is that the reason you hit her on all the previous occasions?"

"I never hit her before. That's the only time. She's made up the rest for your benefit."

"Oh really?" said Milne, with heavy irony.

"Yes, really," said Burnham. "That night she was ... I found her with somebody else. I was jealous. I lost my temper. That's how it happened. That's the truth."

"Yes," said Milne. "Losing your temper, that's certainly the truth. You also lost your temper with your wife, didn't you?"

"No," said Burnham. Milne pressed harder.

"You treated her like a piece of property, didn't you, just like you treated Mrs. Stone?"

"Rubbish," said Burnham.

"You used both of them, turning them into things to suit your convenience. Isn't that right?"

"Certainly not."

"And when your wife began to be inconvenient, she had to be discarded."

"No."

"So first you humiliated her, tormented her, stabbed and raped her. Subjected her to all sorts of indignities."

"This is wrong," said Burnham, his voice louder.

"Is it, Mr. Burnham? We've seen and heard the evidence. Your poor wife bore the marks of your final brutalities."

"Not mine. It wasn't me."

"And I suppose it wasn't you either who made her stand in that room, bleeding, sore, in pain and degradation, while you put your shotgun against her back and pulled the trigger?"

"No, I didn't do it. I wanted ..."

He stopped. Milne gave him a moment to continue but Burnham didn't know what to say. He was lost, totally disoriented by the attack. Milne stared at him, holding his gaze, then nodded slowly for the benefit of the jury and sat down once again.

The final summations took up most of the afternoon. Milne stressed Burnham's volatile character, his abuse of women, his distaste for his wife, the absence of any alibi and the overwhelming amount of circumstantial evidence which locked him to the time, place, items and elements of the deed. He warned them against being misled into considering the involvement of person or persons unknown.

Deliberately, Maunder took rather longer. Apart from a natural desire to undermine some of the more damning pieces of evidence with speculations, he wanted to keep the jury in court until the following day. He made much of the mystery of how the dying Mrs. Burnham could clutch at a sweater which was out of her reach and hinted that her relationships with others made her a very different creature from the one depicted as innocent victim by the prosecution. Burnham the monster became Burnham the put-upon, whose temper had been snapped by the stresses he had been under since the tragedy had struck his house. By the time he sat down, it was too late for any further business.

The next morning, the judge reminded the jury of the verdicts available to them, stressing that the defense had to prove nothing at all and that it was up to the Crown to make a case. He exhorted them to consider what had been presented to them and to ask whether it satisfied them beyond reasonable doubt that the accused had indeed murdered his wife. If at least eight of them were convinced that it did, that was sufficient to bring in a guilty verdict. With a final reassurance that they could take as long as they liked to come to their decision, he asked them to go and deliberate. It was ten twenty-seven.

Carston hadn't been able to justify another trip to Aberdeen. He was sorry to miss the conclusion of proceedings but the heap of paper that had built up on his desk was an increasingly visible indictment of him and it was time to ease some of the pressure on Ross. He'd left a message with the duty constable at Grampian Headquarters in Queen Street to contact him as soon as there was any news. The call eventually came at three-forty. Ross watched as Carston heard the verdict. Carston nodded, thanked the constable and put the receiver back.

"Well?" said Ross.

"As we thought," said Carston.

"Not proven."

"Yep."

It was a familiar experience. The not-proven verdict was being questioned more and more in Scotland. It allowed the jury an alternative not available under other systems. If they weren't convinced

of the accused's guilt but were equally uncertain that he was innocent, they could find the case not proven. The problem was that it
often interfered with rather than helped the course of justice. It was
a cop-out; arguments didn't have to be followed through, juries
could be lazy. They went through the motions and, when they
thought they'd done enough, they decided that not proven would
indicate that they'd done their duty and that it was someone else's
turn to have a go. In the minds of most people, the verdict implied
that, if the police could find more evidence or the prosecution
could present a different case, a verdict of guilty would be possible.
That was why Friday afternoons tended to produce so many not-
proven verdicts. The thought of having to spend the weekend
locked in a hotel arguing about a case they were already sick of
made jurors eager to give any sort of verdict. Not proven meant,
"OK, we're not sure, but have another go with another lot, try a bit
harder and you'll probably get a result." What no one ever seemed
to realize was that, as far as the accused was concerned, it was in
most respects equivalent to being found not guilty. He was freed
and couldn't be retried on the same charges. The police knew this,
counsel knew it and Burnham's lawyer had obviously been counting
on it. By the time Carston received the call, Burnham had already
been acquitted and discharged.

"Sickening, isn't it?" said Ross.

"Maybe not, Jim," said Carston.

"Why? All that work, everything down the pan?"

Carston shook his head.

"I haven't liked this from the start, remember?"

"Aye, but that's your usual cussedness, isn't it?"

"I don't think so. Not this time. And the more I listened to all of
that this week, the less certain I was that we'd got it right."

"OK, so what now then? Start again?"

"Only partly."

Ross had spent too much time recently covering for his boss to
be very tolerant of his musings.

"Well, I don't know what sort of priority you want to give it.
There's a few other things on the go, you know," he said, his impatience edging through.

"It's OK, Jim," said Carston. "I think I know what we're looking for and where to look for it."

Ross's curiosity came briefly back.

"You think somebody else did it?"

"Yes."

"Who?"

Infuriatingly, Carston tapped the side of his nose.

"Read the report of the trial. See what you think," he said.

The fact that he'd been waiting for the call meant that he'd had no option but to sit at his desk and work through the paper mountain. Now that he'd heard the verdict, he was glad that that was the case because he was up to date and he could turn his energies back to Burnham right away.

"I've sorted these case files," he said, getting up and plonking a heap of folders on the desk under the window. "Most of them can be handled by Fraser and Spurle, but the ones I've left on my desk are for McNeil. Draft in some uniforms to help her with the Beverley case."

Ross was making notes of all this. He looked up.

"What'll you be on?" he asked, knowing the answer.

Carston was at the door.

"I'll be at your disposal first thing on Monday, don't worry," he said. "I told you, I know what I'm after with Burnham. I'll sort it all at the weekend."

"Sir," said Ross as Carston was halfway out of the door.

"What?" said Carston, stopping and turning back.

"It's bloody awful sometimes, working with you."

Carston grinned.

"With you, it's bloody awful all the time," he said.

In fact, it took Carston three weeks to bring together the various elements he needed. The time he'd spent in Aberdeen at the trial had made him feel a bit guilty and so he did most of the extra work himself outside office hours. It wasn't always easy because he needed co-operation from others for some of the searching that had to be done, but, as each piece of evidence fell sweetly into its place, he found the occasional late night very easy to take. He correlated the materials he'd collected, prioritized interviews and inquiries and gradually collated it all into a dossier for the chief constable and the procurator fiscal. Fortunately for his marriage, Kath was equally busy working on her commission for the Washington Wilson exhibition and, now and again, they passed one another on the stairs, in the kitchen and once, at the sports counter in Waterstone's bookshop. All these meetings were little occasions. Sometimes they'd look at one another as if they were strangers, sometimes he'd make an obscene suggestion and, in Waterstone's, Kath asked him to stop molesting her and threatened to call the manager.

He spent the first weekend working out the things he needed to know and listing the contacts he needed to make. He started the initial inquiries by phone on the Monday morning. Forbes Grant, at the clay pigeon range, was as unfriendly and unhelpful as he'd been during his first interview with Ross. The information he had was also harder to come by. Carston wanted him to check his receipts for everything bought in the clubhouse shop in the previous July and August.

"You do realize," said Grant, his tone spread with the same tired superiority that had driven Ross to the edge of his patience, "that we're probably busier at that time than any other? You've heard of the glorious twelfth, have you?"

"Yes. Cavalry regiment, wasn't it?"

Silence.

"Anyway," Carston went on, very sweetly, "I'm afraid I can't adjust the dates that interest me to accommodate your sales charts, Mr. Grant. *Nil operat bibendi*, eh?"

This time, the silence was different. Carston had no idea whether the collection of syllables he'd just uttered meant anything, but they sounded like Latin and he was confident of the effect they would have on a satellite of the gentry like Grant.

"Well, yes," said Grant, an atavistic respect for the emblems of learning momentarily suppressing his shopkeeper's instincts. "But can't you narrow it down a little? The books really are rather full for that period."

"I tell you what, would it help if I had a look myself?"

224

"I'm not sure. If there were any breach of confidentiality …"

"Not a chance. I know exactly what I'm looking for. I might even be able to get a credit card number to check it against. How would that be?"

Grant was reasserting himself.

"Just as inconvenient, but if it expedited the process, I suppose that would be the preferred option."

"Good," said Carston. "We'll take the preferred option then. I'll be there at six-thirty."

He heard and ignored the beginnings of Grant's protests as he replaced the receiver. He redialed immediately. This time, it was the Clydesdale bank. He asked to speak to the manager. Frank Creedle was quite accommodating and agreed, without any indiscretion or professional misconduct, to open a few doors that would let Carston get quickly to the credit card information he was after. It was all going very smoothly. The next call set up a meeting with a Dr. Parnell, a consultant psychiatrist at Kingseat Hospital, for the following Wednesday.

After work on Tuesday evening, he forced himself to review the video of the Burnhams' study and supplemented it with a careful scrutiny of the stills that had been taken. With his new conviction of what had happened that day in September, he looked at the scenes and details with a fresh eye. Everything now made so much sense that he was annoyed at himself for not having considered the option before. The wounds and the signs of struggle were even more distressing but they conformed to a pattern that was now glaringly obvious.

At Kingseat Psychiatric Hospital, on the Wednesday, he was met by a small, sandy-haired man in brown slacks and a Marks and Spencer cardigan. Dr. Parnell was overweight and balding but had eyes that smiled and seemed sympathetic. The only disconcerting feature was that the eyes remained open and trusting while he listened but, as soon as he launched into anything longer than a single, short sentence, their lids dropped over them and fluttered on the verge of reopening throughout his speech. The eyes didn't reappear fully until he got near to his final words. The effect was to make Carston wonder why the process of giving his professional opinion made the doctor feel so vulnerable. Time and again, he found himself watching the curtains drop over the eyes and thinking more about the flickering defense they offered than about what Parnell was saying. When the conversation homed in on depressive characteristics, he forced himself to concentrate.

"Yes," Parnell was saying, "with affective psychoses, you frequently get a loss of contact with reality, a tendency to elaborate fantasies, almost a ritualistic impulse to distort the truth." The eyes reappeared. "Or rather, to perceive distortions as the truth. There are often delusions or hallucinations."

"What's the difference?" asked Carston.

The doctor leaned forward. For a moment, his eyes remained steady on Carston, then they were quickly shuttered again.

"Well," he said, "with delusions, the sufferer receives normal sensory stimuli but tends to misinterpret them. He or she makes flawed judgments about people or events. Hallucinations on the other hand are seemingly genuine, legitimate sensory experiences which have no real sensory stimulus to provoke them."

"That's rather a comprehensive state of confusion, isn't it?"

"Yes it is, I'm afraid. The patient lives in a real world but fails to interpret it correctly and adds to it his or her own imaginings which are equally real."

"And what sort of things could bring this on?"

"Anything. But if you're asking about the seriousness of the condition, this isn't just some temporary reaction to a setback or a depressing event. I'd say that, for it to be manifest in any lasting form or for it to affect behavior adversely, there'd have to be a predisposition to an abnormal personality."

"What do you mean by that?"

"Well, it can take many forms, but I'd say the predominant characteristics are ..." As Parnell paused to consider, Carston was gratified to notice that, for a change, his eyes opened wide and were raised to the sky outside the window. He listed attributes, each as a considered opinion. "Dependence ... anxiety ... an obsessional, assertive or hysterical temperament ... a tendency to rapid changes of mood. These people are quite likely to be demanding attention all the time ... Oh dear, there are so many possibilities."

"I see the problem," said Carston, adding, after a pause, "How dangerous could they be?"

Parnell shook his head.

"You keep asking questions that don't have answers," he replied. "They can be lethal, or they can live a lifetime in the community with no problems other than their own misery. Their moral values would be … unreliable at best. Potentially, anyone whose hold on reality changes that frequently needs to be watched."

Carston nodded. Treading the pathways of the mind like this was like walking on a mat of vegetation which could suddenly turn into the buckling pads of water lilies. There were no signposts, no directions. With no obvious trigger, a familiar world of structures, dependences and friends could explode into nightmare. As had happened to him so many times before, he felt a great sadness and compassion at the tiny pains that people were carrying around with them as they caught buses, washed dishes and simply sat on benches in the park. Parnell was watching him and, this time, the open eyes, seeing the sympathy in his face, betrayed the fact that they had seen more than their share of such pain. Perhaps their strange closing was simply to allow Parnell to retreat to a place where he could try to understand things without needing to witness the continual evidence of the damage they did.

In their short discussion, Carston had already heard what he needed but his fascination for the work that went on at Kingseat kept him talking. It was left to Dr. Parnell to look at his watch and remind Carston, apologetically, that he had his rounds to make. Carston was suddenly embarrassed at his own thoughtlessness and quickly left, wondering how people like Parnell went through life surrounded by such distress, dabbling in its manifestations and yet living apparently normal lives. He couldn't know that Parnell was wondering much the same thing about people whose daily experience included bodies, woundings, bludgeonings, muggings and the other undesirable excesses of their fellow beings.

It was the middle of May before Carston had everything he needed. Ross had learned to be patient with him and had continued to ignore the gaps and lapses that were caused by his obsessive pursuit of the Burnham business. It was, fortunately, a relatively quiet time for them all. McNeil was studying hard for her sergeant's exam. Fraser had become a raging Francophile since his trip to France and spent a lot of his time in the squad room trying to educate Spurle, who seemed never to tire of asides that featured snails, frogs or garlic. Crime hadn't exactly stopped in Cairnburgh, but the forms it took were entirely predictable and its perpetrators seemed to be in a particularly careless phase.

When Carston at last decided he was ready to tie things up, he told Ross to pack up early and come for a drink. It was a Friday, the sun was shining and Ross was glad of the chance to get out and start the weekend ahead of schedule.

They were early enough to get the bay window. Carston waved Ross towards it while he went for the drinks. Ross sat down obediently and looked out at the late flowering tulips that dotted the garden. A shed at the end of the path that led round to the car park was covered with a huge mound of pink clematis montana and the shrubs in the borders looked plump and ready to explode with flowers. Ross wondered how long it would be before his own plot was as mature and self-sufficient as this. He spent as much time as he could afford keeping the place in order, planting and transplanting things, weeding, trimming, and he envied the people on 'Gardeners' World' who seemed to have nothing else to do but turn compost heaps and lift things in and out of cold frames. His daydreaming was interrupted by Carston and two pints of lager.

"Cheers," he said.

Carston lifted his own glass and took a small swig from it before sitting down. He'd been quiet all day. Ross could guess at what was coming but Carston still took him by surprise.

"Ever thought how much like GPs we are?" he asked.

"In what way?"

"Looking for symptoms, giving diagnoses."

Ross took a pull at his drink. When Carston got in one of these speculative moods, it could turn into a very trying session.

"Vets do that, too," he said.

Carston smiled.

"No. I mean something else. I had a dodgy knee once. Went to

228

see about it. The first thing the doctor asked, before he even looked at it, was whether it felt hot and swelled up."

"So?"

"So, he was trying to give me symptoms he already had in his head. Instead of asking me things, he went for a ready-made diagnosis."

Ross looked at him.

"You're talking crap," he said, adding, "sir."

"No. Think about it. He must have seen umpteen people with injured knees and most of them would be to do with ligaments or cartilages. I mean, that's what usually goes wrong, isn't it?"

"Well?"

"So he assumes it's the same with me and tries to make me fit the pattern."

"And that's what we do, is it?"

"Sometimes, yes. We sort of assume things, then we start looking for things to confirm them." He paused, took a drink, waited for a reaction. Ross said nothing.

"It's what we did with Burnham," said Carston at last.

"Who says we were wrong? It was not proven, that's all."

Carston shook his head.

"No, Jim. He wasn't guilty. No question. We were off target from the start. I should've gone with my gut feeling on it."

Ross turned from the garden and gave Carston his full attention.

"Is that still what you're going on?" he asked.

Carston shook his head slowly.

"No, Jim. Hard evidence. Better than any of the stuff we had on Burnham. And so bloody obvious once you start looking properly and don't just try to feed preconceptions."

"I don't think that's what we were doing," said Ross, slightly annoyed by the implied criticism of his professionalism.

"Well, I was. I could never come to terms with Mrs. Burnham. Whichever way we approached it, she kept changing. But I never followed that through. I was too busy clutching at straws, matching up those fibers with his jumper, things like that."

"But they matched," said Ross. "We were right. I'm sorry, but I don't see what difference it ..."

229

Carston interrupted him.

"It was the same all through the trial," he said. "She was all contradictions. You'd have thought there were several victims to listen to what they said about her."

The expression on his face told Ross that he was remembering the things he was speaking about, seeing the courtroom and witnesses again.

"She must've fooled all of them. Sleeman, Burnham, Roach, Borney. She fooled us, too. The more they talked about her, the less real she was. Did you notice anything about the people who talked about her at the trial?"

Ross shook his head and shrugged his shoulders.

"None of them was a friend. There were character witnesses, colleagues, husband, lover, but no friends. Who did she go to with her problems? What sort of woman doesn't have any friends? She must have been bloody lonely, Jim."

"So how does that alter anything?"

"She was also a cool, hard thinker. She set up Roach in a scam she could just walk away from, with no risks. When clients questioned her, she more or less told them to piss off."

"Oh aye, very cool," said Ross.

"Maybe not cool, but not just the lonely little wifey either. Who the hell was she?"

Ross's interest was being edged out by an increasing impatience.

"I'm sorry, but none of this sounds like hard evidence."

"No, you're right, Jim. It's not. But it's what started me thinking during the trial. I've got the evidence now. I'm taking it to the procurator fiscal on Monday."

"So?" said Ross. "What is it?"

Carston looked out at the garden and shook his head.

"Stuff we couldn't have guessed at, Jim," he said. "Stuff that none of our preconceptions could have covered. We only scratched at some of the pain that was there last September."

His tone stifled the exasperation that Ross was beginning to feel again. It was quiet, sad and there was no teasing in it. Ross waited as Carston lifted his glass, took a swig, put it down and leaned forward.

"I'll tell you how wrong we got it," he said, and began to recreate what he now knew was the probable sequence of events that had led up to Stephanie Burnham's death.

His reconstruction was accurate in the facts that structured the event but it would have needed more than a chief inspector of police, even an inspired and compassionate man like him, to understand the motives and impulses that led between them.

Burnham was at the door of the study, pushing his shirt back into his trousers and zipping up his fly.

"I'll never understand you, Steph," he said.

His wife was sitting in the chair at the desk, her skirt high on her thighs, watching him. She said nothing. Burnham wanted to say something else, try some endearment or at least some flippant joke to help him understand the reason for the violent sex they'd just had, to bring it into a comprehensible context, make it semi-normal at least. No words came. Her eyes were staring at him, cold, empty. In the end, he just wanted to get away, off to the anonymity of the betting ring.

"I'll be back about six," he said.

Still nothing from Stephanie. No word, no gesture, no change of expression.

In the silence, gunshots sounded from the clay pigeon range. Burnham only noticed them because it was so unnaturally still in the room. He said "Christ" and went out quickly.

She let her eyes fall to her stomach and brought both her hands up to press against the womb that held her baby. Warm tears welled in her eyes as she heard Burnham go along the landing to his room. Minutes ticked by and his bedroom door banged shut. He clattered down the stairs, paused in the hall, then opened and slammed the front door. His car started and the engine noise soon subsided as he drove away.

When there was only silence and the continuing bangs and pops of the shotguns, she said "I'm so sorry" to the life inside her and went downstairs, still crying. In the kitchen, she put on rubber gloves, opened the cupboard under the sink and took out a bundle. From it she took a newly cut key and went to the garage. When she

231

came back, she'd thrown the key out into the canal and was carrying Burnham's 3-inch Tolley Magnum Hammer. She took it and the bundle upstairs again, put everything on the desk, then took off the rubber gloves and laid them on the chair.

The tears had stopped. Her movements were as purposeful and unhesitating as the gin she'd drunk allowed them to be. She went to the bookshelves and suddenly swung her arms against them as if she wanted to punch the books with the sides of her fists. The pain as her forearms struck against the edges of the shelves was sharp and welcome. Michael was flinging her forward into the wall and Bob was making the boom of his boat swing against her to knock her over the side. She started scooping the books off the shelves and the emotion of what she was doing penetrated the studied concentration once more. As she created the mayhem that the police would find, she said the word "bastards" over and over again.

Panting from her efforts, she looked round and saw the knickers she'd taken off before the sex they'd just had. She picked them up, lifted her skirt and forced them savagely between her legs and into her vagina, wiping them roughly around, digging her fingers through the material into her flesh. She brought them out, looked with disgust at the wetness and blood staining them, then tore them and threw them under the desk. She already believed that Michael had raped her, her fiction was taking over. This child which he'd forced upon her, this imposition on her freedom, this parasite that would first destroy her body, then her life, it was natural to want to be rid of it. It wasn't the kid's fault, it was his. He wanted her to be his factory, his bloody production line. She put the gloves back on and, from the bundle on the desk, she took a fork, her anger rising all the time. Deliberately, she opened her legs and jabbed the points into the inside of her right thigh. The first stab was tentative, the second fiercer. She was surprised at how little it hurt. She straightened up, looked out of the window at the canal, then suddenly swung the fork down again, the arc taking it into the front of her left thigh three times in a deliberate, cold, angry rhythm. The pain of the third thrust was acute again. She cried out with it and threw the fork into a corner.

232

Behind her on the desk lay a plunger which had been part of the bundle. It had only been used once, by Michael, several weeks before. Even that long ago, she'd been planning the sour details of this day. She'd seen him forcing it against the sink in the kitchen and decided to wrap it up and hide it when he'd finished. She turned now and picked it up. She looked at its white wooden handle, shook her head and put it back in its place.

Instead, she picked up the gun and walked around the room, banging its butt into the carpet, creating lots of indentations. This, too, was part of her planning and it helped to stoke her anger even higher. The wounds on the front of her leg were smarting more but she was beginning to feel a strange, fierce energy. All her attention and efforts were focused on this room and this resolution of her anxieties. Outside, all the antagonisms were massed and ready to hurt, but here, she was building the structure that would rob them of their satisfactions.

She put the gun back beside the bundle, took one of the super-speed cartridges she'd bought from the bundle and loaded it into the chamber. As she laid the gun across the chair once more, she suddenly stopped. For the first time, a small doubt crept into her mind. She stood and began to pace around the room. She'd thought all this through. Suicides who used firearms always chose what were known as favored sites; the temple, the roof of the mouth or, by leaning on a shotgun, the chest. A wound in the back generally suggested homicide. That was what she wanted. She was going to loop thread around the trigger, fix the gun on the chair and lead the string around its back. But the thread was a problem. She'd teased some long strands from the edge of the study carpet and scattered them over its surface. By using one to pull the trigger, she would simply leave something that would be seen by the police as a part of the general location. But what if it wasn't? What if it got caught during the recoil? What if it stayed around the trigger? Or if it broke and the broken end stayed with her or near her? It would be a tiny shred of evidence, but one which could undo all her other preparations.

She was at the window again, her mind trying to push aside the numbing effect of the alcohol. The canal swept along the house and around the corner of the garden. As she fretted over this sudden new anxiety, her eyes flicked over what looked like a brownish stain against the red of the cotoneaster berries. She looked back at it and gritted her teeth into a hard smile as she realized she'd found the answer. It was Michael's sweater. She went downstairs and out into the garden to fetch it. Loose threads hung from a hole in the elbow of the left sleeve. As she went back upstairs, she pulled them free and tugged at them to test their strength. The single thread broke right away, but with three of them wound together, it took a good pull to break them. In the study, she turned the sweater over. More threads hung at the front. She teased several of them slowly out of the weave and yanked them free. She wound them together into a single strand and, very carefully, laid it on the chair beside the gun. Then, her mind now working with a clarity that excited her, she moved around the room brushing the sweater over surfaces, along the carpet and swinging it against the bookshelves. When she'd finished, she went down to the garden again, threw it into the cotoneaster bushes and ran back upstairs.

There was a sort of exhilaration in what she was doing. As she laid the twisted strands of wool across the seat of the chair, she realized that she was sweating and that the wounds in her leg were beginning to throb a regular pain up through her. But there was more pain still to inflict. She tore at her skirt and let it fall on the floor beside her. She was a clear-thinking woman. Her men had always found her attractive and yet been slightly frightened of the power she displayed when she set her mind to solving problems, taking decisions. If she'd been a man, she'd have made the board-room very early. Instead of that, though, from her days as a girl in and around Stratford, through university in the Sixties and on into her full, prime years, she'd always, in the end, been primarily an object. Her thinking led her back again to the child she was carrying. It was another manifestation of her negative value, her lack of status. She was a combined food processor and incubator, a series of filters sieving life into a blob of pulsing cells which would soon tear itself from her and make another sort of demand, insist on subjugating her into another ego-less role. In the end, she was nothing more than a receptacle.

Her head felt hot with the physical and mental pains that were pounding in it. She reached across the desk and, once again, picked up the plunger. Its rubber cup was cold and seemed to grab at her fingers as she held it. Its white handle pointed at her. Slowly, she lowered it with her right hand. She didn't look down but felt the cold tip of the handle slip across the top of her thigh and through her tangled hair. As it touched her clitoris, there was no pleasure, no sensation except the shiver of anticipation. She angled the plunger and eased it gently up inside her. It made her think of other penetrations. If only they'd been this considered, this thoughtful, this gentle. Bob, on the deck and in the cabin of *Raider*, had always seemed to board her, impale her, wrench his and her pleasure from hard, savage thrusts. And Michael had only ever known one single rhythm. Others had been more or less successful in releasing her pleasures as well as their own, but the lasting sensation with all of them was of invasion, a stiff, scouring intrusion into her followed by a withdrawal to seemingly vast distances. One instant she was clenching her muscles over the foreign flesh inside her, the next she was lying in a chill, seamless emptiness.

The anger returned. She withdrew the plunger and immediately forced it back inside her, further this time. It scraped hard against her soft walls. This was what they had been doing to her all these years. This was sex. This was what she was for. Her thrusts got harder and faster, the pain spreading from each stroke to blend with that of all the others. She heard her own voice shouting "bastards" again in time with her movements. There was blood on the handle and she felt the whole of her vagina as a wound.

It was fatigue rather than pain that stopped her in the end. Her wrist and forearm ached with the effort and she was crying with frustration and self-pity when she eventually let the plunger fall to the floor beside her. She'd gone even beyond her own imaginings now. She wanted to leave, wanted to stop being the object called Stephanie. Through her tears, she heaved a long, long sigh of self-pity. If only she'd been loved.

She picked up the plunger again and, this time, without first probing to find the entrance, jammed it as hard as she could up inside her anus. It was a new pain, ragged and hot alongside all the others. It made her scream for the first time and she could only manage two more quick, excruciating thrusts before she pulled the plunger free and tossed it aside.

She was sobbing now. Fear mixed with the pain as she picked up the gun. She looked at the long barrel, lowered it in front of her and, with a final, defiant thrust, pushed it up into her vagina. The pains became one single furnace inside her. She slid the gun out, picked up her skirt and wrapped it around the stock. Carefully, she arranged the gun on the seat of the chair, jamming its stock against the back and using the skirt to protect the wood. She wanted no telltale splinters knocked freshly away for some smart-arsed detective to start getting clever with. She took the loop of wool and lifted it around the back of the chair and over the trigger. She stood, the fire of her wounds spreading through all her flesh. As she took the gloves and the rest of the bundle down to the kitchen to store them away, she was beginning to tremble. On the way back up the stairs, she had to stop twice because her legs were so weak.

She closed the study door and stumbled forward to the chair and its simple little arrangement. She no longer wanted to think or feel. She fell to her knees, took the end of the wool in her right hand and turned away to face the wall. She leaned slowly back until she felt the muzzle of the shotgun against her blouse. She raised her head to the ceiling, opened her mouth and repeated the words "Stephanie Burnham" twice before pulling hard on the wool.

The shot threw her forward as the gun kicked upwards and back off the chair, taking the skirt with it and knocking the chair itself sideways. The butt of the gun made another indentation in the carpet as it bounced clear of the skirt. Stephanie really had thought of everything. Her body was left, its warm blood spreading into the scenario she'd constructed, with an added bonus she could never have foreseen. The recoil had broken the woolen loop, throwing some of its fibers to mix with those already on the carpet. But its end had stayed with Stephanie. In the paroxysm of her suicide, the spasm of the muscles of her right hand made sure that the investigators would find the evidence they needed to accuse the husband she so much wanted to punish.

◆◆◆

"Christ, she must have loathed him," said Ross, when Carston had finished his version of the suicide. "Setting him up like that."

"Who knows, Jim? We can't even guess at the state her mind was in. The boozing, the moods, they were all part of a deepening state of depression. Dr. Parnell said that morality and judgment had probably long gone. She didn't know who she was any more."

Ross shook his head, saddened by the thought of the lonely, distracted woman playing out such a deadly charade in a rich, middle-class street surrounded by the ordinariness of living.

"You see what I mean, though, about our preconceptions closing our eyes?"

"Oh come on, sir. Death by firearm, contact wound in the back. Suicide isn't an obvious line to follow."

"No, but the facts didn't add up the other way so we should have at least explored it."

"Maybe," said Ross.

Their glasses lay untouched on the table in front of them. Outside, a small evening breeze set the tulips waving and rippled across the clematis.

"She couldn't have been nuts all the time, though, could she?" said Ross. "Some planning went into it all."

"Yes. From way back, too. She's been keeping these things with his prints all over them for a while."

There was a pause.

"Poor sod," said Ross.

"Yes," said Carston.

He reached forward and turned his glass round on the table. The silence spread between them until Carston said, "I'm going round to tell Burnham myself."

Ross looked at him.

"You don't have to," he said.

The glass turning continued.

"No, but we owe it to him, I reckon."

"Maybe," said Ross. "D'you want me to come with you?"

Carston sat back.

"No, Jim. No need. Get back to Jean."

He remembered the baby.

237

"How is she?"

Ross picked up his glass.

"Great," he said, disinclined to let Carston into the secret that pregnancy tended to make her even hungrier for sex than she was before. Other women might want lobsters stuffed with bananas and other weird things; Jean wanted long, intense sex. It suited him very well.

The revelations about Mrs. Burnham had left no room for any small talk. Each of them had sunk into thoughts and associations that drew them deeper into their own private despairs and sympathies. They'd had two pints each and neither wanted another.

Carston used the phone in the entrance hall of the pub to ring Kath and warn her that he'd be home late. Then, with Ross saying he'd give Jean Carston's love, the two men parted on the pavement outside and Carston set off for the bus stop to go across town to Dyson Close.

He wasn't surprised to see that Burnham, when he answered the door, was carrying a glass of whisky, but he was surprised at his placidity. He'd expected some reaction from him, anger perhaps, frustration at a further invasion of his privacy. Instead, Burnham looked at him without expression. The aggressive moodiness that had marked him before had been suppressed or simply discarded. The outbursts during the trial had been his last demonstrations of willfulness. The whole experience had drained the passion from him. He was innocent, but the law had failed to show it. Everyone still believed that he'd killed Stephanie. There was nowhere for him to go and certainly no one to go to.

"Can I come in, Mr. Burnham?" asked Carston. "I've got some news I think you ought to know."

Burnham simply turned his back, waved an arm at him and walked back into the house. Carston followed him and closed the front door. They went through to the same clinical room they'd used during the last visit. The knowledge that Carston was carrying affected his perceptions. On the previous visit, he'd judged that the brown leather of the chairs and the textured wallpaper had been intended to soothe; now they seemed only oppressive, brought the room in on the two of them.

"Drink?" said Burnham.

The two lagers were still washing uncomfortably about in Carston's stomach so he declined. Burnham waved him to a chair and the two of them sat down. Burnham wasn't drunk but he seemed to have shriveled. His clothes were creased and nondescript, his back bent forward, his face had a grayness that hadn't been there before.

"How are you?" asked Carston.

Burnham shrugged.

"No idea," he said, adding, without a pause, "what's the visit for?"

Carston had wanted to approach the news in his own way but the directness pre-empted him.

"I've been looking at the case again. Looked at things we should maybe have considered before."

Burnham waited.

"I know what really happened now. I thought you should know ... before it's in the papers again."

"I don't care about it, Carston," said Burnham. "It's too late to do me any good, isn't it?"

Carston nodded. He wanted to get it over but without crushing Burnham any further.

"Who did it then?" asked Burnham at last.

Carston brought his hands together in front of him and interlocked his fingers.

"I'm afraid it was suicide," he said.

Burnham nodded his head as if in calm acceptance of the news then, suddenly, its impossibility struck him. His head came up and his features came to life.

"Suicide? How the bloody hell could it have been suicide? She ..."

Carston held up a hand to stop him and, as he had earlier with Ross, he explained what Stephanie had done and the planning that had gone into it. He left out the more painful details of her self-mutilation, but Burnham's imagination was already at work.

"The splinters they found ... the rape ... all that. She did it all herself?"

"Yes ... I'm sorry."

Burnham's head was shaking slowly. His hand brushed back and forth across his right knee, smoothing out the folds in his trousers.

"And making you think I did it. Setting me up for murder. Unbelievable … Amazing … What for?"

"She was badly disturbed. Who knows how these things happen? What people think and do when they lose their way?"

The movements Burnham was making slowed and stopped.

"Christ, she must have hated me. Doing all that. Going through all that …"

"Not necessarily. She didn't really know what she was doing."

Burnham wasn't hearing him. His voice went on as if in a monologue.

"I suppose it was the baby. I thought it was mine. Didn't know it was that other bloke's. Didn't even know he existed. So we argued about it as if it was ours. I thought it was me, my future. A chance."

He got up and went to the window which looked out over the garden to the left and the canal to the right.

"I sat out here one evening last summer. After we'd had the row. After she'd said she wanted the abortion. There were bees, wasps, insects everywhere, all busy as … well, bees. Not socializing, not entertaining themselves, not doing anything in fact. They were just rushing about breeding and feeding. Reproduction, all over the place. Single-minded, all of them."

He turned back into the room.

"You ever wondered about that?"

Carston didn't know where he was leading.

"What?" he asked.

"Why anything bothers. Evolution and all that stuff. If the idea's just to replicate yourself, why do it? Where the hell's it going? What are we evolving towards?"

"Big question," said Carston.

Burnham nodded and turned away again.

"Yeah," he said. "Still, they're all better than us, aren't they? Right bloody mess we make, don't we?"

He turned back suddenly, taking Carston by surprise.

"I mean, what sort of creature decides to destroy his offspring because it'll get in the way of his pleasures? Grotesque, that is. Isn't it?"

Carston was inclined to agree with him, but he wanted to lead him back from the depths that that sort of thinking could open up.

"That's probably only part of the story. How do we know what your wife thought about it? She was the one who was pregnant. It's easy for us, isn't it?"

When Burnham replied, there were tears in his throat.

"No. It's not easy, Carston. It's not easy for anybody."

Outside, in the distance, they heard a siren.

"Your lot on the lookout again," said Burnham, trying to bring himself back.

"No," said Carston. "Sounds more like an ambulance."

Burnham nodded.

"Some other poor sod, then."

He came back to his chair and sat down.

"Know what we used to say as kids when we saw an ambulance?" he said.

"What?" said Carston, surprised again at the change in him.

"'Touch your collar, be a scholar, never get a fever.' Then you had to hold your bloody collar until you saw a four-legged animal."

Carston smiled. The little rhyme had triggered a memory he'd long forgotten.

"We had a different one in Brixham," he said. "'Touch your nose, touch your toes, never go in one of those.'"

It was Burnham's turn to smile.

"You're right," he said. "Simple, isn't it?"

"Yeah. It is really," said Carston.

Bill Kirton

Bill Kirton was born in Plymouth but has lived most of his life in Aberdeen. He was a lecturer in the French Department at Aberdeen University, is an award-winning translator, and was one of the first RLF (Royal Literary Fund) Fellows in Scotland.

His theatre experience includes directing, acting, and writing. His radio plays have been broadcast by the BBC and the ABC (Australian Broadcasting Corporation) and his stage plays have been performed in Scotland and the USA. In the late seventies, he and his wife, Carolyn, performed Bill's revues at the Edinburgh Festival which led to invitations to perform, direct, and teach in the USA. Sketches from the revues were also shown on BBC, ITV, and French Television. Bill has also been a television presenter and has written, presented, and directed both commercial and educational videos and has written hundreds of video scripts on a variety of subjects and themes.

Since taking early retirement from the university, Bill has concentrated on writing fiction mysteries. He is married and has four children.

Bloody Brits Press

PAYMENT DEFERRED
A Fizz & Buchanan Mystery

Joyce Holms

When solicitor Tam Buchanan first encounters "Fizz" his heart sinks. The young woman with the guileless expression sitting outside his Legal Advice office looks too young to stand the pace as his assistant. But Fizz's innocent appearance belies the reality. Soon to be a mature student of Law, she's very bright, utterly single-minded, and has the rare talent for making people talk—people like Murray Kingston, who Tam, to his horror, finds ensconced in the office late one morning.

As far at Tam's concerned, his friendship with Murray ended the day Murray was convicted of molesting his daughter. But Murray's desperate plea of having been framed has persuaded Fizz, and somehow Tam finds himself digging into the past while Fizz undertakes to interview old witnesses. But soon Fizz begins to wonder if her confidence in Murray's innocence is entirely justified …

Set against a backdrop of busy Edinburgh streets and Scottish Borders countryside, *Payment Deferred* is an irresistible and utterly satisfying novel, introducing two unlikely sparring partners whose conflicting approaches to sleuthing make sparks fly—but get results.

Payment Deferred is the first Fizz & Buchanan Mystery.

ISBN 978-1-932859-31-7 $13.95

Bloody Brits Press

NIGHT VISIT

Priscilla Masters

"It is always a joy to discover a new crime writer with a sure touch and the capacity to shock." —Peter Lovesey

Dr. Harriet Lamont has a superstition: that the first few hours of a new year set the tone for the coming twelve months. And 1998 does not begin well. During a New Year's Eve party, Harriet is called away on an emergency night visit—fatefully leaving her husband Robin to meet the alluring Jude …

Harriet's patient that night is Reuben Carnforth, an old man who lives on the edge of the forest. As he is taken to hospital for the last time, Reuben begs for Harriet's help. But his plea has nothing to do with his illness: a decade earlier his six-year-old granddaughter Melanie vanished. His final wish is for her disappearance to be solved.

Two months later, Harriet's marriage is over. As she struggles to overcome her own heartache and that of her daughter Rosie, Harriet finds herself becoming obsessed by the image of a child in a red dress wandering lost in the woods. With Reuben's dying words still clear in her mind, she vows to find the body—and the killer—of a little girl they called Melanie Toadstool …

ISBN 978-1-932859-36-2 $13.95